CELESTE

CELESTE

by Colette Snowden

Bluemoose

For my Mum

First published in 2025 by
Bluemoose Books Ltd
25 Sackville Street
Hebden Bridge
West Yorkshire
HX7 7DJ

www.bluemoosebooks.com

British Library Cataloguing-in-Publication data
A catalogue record for this book is available from the British Library

ISBN 978-1-915693-35-8

Printed and bound in the UK by Short Run Press

1

Celeste

As Celeste walked towards home a whisper before midnight, all she could hear was the clicking of her small heels on the hard pavement. The rain had stopped. The cars had stopped. In every house the curtains were drawn, and only a very few still had their lights on.

One of her brown ankle boots needed re-heeling, making the sound shift from left to right as she walked at a good pace but with no hurry. Click. Clack. Click.

Hearing only the sound of her own two feet in the quiet, Celeste began to listen. Click-clack, click-clack. The sound bounced around the empty street, off the walls of houses and the metal shutters of the shop she visited almost every day to buy milk and top up on the things her mother had run out of or forgotten to buy.

Click-clack, click-tick, tick-tock, tick-tock. The rhythm of her footsteps on the pavement became the ticking of a clock counting Cinderella down to her curfew. She slowed her pace to stretch out the minutes. Time had stood still for her since she'd left university, and that had been almost a year ago now.

While her friends had moved on to careers or PhDs, or new lives abroad, or new towns where they were busy setting up love nests furnished with second hand finds and hand-me-downs with their so-called 'other halves', Celeste was reluctantly, aimlessly wandering around the streets that had been familiar to her all her life. She was back in her old bedroom, with the marks still on the wall where she'd crayoned her name framed by a rainbow. That had been well over a decade and several lifetimes ago now, but she still remembered kneeling on the carpet to make her mark on the space and enjoying the feeling that she was making the place better. In that moment, she'd thought she was creating a work of art that her parents would admire, just as they gushed over the drawings she brought home from school or worked on at the kitchen table.

She remembered the punishment at the end of that rainbow too. How her dad had taken all her pens and crayons away and ordered her straight to her room, with no TV for a week. She recalled how her mum had brought up a drink and a biscuit and told her she'd speak to Dad and get the punishment downgraded. Her mum had promised she'd try to get at least some of the pens back by the following day, if only for the making of a card to apologise. Celeste replayed the row it had all caused.

There had been tears. They hadn't been Celeste's tears. It had been the start of her dad's slow drift from father and husband to unfamiliar middle-aged man, living miles away and occasionally phoning or turning up on the doorstep with plans for an impromptu trip to the seaside or Sunday lunch at a carvery.

For years, he'd been an occasional and unpredictable figure in Celeste's life. Turning up to his own timetable and agenda and expecting her to be delighted that he'd appeared. In the same way she might be excited to see a rainbow on a rainy day, maybe, or an urban fox as she walked home. There would always be gifts or treats, but the ice creams and felt tips had become a less convincing compensation for the long absences as she had got older. And her mum's stony-faced hurt had become less easy to unsee after Celeste had invited her father to her graduation and, despite saying he would come, he had decided not to, without a word to her or her mother. She'd tried to call him twice before she went into the building for the ceremony, and reached only his unconvincingly chirpy voicemail message *'you've reached Robert, but it's not really me, leave a message!'* She'd left a message, knowing that he never listened to them, and sent a text even though he rarely had his phone switched on. She'd spent the entire thing looking at the door to see if he'd snuck in late, scouring the crowd in case he'd sat in the wrong seat, and looking over at her mother, with an empty seat next to her. She'd imagined him on the floor, mid heart attack, or being cut of out of his car as traffic queued up behind his accident. It had only been when she'd switched her phone back on after everyone had left the hall that she saw his reply to her text *'Sorry. Flat tyre. Can't make it. Have a great day and see you soon xx.'* It had been a relief to both Celeste and her mum that it was just the two of them in the photos in the end.

Celeste had seen her dad just once since then, when he turned up with flowers a couple of days after her birthday. He'd handed her the supermarket bouquet and ambushed her in the doorway with a hug she couldn't escape, crushing her with the weight of his guilt and the overpowering scent of lilies. He had given no explanation for the late arrival of his birthday wishes, and made no reference to her graduation or his absence from it. Celeste hadn't mentioned it either. She had gently stepped back from his embrace, thanked him for the flowers and wandered into the kitchen to find a vase. Returning to the living room to place her gift on the mantelpiece, she'd had to wade through her parents' viscous silence to reach the other side of the room.

She stopped walking to breathe in the quietness and the greenness of the garden hedges after the evening's downpour. With the exhale she tried to flush out the discomfort of her anti-nostalgia. Was there a word for that? For indulging in painful memories, reliving moments that gave you the meagre succour of being justified in your unhappiness. It was her worst habit. Her everyday method of torturing herself and taking small steps backwards to retreat from a future where she would have no-one to blame.

Breathing in deeply for a second time, she enjoyed the sound of the intake of breath through her nose, and the huge exhale through lips which were still coated in dark red lipstick, the kind that says it will last for 12 hours and stains deep into the flesh. This was the way she'd been taught to breathe at yoga, an exercise for body and mind for which she'd had a brief enthusiasm at university, when she'd discovered that the skinny boy in the oversized yellow jumper taught a class at the church hall at the end of the road where she'd shared a large house and a filthy kitchen with friends she'd assumed would be for life.

Celeste had noticed the skinny boy soon after she'd moved into the student house. He was sharing with a mixed group of boys and girls, all of whom left the lingering sweetness of incense and patchouli in the street whenever they walked past. She'd rarely seen him without the yellow jumper, and he had a collection of hats to complete the look, varying from wool to straw, depending on the weather. She'd watched him chatting easily with friends and acquaintances around campus, or in the local vegan café where he drank green tea, stirring it with elegant fingers and listening with practised intensity to whoever was talking.

For Celeste, this was love at first sight. He was perfect in his otherness; the antithesis of the homogenous track-suited, short haired boys she'd gone to school with. He was exotic and individual. He looked like he was in need of nurturing, with his one jumper, skinny frame and hair pulled back into a bobble just like hers, while sections that had effortlessly escaped from their tether tumbled over his right eye.

She'd tried several times to find a reason or excuse to speak to him, and had managed it more than once, but not in any meaningful way. She'd commented on the queue a mile deep at the local pub on a Saturday night, then casually wandered past the jukebox so she could make some small remark about his great choices. She'd loitered outside the department of Archaeology, Classics and Egyptology, waiting to bump into

4

him as he came out of a tutorial, but he'd walked out chatting with friends and acknowledged her only enough to apologise when they'd accidentally danced by both stepping aside for each other, each choosing left then simultaneously correcting it with a step to the right. She'd dropped her spoon on purpose in the vegan café and he'd dutifully picked it up for her with a smile and a 'there you go' just like she'd planned. But when she'd commented on his excellent choice of macadamia nut and carob brownie, he'd smiled and said it did look good, but it wasn't for him, before standing to greet a willowy, exotic-looking woman with a chain round her ankle that chimed as she strode across to him from the door. The heavy clack of the woman's flip-flops had slapped Celeste right back down as she'd watched them hug enthusiastically and heard the intruder congratulate the boy on remembering her favourite cake.

Orson. She'd found out later that it wasn't his real name, but Orson sounded more original than his actual name Michael, he'd explained, or the Mike, or Mick, or Mikey options that offered him. He'd claimed the name had been foisted upon him by a girl who'd remarked that his prominent philtrum reminded her of Orson Welles. The name had 'just stuck' Orson had eventually told her over a green tea after her fourth yoga class.

It had been completely by chance that she'd spotted him putting posters up about the class. He was fixing them to trees rather than noticeboards, as though the trees themselves would make a better advocate for his promise that he would connect you with your inner chi and help you find peace in your surroundings, no matter where you were or what stresses your studies might put you under. She'd stood behind him to read the home-made poster as he pinned it up without acknowledging there was anyone behind him. The thought of it gave her a touch of the pounding heartbeat she'd experienced at the time, which had made her quite breathless.

He'd spun round energetically to ask her if she was going to join the class and she'd nodded a silent yes, then mustered a comment about how she'd been looking for a class. She'd swooned at the grin he'd given her in response and the 'fab, see you there', that came with it.

But he hadn't seemed to notice her at the first session or the second, so at the beginning of the third class, when Orson had asked were there any ailments or illnesses he should know about, Celeste had raised her hand and her concerns about whiplash she'd suffered in a fabricated minor incident during the week. Her fake injury earned her some special one-to-one attention and the prize of his right hand on her upper back, while his left was placed gently on her stomach as he helped her maintain a straight posture and stand shakily on one leg. It had been even harder not to wobble with the warmth of those long, elegant fingers spread across her shoulder blades.

She'd told him her whiplash was still a problem the following week and, feeling she'd made sufficient connection with her teacher through the intimacy of his special attention during class, she'd asked him if he was free to go for a drink, as a thank you for giving her extra help.

His assurances that it was all part of his duty of care as a yoga teacher hadn't put her off insisting, so he'd agreed, but only to green tea because he never touched alcohol or caffeine after a session. His body and spirit were refreshed, he'd explained, and he didn't want to undo the benefits.

It had turned out she hated green tea, but she drank it anyway, sweetening the earthy wateriness of the hot liquid with her daydreams of where their evening of sipping and chatting might take them. And it did take them back to her room and her bed and his yellow jumper on her bedroom floor. Not just after her fourth class, but after her fifth and her sixth too. Yoga followed by green tea and sex became her Thursday evening routine until they both forgot about the whiplash and she developed a stoic affection for green tea.

But they never spent any time together between Thursdays. When he saw her in the street or at the pub he would smile and acknowledge her as he would anyone else from his class. But there were no enthusiastic hugs or carob brownies. There were none of the evenings out and afternoon picnics she'd offered him. When she woke up on a Friday morning, it was usually to an absence in the bed or a swift peck on the lips and see-you-later.

Eventually, in Celeste's second term of yoga, the woman from the vegan café had turned up beside her at the class with her long, supple limbs and perfect posture. She'd introduced herself as Mimi, with a broad smile of perfect teeth and insincerity. As they rolled up their mats at the end of the class, with Celeste's imagination already skipping past the green tea to planting kisses down Orson's back, the woman had told her to be realistic about what she expected from someone as special as that.

The memory of watching Orson saunter from the church hall arm in arm with Mimi, in step with the easy melody of her laughter, dragged Celeste back to the dismal surroundings of red brick terraces and litter-strewn pavements. She filled her lungs with a deep dose of cold, damp disappointment as she remembered Mimi's words: 'Orson can have any girl he likes, you know. And he often does', but the freshness of the here and now did nothing to erase the burning feeling at the back of her throat. It was just the same as it had been that evening, as she'd imagined where Orson and Mimi might go together as they flowed like water down the street, while she went home alone for a hot mug of cold solace; chocolate digestives dunked in Yorkshire tea.

Celeste pulled on the small star-shaped pendant around her neck as she tried to exhale thoughts of Orson into the evening air. Letting go of negative energy he had called that. The alcohol she'd drunk earlier, courtesy of whatever his name was, had lost its comfort, and she pushed the tiny points of the star into her index finger as she walked, an unconscious habit she'd carried from child to teen to adult. Whatshisname had tried his luck with both Celeste and her friend Esther before

7

finally plumping for Esther's ample cleavage and pleasant lack of sarcastic attitude. Esther had whispered that they'd shake him off, but she'd seemed less and less inclined to do so as the evening wore on and the drinks convinced her that he was funny and quite cute actually.

Eventually, Celeste had decided that getting the last bus home alone was preferable to any awkwardness in the taxi queue later. She'd sat on the bus, trying not to see her own reflection in the window or catch the eye of the one other passenger on the top deck, who'd watched her walk to her seat three rows ahead of him and offered her an unreciprocated smile as she'd sat down. She'd taken her phone from her pocket and scrolled aimlessly past videos of people she didn't know saying things she didn't care about as the bus made rapid progress along empty roads.

She'd counted the stops to home and tried to feel triumphant that she'd not been willing to settle for whatever no-hoper presented himself. It wasn't an easy thought to hold on to. Esther's easy ability to connect with a stranger and be liked clawed at the sides of Celeste's positive spin, fraying the edges of her fragile self-esteem.

'Envy is a fast track to unhappiness' Celeste declared to herself out loud, repeating an affirmation she'd learned from a self-help book. And anyway, he wasn't all that. Esther was welcome to him because Celeste was going to find the man of her dreams and the job of her dreams. Any day now. And move away. Possibly abroad.

Celeste began walking a little faster. Click-clack, click-clack, click-clack. 'And buy new boots', she said to her feet. Her legs aching and her feet sore from standing up all evening in the crowded bar, she looked accusingly at the boot that needed re-heeling because there was something inside it, biting into the soft flesh of her heel, making it painful to take each step.

She was nearly home. She paused. Could she wait the extra steps to get there before sorting out her boot and checking what was attacking her from inside it? Click-clack, click-clack. No, she couldn't. Clack, clack, clack. She hopped to the bench in the community garden they'd built on the corner by the church. The 'Togetherness Garden' they'd called it, probably not because they'd anticipated it would be the place that the neighbourhood stoners would sit together for a smoke. But not tonight. If they'd been there, they must have gone home already and would be busy emptying cupboards of biscuits by now.

On the wall at home there was a picture of Celeste and her mother at the party to celebrate the garden's 'grand opening'. In the picture, she was holding the plant that all local residents had been given to take home for their own garden. They were supposed to nurture it to mark the beginning of this new community space and the efforts of the church to bring nature into the lives of the city dwellers in the surrounding streets. She was immortalised in another time in that picture, smiling against a background where everything was completely new and in bloom. In the present, as she sat down on the bench avoiding the stains that the pigeons had left, the plants were still thriving, mostly, but in the still evening air, she could smell the dog shit that had been left to fester on the carefully laid pebbles and could see where it had been trodden in, smeared and scraped off on the edge of the raised bed. The scent mingled with the odour of vomit and the lingering mustiness of marijuana, smoked by local teens who treated the bench like a living room sofa where they could sit together to get high at a comfortable distance from their parents' disapproval.

This place had been intended as a catalyst for community cohesion where people could sit on the heavy curved bench on sunny afternoons and read a book or chat with friends. At one point there'd been wind chimes as part of a half-formed idea of a sensory garden, but the house opposite had complained that the noise kept them awake at night, so the vicar had removed them.

The space was a nice idea though, Celeste had always liked it. And it came in handy for things like checking your shoes for stray stones on your way home from a night out. The old lady who lived three doors down from Celeste definitely appreciated the bench whenever she over-estimated how much shopping she could carry from the little Tesco or the round-the-corner shop and had to rest on the way home. But mostly it was used as a space to take your dog for a quick toilet stop before work or bed, or for boys in expensive trainers to shake hands and smoke.

Celeste unzipped her offending boot. She raised her bent leg and rested the ankle on her other knee while she took the boot off. There was just enough light from the lamppost for her to see that the heel tip was almost completely gone, and the heel was wearing down at an angle, creating a unique contour tailored to her step. She kept her leg bent and foot off the ground while she shook the boot upside down, and thought she heard something fall to the ground but she wasn't sure. The light was good enough for her to see the boot in her hand, but not to see anything tiny that might have tumbled out. Even if she could be bothered to use the torch on her phone, she'd be unlikely to see it.

Instead, just to be certain that she'd got rid of any irritations, Celeste put her hand inside the boot and felt for any stones or anything loose. There was a hard ridge where the insole had scrunched up to create an uneven surface. Perhaps it was just that making her heel so uncomfortable. She placed the boot on the bench beside her while she massaged her poor, sore heel, considering whether to put the boot back on or carry both boots and walk the short remaining distance barefoot.

The choice between putting the boot back on or walking the last few yards with both boots in her hands was a decision Celeste didn't quite get as far as making. Sensing a presence next to her, she looked up. It was a small action that was more of an instinct than a conscious choice.

With one boot on and one sitting on the bench next to her, she was ill-equipped to run.

2

William

William had known Anne Mitchell since primary school, but it was only in the past six or seven weeks that he'd set about trying to get her to notice him so that they could be together.

Everyone had called her Mitch-the-Titch at school, apart from William. Even after she'd shot up and filled out in her teens, she'd hung onto Mitch and dropped the titch. But she had always been and would always be Anne to him. Classic. Homely. Respectable.

She'd ranted at him once, back in their school days, when he'd called her Anne to her face. She'd declared that Anne sounded like someone's mum's name or the kind of name you'd have if you were a nursery school teacher, or a dental hygienist. 'Do I look like I want to be a dental hygienist?' she'd protested to her audience of friends and groupies in the classroom. 'My name is Mitch. One word. Like Madonna, or Björk, or Drake, or Adele.'

Indeed, she hadn't become a dental hygienist or a nursery school teacher: she worked the late shift in the local Tesco Metro, 4pm to 11.30, five days on, two days off. It was just while she saved up enough air fare to go to India and be an activist and a blogger, she'd explain to any colleagues or customers prepared to listen. William had heard her many times declaring her plans as she stacked the shelves.

The sight of Anne arranging tins, label facing forwards, pained William almost as much as the idea of her moving to India. He knew that her job wasn't making the most of who she was, but it suited him. It gave him a routine knowledge of where she would be every afternoon and evening and an excuse to see her there.

No matter how often he saw Anne wearing her Tesco name badge, he could never think of her as Mitch. She was Anne. William and Anne sounded good together; they had been names paired as married couples down the centuries, since forever. Her name was a sign that they were meant to be together, and they would have similarly traditionally-named children in a life where he would pay the bills and she would shop for their tea at Tesco, instead of working there. They'd have a boy named William, known as Bill or Billy at home, like William's own father, to make it easier to work out who was talking to whom. And a girl named Anne-Marie or Sarah-Anne, who would look just like her mother but sound a little different to avoid any confusion in their perfect, happy home.

William had it all mapped out, he just needed to wait for the right opportunity to broach his vision with Anne, and find the right thing to say in the lead up to that special moment. While he worked his way up to it, he'd bought a lot of things from Tesco. Small, normal things, like packets of pasta and loaves of bread. He never bought alcohol at her Tesco; he didn't want her to think he was a drinker.

If he got to the cash desk and found that she wasn't serving, because it was her day off or she was on a break, he'd just dump his items on the nearest shelf and go back the next day. No point spending money on things he didn't need if it didn't buy him an interaction with his future wife. And he never used the self-checkout, despite having it politely suggested to him by members of staff, including Anne (who was just doing her job when she suggested he pay using a machine instead of talking to her, he was sure).

He had spent the past six weeks learning Anne's routines. He'd found excuses to walk past Tesco and glance in at the window to see whether she was there, discovering within the first few days that she almost always worked later on. He'd gone inside and browsed the shelves without buying anything several times, waiting for her to say she recognised him, and ask what he was up to these days, but she never did.

Once or twice he'd even brushed past her while she was arranging new stock, breathing in her scent, his heart a piston threatening to beat out of his chest. He'd kicked himself afterwards for lacking the courage to accidentally-on-purpose bump into her so that he could apologise.

She had even spoken to him once. He'd stood in rapture, eyes darting from pre-packed sandwiches to take-away salads as she scoured the fridges for items about to go out of date, removing any offending articles onto a trolley and replacing any that had a reprieve until the next day. She'd reached across him with an 'excuse me' to pick up and check the sandwiches directly in front of him. He'd grasped at the initiation of a conversation, asking her if some of the sandwiches were going to be reduced.

'I've just got to get them off shelf for now, love,' she'd replied. 'We'll mark them down and put them back out in a bit. Are you looking for something specific?'

He'd wanted to find something witty and intelligent to say but his mind was almost as empty as the shelf she'd just unburdened of its salads. She'd called him love. She'd called him love and then apparently offered to do him a favour by checking for his preferred convenience food on her trolley of soon-to-be-marked-down items. She must recognise him as a regular customer. Maybe she looks forward to seeing him. Maybe she'd come over to take the limp salads and dried-up sandwiches out of the fridge as a way of getting close to him?

He'd felt the heaviness of silence as his mind raced to come up with a word or even a smile to acknowledge what she'd just said. He'd stared blankly past her discomfort at her breasts and said nothing until she interrupted his lack of words by retreating with her trolley and an uneasy, 'about half an hour till the marked-down stuff goes out.'

The mark-down episode by the fridge had been over a week ago, though to William it felt much longer. Much, much longer. Since then, he had been in the shop six times and managed to be served by Anne at the checkout on five of those occasions. On the sixth, she'd been at the other till, serving someone cigarettes and flirting with them when she couldn't find the right brand.

'They all look the same, apart from the hideous disease top trumps on the side of the packs,' she'd laughed, finally handing over the right packet.

'A bit like your customers, eh love?' the man had replied. He'd been old, too old for Anne, William assured himself, but dressed as though he still thought he was in with a chance with someone as young and lovely as her.

William had smiled at Anne, trying to muscle in on the joke. Trying to communicate without speaking how awful it must be for her to have aging rock star wannabes like this guy chatting her up. But she didn't even look at him. She simply gave the man his change with a friendly 'see you soon' and a sigh of 'next' to the ill-formed queue.

William had followed the man outside with an idea that he might start a fight with him or let down the tyres on his car, but the man was on foot and already striding away to the pub a few doors down. William followed him to the pub and stood at the bar while the man ordered a pint, ordering a Coke for himself and a packet of dry-roasted peanuts. Why not?

When the man took a seat and started scrolling through his phone, William moved over to sit at the table next to him and ate his peanuts slowly, sucking the salt from the outside before crunching. He watched the man sip and scroll, sip and scroll.

Around half-way through William's packet of nuts, the man stood up and asked William to keep an eye on his pint while he nipped to the gents. William nodded and watched the man as he made his way across the room, navigating the tables and the people to reach the toilets. As the door closed, William stood and carefully, making sure he appeared more clumsy, or drunk even, than malicious, knocked over the man's beer with his elbow, making sure it spilt onto the seat and the jacket the man had left there. Leaving the pub with the remainder of his peanuts still clutched in one hand, and a Tesco bag containing a punnet of strawberries in the other, William smiled at his triumph. An empty glass, a damp seat and a soggy, smelly jacket should teach that old Lothario a lesson.

William had walked past Anne's workplace more often than he could count, but he didn't need to keep count because kept a record in his diary. Every time he went into the shop, every time he wandered past and glanced in through the window, he noted whether Anne was working or not. He tracked her shifts and break times, returning later if she wasn't there and making meticulous notes until it was clear that she worked five days on and two days off in a rolling cycle. It was harder to narrow down when she took her breaks. He'd come to the conclusion that it depended on too many variables to be predicted. But he'd learned that she was always in the shop for the first couple of hours and the last hour of her shift, so these became his regular hours too.

He logged times and dates she served him, marking with a big asterisk the day she talked to him about the sell-by-date sandwiches. He noted how she was wearing her hair, if she was wearing make-up or earrings, whether she spoke to anyone else while he was there, jotting down as closely as he could what she had said to them.

For the past three nights he had followed her home from work. Each time, he'd arrived at the shop just before the end of her shift so that he could watch her leave and follow her at a distance to her home, an ordinary-looking semi-detached where she lived with her parents and her brother. Just to see she got home safe. There were weirdos about, after all, and it was late and dark when she walked home.

He'd discovered that she walked home the first few streets of her journey with a colleague. They chatted and laughed as they made their way home. He couldn't hear what they said to each other, but he liked the sound of their to and fro, there was a rhythm to it; irregular and unpredictable but always a sound in response to sound. The friend was taller than Anne with a blonde bob and fake nails in neon colours, like glow-in-the-dark bear claws. William assumed this poor girl must feel so ordinary she had to add the nails and the hair to make herself more noticeable. He recoiled from her and saw Anne as even more extraordinary by contrast. But he was glad that Anne had a friend like that, someone to chat to on the way home. Someone she could compare herself to and see the chasm of difference between them, like he did.

Each time he followed Anne home, he watched as she hugged her friend goodnight when they parted, envious of the blonde girl and imagining what would it be like to be her for that ritual parting moment. He watched as Anne waited while the blonde girl walked up her street. Anne would wait, watching her friend complete the last few steps home, where William could envisage nothing but nothingness for the nameless girl as she vanished from his sight, ceasing to exist.

He had followed Anne the rest of the way home then. Past the shop with its shutters closed for the night, past the community garden, then up the third street on the right to the house with the huge horse chestnut outside, getting ready to burst into flower any day.

For the past three nights, William had followed Anne and made no attempt to make himself known, even when the blonde girl was safely out of the way. For three nights, he had followed her, and she had given no indication that she knew he was there.

But tonight, he noticed her pace quicken as she walked past the shop with its cardboard boxes folded up outside ready for the bin men. He walked faster to keep up at the same distance. And then she stopped without warning, as though obeying a traffic light, pausing under the streetlight next to the community garden to rummage in her handbag.

For a moment he stopped too, unsure what to do next. He could wait until she continued and follow her as before. He could carry on walking and saunter past her as though he were just on his way home himself and their two journeys were unconnected. Or he could finally make his move, actually talk to her, declare himself. It had to happen sometime; why not now?

The silence of his short hesitation had already punctuated their walk home like a full stop. He took in a long, thoughtful breath to slow his racing heartbeat and order his chaotic thoughts. Why not now?

He walked more quickly and more purposefully than before towards where Anne was standing, her face illuminated now by the light from her mobile phone. As he reached her, he raised his arm to tap her on the shoulder. He didn't want to spook her by just appearing out of nowhere, he needed to let her know that he was here to talk to her. He wanted to tell her how he'd been walking her home to make sure she got there safe. He wasn't expecting a thank you, but it would be nice. It would be good to start with her smiling her thanks for his knight-in-shining-armour protection.

But she turned sharply before his hand reached her shoulder and she scowled accusations at him. Didn't he understand that following people home was creepy? Didn't he know that she could get him barred from the little Tesco if he was just coming in to perv at her and not buy anything? Didn't he know that she could get him done for stalking? Or she could get her brother to come round and have a word? Did he know her brother? He didn't want to mess with her brother.

She held up her phone with her left hand and William could see the picture of a young man with the number and a call icon below it.

She could call her brother right now and he'd be there in seconds, Anne told him. 'In fact,' she said, 'I'm calling him and you're going to wait here while I walk the rest of the way home on the phone to him. You're not going to move from here. You're not going to come back into the shop, and you are never, ever going to follow me again. Otherwise, it will be the police I'm calling next time.'

She touched the dial icon, held the phone to her ear and started walking away backwards, telling the voice on the other end of the line how some weirdo creep had been following her home.

William stood watching her go. The blows her words had rained down on him halted his breath and bombarded his brain with thoughts he couldn't control. He couldn't have followed her, even without her threats and accusations. He couldn't move. He couldn't think. She hadn't understood what he meant. She hadn't given him time to speak. Not. Even. One. Word. She hadn't even given him the chance to tap her on the shoulder and explain. Why was she like that? Why hadn't she given him a chance? What was it with girls like that? What kind of a girl was she anyway?

He watched her walk away quickly as the hurt raced towards him. Her phone held tightly to her ear, she was striding forwards away from him now, glancing back at him every few seconds. He could still hear her footsteps. He could still hear her muttering into the phone: 'yes he's still there', 'no he's not moved'. William watched her until she turned into the third street on the right and was gone.

She was gone, and it was as though she had never been there. There was nothing. No sound. No exciting times ahead to look forward to. No hand to hold as he walked her the rest of the way home.

William felt sick. Anne had poisoned him with her accusations and her nastiness. He tried harder to breathe and darted into the community garden to vomit into the bin. But he didn't make it that far, leaning over instead to empty the contents of his stomach onto the roots of a tree, from where they splattered back onto his trainers.

He felt tired. Not the normal kind of ready-for-bed tired, but the kind of tired he usually only felt when he was ill. He heard his mother's voice in his head telling him he must be coming down with something. Perhaps he'd imagined the whole thing? Perhaps he was feverish and delusional? He sat down on the bench in the community garden to calm down and think through it all, placing his hand on his head to check for a temperature. It felt warm. He felt warm all over. Perhaps he really was coming down with something. Maybe he could go and explain to Anne tomorrow that he'd not been well, and she'd understand and ask him to walk her home properly this time?

But as he sat, he knew that wasn't how it had happened or how this was going to go. He hadn't imagined the contempt on her face. He hadn't imagined her accusatory tone or her clear instructions to stay away. Her threats. She'd probably been waiting all this time, letting him build up the idea of the two of them together so that she could batter it back out of him in one cruel, killer punch.

He could smell the stench of his own vomit rising from his trainers and the sourness in his mouth as the foul aftertaste was seasoned by fury at the way Anne had behaved. How dare she lead him on like that? Who did she think she was? No-one important. No-one very attractive. She was nothing. Worthless. A whore. A fucked up little bitch.

He got up to leave, thinking about whether to put his trainers straight in the washing machine so his parents didn't ask any questions, or just leave them outside and hope for more rain.

As he stepped away from the bench, he heard footsteps. For a moment he assumed it was Anne coming back. She wanted to apologise. She'd realised she'd misjudged him. He stood, listening to the footsteps and considering whether he would forgive her warmly, begrudgingly, or not at all.

But the footsteps were coming from the opposite direction, tracing the same path he'd just taken to follow Anne home. And they were different; uneven. The sounds alternated between a dull tap and a sharp one. As they got closer, they slowed down, then paused.

William waited for the sound to start up again and stepped into the darkness behind a tree so that he could see whose feet were approaching.

He watched as a girl entered the garden and sat down, glancing at the ground as though she had lost something and coughing as if clearing her throat to speak. But she didn't speak. He could just make out her silhouette in the dim light cast by the nearby lamp post. She lifted her leg to place her left ankle on her right knee, and took off her boot, shaking it upside down to release whatever might be in there.

He watched her concentrate on this small task, listening out for something falling, placing her hand inside the boot to feel for anything that might have strayed into it. His eyes traced the shape of her long legs, covered by dark tights, with her modesty barely obscured by her tiny skirt, framing legs opened in a teasing, shameless triangle.

He watched her face. Her dark mouth contrasting with the paleness of her skin, and her tongue peeping out as she concentrated on clearing the boot of debris. She was a slut, just like Anne. She'd been out leading on men like him all night with her red lips and short skirt.

As though she could hear what he was thinking, she began teasing him even more to prove it, setting the boot down on the bench and massaging her foot provocatively. William thought about Anne, about how all he'd ever wanted to offer her was devotion, and how she'd stomped on his good intentions with her arrogance and conceit.

He looked at the girl and thought about Anne. He looked at the girl and thought about all girls. He carefully, silently stepped out from behind the tree and stood beside the bench waiting for her to notice him until, after long seconds, she looked up.

3

Yvonne

Yvonne was woken by the church bells ringing out to call the faithful to Sunday morning worship. She was disoriented, wondering for a moment if there might be some terrible disaster and the bells were being used as a signal to raise the alarm.

She had to concentrate to work out why she could hear the noise as it clanged in her stomach as well as ringing in her ears. She was too hot, the light of the sunny May morning coming through the curtains was too bright and the duvet was wrapped tight around her ankle, anchoring her to the mattress. As she kicked her way to freedom, and cooled down by fanning herself with her newly loose covers, she realised she'd slept in. She felt groggy, as though she were waking from a concussion rather than a good night's sleep in a comfortable bed.

Her eyesight was too poor to see the clock plugged in on the other side of the room without the help of her glasses or contact lenses, but the bells rang at 9.15am every Sunday so it must be 9.15. Time to alert those who were both pious and lazy that they had just 15 more minutes to pull on some clothes, brush their teeth and take their pews for the 9.30am service.

It had been a while since Yvonne had slept in so long. Usually, she was awake by 7am on a Sunday, just like every other day, no matter how tired she might be. No matter how much empty time filled every room in the house with nothing to do but tidy and potter. Most Sundays she'd wake early with a jolt, assuming she'd forgotten to set the alarm or slept through it, then she'd slowly realise that she had no bus to catch for work and her daughter, though home again, was old enough to make her own breakfast and pick out her own clothes.

Relieved it was Sunday and there was nothing more pressing than the taste of coffee to call her from her bed, Yvonne would tell herself to go back to sleep. She would make a nest with the pillows, sink into the middle of it with a deep breath, close her eyes and wait for sleep to come to her. But it rarely did. Her mind would wander to the jobs that needed doing around the house, or a remark someone had made in passing at work last week, which could have been barbed but might not have been, she couldn't decide. Or she might replay memories from further back, from when Celeste was a baby or a busy little girl, into everything. From the times just before and after Robert had left, or from the months after Celeste had gone to university, when she'd had to stand in front of the mirror when her daughter called home so that she could force herself to form a smile that Celeste would be able to hear down the line. Sometimes, she would even rehearse whole conversations, reinventing events that had already happened with a new script, or mapping out future events where she always said the right thing and was in full control of everyone else's responses.

No matter how hard she reminded herself to relax and empty her brain of all these things, she couldn't persuade her mind to rest. Her determination to go back to sleep rarely lasted for more than half an hour or so. She would heave herself from the bed, feeling more tired than she had when she first opened her eyes at a time she'd defined as too early, regretting the waste of minutes that could have been better spent.

But this Sunday morning, as the bells ceased suddenly, leaving a quieter silence than when they'd begun, Yvonne didn't feel like she'd been cheated of extra sleep; she felt as though she'd triumphed over sleep. She'd claimed her rightful rest quota. She felt tired though, weighed down from the cumulative exhaustion of years. The gnarled duvet and clammy sheets were evidence that her sleep had not been as restful as she might hope for. They were the trigger for a slow unravelling of her dreams as she raised herself onto her elbows to think and blink at the sunlight searing into the room, highlighting the dancing dust motes over the bed.

In the dream she'd been eating toast in the kitchen, standing by the toaster in her dressing gown so that she could collect each piece as it popped up. She'd felt full but kept on eating and eating, never having to refill the toaster with bread because it just kept producing more toast all by itself. And when the toast appeared she had to eat it. As she ate, she got fatter and fatter, like a balloon being inflated puff by puff and, as she expanded, she found herself less and less able to eat any more, until the toaster was popping up new slices before she'd moved the previous pieces, until there was toast all over the floor.

Back in the room, Yvonne smiled to herself. Why had her sleeping self not just unplugged the toaster to stop it producing more toast? She hadn't thought of that in the dream.

There was more to remember. The kitchen in Yvonne's dream was not her actual kitchen, the toaster looked the same, but the cupboards were different; her subconscious had given her an upgrade. She'd stopped trying to eat the toast and just let it fall to the floor, but her belly had carried on getting bigger and bigger until she'd realised that she wasn't fat with too much toast, but pregnant. The nice man from the shop who always asked her *'how are you today?'* filled the kettle and got some mugs down from the cupboard. *'This is not for your clean towels and hot water,'* he said, *'people don't actually do that. This is for a cup of tea. Don't you think you should ring the hospital? You're having a baby, you know?'*

She'd looked around for her phone, but she couldn't find it. There was toast everywhere and, as she searched through it looking for her phone, the toast carried on making more and more mess. It smelt delicious as each piece catapulted out of the toaster, but it was making the room very warm, and Yvonne had been unable to reach the window or the door, which were in the wrong place, anyway. She'd felt panicked and turned to ask the man from the shop whether he had a phone she could borrow but he'd disappeared and her friend Janine from work was calmly stirring the tea. Of course Janine had a phone she could use to call for help or ring an ambulance. '*But don't worry,*' Janine had said, '*we just need to do this.*' And Janine reached out to Yvonne, opened the front of her bulging belly as though reaching into a cupboard, pulled the baby out and shut the door. The baby was a fully-clothed toddler and Janine put her on the floor, where she quickly crawled around eating up the toast.

Yvonne blinked in the sunshine. Her dream felt so real that she reached down to feel her belly; it was far from flat but certainly not bulging. She was sure she could smell toast though. Perhaps she could smell it because Celeste was up already? It seemed unlikely, given that her daughter been out the night before and routinely slept until breakfast was a late lunch, but it was after nine, so not all that unfeasibly early, and there could be no-one else making toast.

Wrenching herself from the bed, Yvonne put on her dressing gown, feeling vaguely aggrieved that her real-life fleecy robe was nowhere near as nice as the flowery cotton thing she'd worn in the dream. She even wondered for a moment where she'd put that floral one, before dragging her brain back into the real world where her dream nightwear didn't exist.

By the time she reached the landing, there was no longer any hint of the scent of toast, all Yvonne could smell was the 'Ocean Fresh' bleach she'd put into the toilet the night before. She stepped quietly past Celeste's room, resisting the temptation to pop her head round the door. It had been a life-long habit, checking on her chick on her way to bed in the evening and again on her way downstairs in the morning.

For so many years she'd lingered in the doorway of Celeste's room to marvel at the girl's luminous face in the lamplight as her daughter had slept in complete stillness, with her barely audible breath the only sign that she was still living. Indeed, more than once, Yvonne had crept in to kneel by the bed and feel the warmth of her daughter's breath on her cheek, checking that all was well. In the mornings, she'd often found early-teens Celeste reading a book, drawing a picture, or scribbling away in her diary. Sometimes she'd been able to smile at her unnoticed thanks to Celeste's internal world of headphones and concentration. Sometimes, she'd been greeted with a sigh of 'finally, what's for breakfast'. Until eventually, Celeste's enthusiasm for enjoying time in her own sugar pink world on weekend mornings had evolved into long lie-ins and monosyllabic greetings. Into piles of black clothing and empty crisp packets on the floor. Into 'KEEP OUT' signs stuck to the door and 'DO NOT TOUCH' Post-it notes on her diary and her laptop.

Celeste's transition from fairy princess to grumpy teenager had been a painful bereavement for Yvonne, and it was mostly while the girl was asleep that her mother could see the shadow of the child she'd lost, still lingering, but out of reach. Yvonne had reminded herself that a chrysalis was an ugly but necessary phase for a butterfly to take flight. She'd clung to the hand-drawn, carefully composed pictures, still stuck to walls and cupboards around the house, and the rainbow, framing '*Celeste*' in the girl's childish writing on the wall. She'd taken refuge in her memories of weeds picked and presented as flowers, to the feeling of her daughter's weight on her lap, and the shared warmth of snuggling up like that, reading a story or watching a film.

When Celeste had gone off to university, she'd still been stuck in her chrysalis and Yvonne had hoped that she'd meet people there who would help her peel off the layers right down to the woman beneath. Not like that awful Esther who'd always fed Celeste's insecurities and encouraged her to retreat further and further away from the world.

Even since Celeste had completed her studies and returned home to live – who knew for how long – the metamorphosis was still unstable. There were days when Yvonne's daughter was her sweet childhood self; others when she was a thoughtful and insightful young woman, but still some when she was stuck in the murky swamp of her teenage moods, weighed down by the chip on her shoulder and the expectation that the world was way behind schedule in paying up what it owed her. Yvonne's joy at the prospect of her chick returning to the nest had frequently been punctuated by a silent prayer to a God she didn't believe in that her daughter would go out and find her own way in the world. On good days, she hoped that Celeste would stay close by for ever, but there were times when she questioned why she'd ever been foolish enough to have a child at all.

Yvonne had fallen back into the habit of peeking into Celeste's room to inhale a brief moment of affection for her sleeping daughter since the girl had returned home from university, confident she would be dead to the world until at least 11am on a Saturday or Sunday. Until the weekend a few weeks earlier, when she'd pushed the door quietly to find her daughter engrossed in the naked body of a lithe young man who was equally oblivious to the presence of his host in the doorway. Yvonne hadn't mentioned it and had abandoned the habit of looking in on her daughter, morning or evening, unless she knew for certain Celeste had retired to her room alone. One more milestone of a ritual of parenthood unwittingly done for the last time and then gone forever.

This morning, Yvonne avoided flushing the toilet in case the noise might disturb Celeste's sleep. She paused for the smallest of moments outside her daughter's bedroom door to reach for a connection with her sleeping child, even from a distance. As she stepped quietly down the stairs in stealthy slow motion, the bells started up again to mark the beginning of the service, a final call to heed to word of God, and sprint to the church. Yvonne smiled at the ridiculousness of her tip-toeing for the sake of Celeste's sleep against a soundscape of the clamouring call to wake up and rejoice.

The bells rang for a briefer spell. By the time Yvonne reached the kitchen, they had stopped, and the silence rushed in to fill the space with alarming efficiency. Yvonne turned on the radio to push the quiet back to the edges of the room. Elton John was singing that *'you can tell everybody this is your song'* on the Sunday morning love songs programme and the kitchen was back to its usual battered self, with the extractor fan that hadn't worked in years and the tea towel drawer that was carefully held together with duct tape.

Yvonne switched on the kettle, took a mug off the draining board and opened a new box of tea bags, putting two in the teapot and the rest in the almost-empty jar marked 'tea' that Celeste had bought her from a jumble sale as a Christmas present years ago. She eyed the toaster and decided on cereal.

As she took the milk from the fridge festooned with souvenir magnets, Yvonne scanned the counter for Celeste's empty milk glass. Her daughter still insisted on a glass of milk before bed, a habit that had endured from bottle to sippy-cup, to plastic beaker and finally glass. A routine Celeste had extended to eke out the time before bed and add on five precious minutes, that had become a habit she couldn't leave behind. But there was no empty glass on the counter.

There was a rule about milk in the bedroom, ever since a spill that had been vehemently denied, even after the sourness in the air had crept across the landing and down the stairs, lingering for days after the carpet had finally been scrubbed clean. But perhaps Celeste thought herself too grown up for child-proofing rules these days. She was twenty-two now, Yvonne reminded herself, almost the age she herself had been when Celeste was born.

'And this one is for Judith, Susie and Russell, from your mum, Margaret in Hastings. She can't thank you enough for all you've done for her since she's been ill and she knows your dad, Bob,

would be really, really proud of the way you've looked after her.'
The tune started playing as the DJ finished the dedication. It was one that Yvonne didn't recognise, full of high notes and violins. She had an urge to call the radio and request a song for Celeste but there was no one ringing in; these were all songs that had been requested by email or letter.

Yvonne sat at the kitchen table, eating her cereal and sipping her tea, listening to the sentimental songs and dedications of love, thanks and loss that bookended them. When she'd finished her breakfast, she cleared her bowl into the sink and hunted through the odds and ends drawer for a pen and pad while the kettle boiled for water to top up the tea pot.

Then she allowed her hot tea to cool while she composed a note to the familiar voice on the radio. *'I'd love you to play a Sunday morning love song for my beautiful daughter, Celeste, who has been a gift to me since the day she was born. She has no idea how lovely and precious she is, and I just don't tell her how much I love her enough.'*

Yvonne paused to think carefully about which song she should choose. It needed to be a song Celeste would like, but something with the right words; not a romantic love song and not one of those warbling epics with a surfeit of key changes and saccharin sentimentality. She chose Stevie Wonder's *'Isn't she Lovely',* a song she could remember singing to her little girl every time she'd helped her dress up for a party. The chorus played in her head and brought back a scene of Robert dancing Celeste around the living room, with the girl wearing in a pink princess dressing-up outfit and her ex-husband lifting their daughter high in the air every time the word 'lovely' rang out, releasing a peal of giggles.

There was something delightfully old-fashioned in signing her note *'yours sincerely'* and hunting around for an envelope. She found one in the bureau of ancient correspondence and important documents that had stood in the chimney breast alcove of the dining room since the day she'd moved in. The envelope's self-seal had lost its stickiness, directing Yvonne back to the odds and ends drawer to find Sellotape.

Although it was Sunday and the postman wouldn't collect until the morning, Yvonne wanted to be sure her letter made it to the post and arrived at the radio station in plenty of time for her request to make it onto next week's show. And if she could send it off without Celeste seeing, so much the better; it would be much more special if the dedication came as a surprise, not for a birthday or occasion, but just because.

Yvonne looked around to locate her handbag, frustrated as always that she couldn't remember where she'd left it the day before. It was on the sofa, where she'd let it slip off her shoulder on her way in from the supermarket. She extracted her purse and found the stamps she'd kept in there since Christmas when her enthusiasm for sending Christmas cards had waned to a dutiful response to the few she'd received.

Her note written, enveloped, stamped and safely stowed away from prying eyes in her handbag, Yvonne tiptoed back upstairs and past her daughter's bedroom to get dressed so that she could pop out to the post box, dispatch her request and get back for a second cup of tea before the pot was too cold. It felt just like hiding Christmas presents or arranging surprise tickets for a show, a small act of love. A token.

Yvonne left the house smiling to herself, delighted with her secret, and walked past the church and the community garden where two girls were playing. She felt a pang of nostalgia for her own little girl, too old now to be wide awake and full of curiosity at this time on a Sunday morning. She reminded herself to nip into the shop for more milk on the way back because Celeste was certain to need some for breakfast when she got up.

I

Celeste

I can hear a waterfall. I'm listening to the relentless shhhhhh of gallons of water moving. Tonnes of water. How do they measure water? It's too much for pints or litres. It's a river full. Centuries of water moving past me, moving past me, racing past my ears. And when it gets to my ears it speeds up. It sounds up. It greets me louder and faster and then rushes away again.

It sounds like a waterfall, but then it doesn't. The flow fluctuates, adapts. I am trying to focus on the noise and just the noise. Where is the waterfall? If I can hear it, where am I? There is no waterfall near here. But where is here? It must be real because I can feel water. The spray has covered me. I am wet. Cold. I am cold and I am wet. I can hear the deep sigh of water being exhaled, vomited out behind my head.

I could look. If I look, I might get my bearings. But I'm struggling to tell my eyes to open and I am separate from my body. I can feel that body exists. It can feel the wetness on my skin. My skin is prickling in defence against the damp and the air, but it doesn't seem to be part of me. I belong to the sound of that waterfall. Its white noise is in my ears, in my head, behind my eyes, in my eyes. I am the waterfall. Am in the water? If I'm in the water, why aren't I drowning? Am I drowning? Is this what it feels like to drown?

I must focus. I have to think about breathing; how do you do that? My eyes still shut, I picture my nose, two nostrils both open. I concentrate on my mouth. My tongue is still there, I can move it, I can trace the contours of my teeth and feel them all there, solid, hard pieces of me, still strong and immoveable. I open my mouth a little and bring my jaws together to clash the teeth and make a sound. A feeling. All of that is still there. I can move my mouth, I can feel my bite, I can hear the sound of my teeth connecting with each other from inside my ears. Back to my breath. In: long and slow through my nostrils. Out: soft and steady through my mouth. It's moist and energizing. I am alive.

If I can breathe, surely I can open my eyes? This is my breath, and I am in control of it. These are my eyes, and I can tell them when to open and when to stay shut. I command them and, slowly, nervously they listen. The eyelids rise like a theatre curtain.

I can see nothing but grey, so I tell my eyes they must blink and focus. They blink. They focus. The view is still grey. I cannot lift my head and turn it to look for the waterfall; that's too much to ask of it just now. The eyes need to do the work. The eyes need to work with the ears to tell me where this water is coming from and where I am.

I tell them, and gradually they listen to the instruction and send me the information I've requested. There is green. It is soft green grass with daisies waking up for the day, hiding away their pink bellies and undoing their petals for the sunshine. There is grey. A pillar of concrete rising like a cliff face. There is no waterfall, just engines whizzing past below me, duping my ears with their shhhhh. I can't turn my head to see the cars and lorries as they flood past me on the road. Can they see me?

4

Sophie & Laura

Sophie could never understand why Laura liked staying over with Grandma so much. The treats were nice, but going to church on Sunday morning with a no-screens rule until after they'd got back, had lunch, and cleared the table was just mean. It was pointless even trying to sneak the iPad into their overnight bag because Grandma's Wi-Fi was never even switched on.

Grandma said the no-screen rule was to make sure the girls didn't make her late by being distracted by Tik Tok, You Tube and TV instead of getting dressed and brushing their teeth. But it was always Grandma who made them late by losing her keys and stopping to put on her lipstick when the sisters were all ready to go, with their coats on and their hair brushed.

This weekend was Sophie and Laura's first weekend with Grandma for a while. Mum had to work and Dad wasn't feeling well, so Mum had said there was no point in moaning because there was no other way round it. It was either stay with Grandma and bake cakes and have chocolate bought for them, and generally be spoilt rotten, she'd said, or stay at home and fend for themselves while she was at work, listening to Dad make constant trips to the toilet to throw up or, *'you know, the other thing!'*

Grossing them out was a tactic the girls' mum used a lot to shut them up and get them to do as they were told. 'I see more puke and poo in a single shift on the ward than most people see in a lifetime', Faith was fond of saying to her daughters. Sophie had already decided at the age of ten to take her word for it and opt for an office job. Laura was sure she could cope with any amount of blood, guts and bodily functions and, at the age of seven, was quite determined she would follow in her mum's comfortable-shoe-wearing footsteps. She liked the uniform and the idea of bossing people back to bed.

It was one of the many things that marked the sisters out as different from each other. Tall and long-limbed like her mother, Sophie combined her dad's blue eyes with her mum's raucous humour and defiance, and a kindness that made her everyone's favourite, though no-one would say so out loud. Laura had her dad's unruly hair and quick temper, her grandma's impatience, and an impulsive streak all of her own, which often got her into trouble at school.

Despite their differences, the girls were a unit that couldn't be divided, either by the differences in their personalities, or by the three-year gap in their ages. When Laura complained that Grandma had turned up the heating too high and she was struggling to breathe, let alone sleep, Sophie opened the window for her and made up a story about a polar bear to help her sister cool down. When Sophie whinged about bran flakes for breakfast, the weird smell in the fridge and the prospect of spending forty minutes in church, Laura reminded her they would be going to the shop on the way back from the service and that Grandma would let them have a big chocolate bar *each*, instead of making them share like they always had to at home.

They were late for church of course. Predictably, Grandma had reminded them eight million times to brush their teeth after breakfast but, as they'd stood by the door with their shoes fastened and their minty fresh breath, she'd remembered that she still needed to brush her own. Then paused to use the toilet, put on some lipstick and look for her keys.

The second set of bells stopped as they left the house and run-walked all the way. The first hymn had already begun as they quietly, cautiously closed the heavy door behind them and found space on a pew towards the back where they could all sit together and catch up with the second verse. Sophie had been glad that she'd been forced to bring her coat, despite her protests that it was May and it wasn't raining. It was cold in there, and dimly lit like winter, just as it always was, and she breathed in the dampness. The smell reminded her of something, but she couldn't remember what it was, mixed with the heavy floral scent of the large woman sitting in front of them, whose bright red hat and shaky soprano matched each other in scale and unpleasantness.

Laura mimicked the operatic warblings of the woman on the pew in front and Sophie had to focus hard on her hymn book to avoid the giggles. Grandma, relishing the opportunity to open her own lungs in worship, seemed not to notice that Laura's singing was driven by parody rather than enthusiasm. She glanced across proudly at her granddaughter's newly discovered zeal.

The service dragged for Sophie. Laura was good at finding little things for amusement and, between hymns, she occupied herself by watching the other churchgoers, noticing the detail of what they were wearing, how they behaved and who they were with. Most were familiar, but not all, and Laura became particularly engrossed in a couple sitting across the aisle with their toddler. The mother was pulling faces at the little boy to make him laugh, stopping now and then to release her hair from his grip. Her husband was scrolling through the phone he'd placed out of sight on his lap, apparently without realising how much the light from his screen gave him away in the gloomy church.

Sophie was much less able to sit still and occupy her brain. As the vicar explained that peace is a shared responsibility for which everyone, including all those present, must play their own small but important role, she twisted the button on her checked shirt. She twisted it first one way as far as it would go and then the other, repeating both actions again and again until the button came off in her hand and she looked at it as though asking the button why it had jumped off her top like that.

Sophie glanced at Grandma, who was completely absorbed in the sermon. She held the button against the button-hole, already practising an explanation of how it had been loose and had just fallen off. She amused herself by balancing the button on its side on the seat next to her and pushing it gently from side to side like a wheel.

Eventually it was time for the final hymn and one last round of mimicking the lady in front. Sophie opted to join in with the joke this time but was quickly silenced by Grandma's stare of disapproval and reverted to mumbling the words into her hymn book. As the vicar walked back up the aisle towards the door, greeting people warmly and pausing to pat a toddler on the head, the congregation collectively gathered up their coats and bags as though following an unspoken choreography, and began moving as a swarm towards the door and the vicar's firm handshake.

The woman in the red hat smiled a *'lovely singing'* at the girls and, recognising their grandma, paused for a conversation about their health, their families and the weather. Sophie and Laura stood awkwardly waiting, unsure if they were supposed to join in with the conversation or stop eavesdropping.

'Can we go outside, Grandma?" asked Laura. "We can stay in the garden and wait for you by the bench. Can we? It's not raining. We won't leave the garden. Can we?'

Grandma waved them off, barely glancing towards them and echoing her agreement with their plan to stay in the garden.

She continued her conversation as though it were all part of the same train of thought.

It was warm and bright when they stepped outside, as though someone had turned on the heating and all the lights to brighten the place up after the rain of the previous night. The world smelt fresh and green, with spring foliage bursting from every corner following weeks of constant switching between sunshine and heavy showers.

Having won their freedom more easily than expected and edged their way through the small but tightly packed bottleneck of congregation stragglers loitering outside the church for a word with the vicar or a chat with a friend, the girls were unsure what to do next. They were unused to empty minutes with no adult instruction and no screen to occupy them.

Sophie felt lost for a minute and had to reassure herself that they were only temporarily alone. Their grandma would reappear at any moment to stand with the other churchgoers as though at a party, hovering near the snacks while they mingled.

Laura was eager to do something as soon as possible to make the most of their freedom while it was theirs. She wandered confidently into the community garden, expecting Sophie to follow. And Sophie, just as she had every day of her life since the day her younger sister had learned to walk, followed Laura.

The girls copied one another, walking around the edge of the garden slapping leaves in relay to make droplets of rain that had fallen during the night bounce off them, hitting the foliage harder and harder as they walked around the garden to make the rain splash back at themselves. When they hit a leaf sharply enough, the rainwater jumped upwards, as though the rain were rewinding.

With giddy faces glowing with laughter and a thin veil of rainwater, the girls made their way to the bench to wait, but Sophie could see her Grandma deep in conversation with two other women, one of whom was leaning in close to whisper. It was clear they were going to be left to their own devices for a

37

while. She sighed. She hated waiting. She hated being bored. She looked to Laura to come up with another idea for what they should do next, while Grandma's two minutes stretched out into half an hour.

But Laura was engrossed in looking at the brown boot she had found on the bench next to her. She was turning it round in her hands, pulling the zip up and down and picking at the heel where the plastic cap had worn almost completely away and was ragged at the edges, revealing a hollow space inside. She poked her little finger into the hollow and grimaced as she plucked it back out.

'Look at this. It's a nice boot. Who would leave a nice boot like this here?' She said, turning to present the boot to Sophie.

'Maybe someone lost it?'

'How can you lose just one boot? How could you not notice that? You'd have to hop home. It's not even the kind of boot that could fall off, look.'

Laura pulled the zip up and down several times in front of Sophie's face to demonstrate the secure fastening and the unlikeliness of it falling off someone's foot by accident.

Sophie took the boot from her sister and tried the sole of it against the sole of her own trainers for size. It was similar.

'Try it on.'

'I'm going to.'

Sophie handed the boot to her sister while she took off her own shoe, then took it back and placed it on the ground so that she could step into it like Cinderella. It was too big, but not by much.

'It fits you. It actually fits you!' Laura clapped and bounced up off the seat.

'It's a bit big. But I like it. I wonder if we can find the other one.'

Sophie took a stroll around the bench, limping with her one heeled foot and one flat trainer and scouring the paving slabs and under the bushes to see if she could spot the other boot. If the matching boot turned up, she planned to take them home and tell her mum that a friend had given them to her. But there was no sign of the other boot.

Sophie sat back down and switched from the boot back into her trainer.

'It's no use to you if there's only the one,' Laura pointed out. 'And anyway, we don't know where it's been, it might be full of germs. A dog could have weed in it...'

'Or a squirrel.'

'Or a rat!'

Sophie gingerly sniffed the boot.

'It smells OK. But I'm not keeping it, there's no point.'

'No point.'

Sophie continued to hold onto the boot while both girls looked at it. She was unable to think of a use for it but unwilling to let it go.

They were still and quiet for a moment until Laura suggested they play hide the boot with it.

'Like hide and seek, except instead of looking for each other we hide the boot, and the other person has to find it.'

Sophie looked towards Grandma, who was now nodding and smiling, deep in conversation with the vicar.

'OK, you close your eyes while I hide it then.'

They took turns hiding the boot. First in the bushes, then under the bench, then behind the bin. 'It stinks near that bin,' complained Laura. 'Euurgghhh! There's puke on that tree. Disgusting!' They moved the boot again, taking it in turns to close their eyes and count or be the hider. There were limited options, but enough to keep them going until Grandma came over to ask who wanted to pop to the shop on the way home and get some chocolate for later.

Released from the need to entertain themselves, the girls instantly abandoned their game and the boot was left in its hiding place, concealed by vibrant red geraniums, while they twirled and skipped ahead of their grandma down the pavement towards the shop.

Grandma smiled at the girls as they enjoyed the sunshine and the freedom of being young enough not to edit their behaviour or question what their bodies could do. She remembered watching her own daughter skip the same route to the shop to buy a treat after church and wondered where the years in between had disappeared to. She clung to the sight of her granddaughters as they jumped off and on the kerb, knowing that this wouldn't last forever either. One day, in the not too distant future, chocolate would no longer be a sufficient incentive to persuade them to accompany her to church, or wait for her while she caught up with the friends she never saw except on Sundays after the service.

The shop was busy with people who'd pulled on jeans or tracksuit bottoms over their nightclothes to pick up supplies for a lazy breakfast. Grandma soon lost sight of the girls as they disappeared behind the queue to choose their treat. She elbowed her way through the rows of dishevelled Sunday morning shoppers, collecting tuts and dark looks of disapproval as she navigated her way through the shared assumption that she was trying to push in. She found the girls, each clutching a bar of chocolate, and looking for her.

They greeted each other as though they'd been searching for hours, the girls and the grandma both blaming the other for their disappearing act.

In the queue, clutching her bar of chocolate while her sister stood surreptitiously peeling the wrapper off the corner of her own bar next to her, Sophie eavesdropped on her grandma's conversation with the woman standing behind them in the queue.

She hated it when people remarked on how big she and Laura were getting. As though growing up was somehow a surprise, or an act of defiance. As though she could choose not to if she wanted.

'It soon goes, doesn't it?' she heard her grandma remark. 'It doesn't seem two minutes since they were born. It doesn't seem two minutes since you were pushing your little one round in her buggy trying to get her to sleep. What's your daughter called again?'

Sophie cast a critical eye over the woman's shabby green cardigan and tried to imagine what she would be like to have as a mum.

'Celeste,' the woman replied.

Grandma was finally at the front of the queue. Laura already had the corner of her chocolate bar in her mouth and was busy trying to make the wrapper look like it hadn't been tampered with, so Sophie started to peel back the paper from her own treat, until Grandma took it from her to be scanned at the till.

'That's right. I remember. A lovely name. A gift from heaven,' Grandma smiled as she handed the chocolate back to the girls.

'She's twenty-two now,' the woman added as Grandma paid. 'She'll be twenty-three in September. It's funny how pushing her in the pram seems like two minutes ago and a lifetime ago all at the same time.'

The older woman smiled. 'I know, love. I know. You take care.'

Sophie tore the wrapper from her chocolate bar and snapped off a row of squares. She repeated the name Celeste in her head. Nice.

5

Moira

Moira was struggling to sleep in the light mornings of spring. She'd been woken early, around five, by the rain hammering down outside; a downpour that had hosed down the world ready for a new day, like the outdoors taking a shower before work. She'd told herself to let the sound lull her back to sleep. She'd reminded herself that the sound of rain outside when she was cosy and dry inside should be comforting. It was comforting, but it didn't help her sleep.

Sleep had always been a problem for Moira, and she'd been tired for as long as she could remember. As she lay in bed, inert from the massive sleep debt she'd accrued over decades, she tried to recall the last time she'd slept through a whole eight hours without waking. It was before the boys were born, certainly. She remembered how she'd slept like an invalid in the early days of her pregnancy with William, always nodding off if she so much as sat down. Back then, she'd taken herself off to bed with a book and a glass of milk by 9 o'clock every night and never managed to read more than a page or so before abandoning her book on the bedside table with the dregs of her milky nightcap. She'd slept through the night then, alright. They'd even joked about it. Bill had said that the baby would be born wearing a pair of pyjamas. He couldn't have been more wrong. William hadn't slept for more than two consecutive hours from the day he was born until he was what? Two? Three maybe? It was a long time ago now; her bundle of sleeplessness would be twenty-two in a few weeks' time.

There'd been no chance of sleep when she'd been pregnant with James two years later, she'd just had to get on with it. *'Sleep when your baby sleeps'* they'd told her when she'd been anaemic and struggling to cope. The irony was that James had slept. She'd been able to lay him down anywhere - in his cot, in his pram in the middle of a busy shopping centre, in the garden while his brother made a din with toys and wailing around him; he'd napped for hours. But the health visitor had had no advice for when to sleep if your toddler won't let you close your eyes even for five minutes.

James was still the easy one, away at university in Newcastle now and sending pictures here and there to let her know he was fine. But William was still causing her sleepless nights. Her eldest son had been a high achiever at school. Top of the class throughout primary and a walking encyclopaedia, one of his teachers had said. The only negative feedback at parents' evenings had been that he needed to give the other children a chance to contribute in lessons. Just because his hand shot up every time the class was asked a question, they'd told her, it didn't mean he could always be the one picked to give the answer. She remembered how William had got angry about that sometimes, ranting about how the stupid kids were picked to give stupid answers and congratulated by the teacher for a 'good try', when he'd known the right answer all along but never got picked. He'd been angry at the unfairness of it, and would accept no alternative definition of fair from her.

Moira turned, berating herself for letting her mind wander instead of focusing on getting back to sleep. What's the point in mulling over what you can't change? Regurgitating the past made it no easier to digest, so best just leave it where it lay to settle.

43

She could feel Billy's breath too close to her face and turned again. Eyes back towards the window, she reminded herself to focus on sleep, but her thoughts drifted back towards William.

Secondary school had been more challenging for her elder son: a bigger pond with smarter fish. He'd been in the top set for everything and tackled his homework as soon as he got home every evening. But his friends were also his rivals, and he could barely contain his loathing for them if they scored better than him in a test. Moira had found a notebook in his room with tables of end of term exam results where he'd noted down his own mark and those of his peers. If someone else had scored higher than him it was circled in red and there were notes at the bottom of the table, with reassurances and action points William had made for himself. *'Anthony scored 2% higher in geography but I did better in English, French and History so still better overall', 'Marcus has exactly the same score as me in English and History – need to be careful re cheating', 'Olivia got higher in French, English and Geography AGAIN!!! Make sure she's aware of my results in Maths and Science'.*

Moira had been disturbed by the notebook and the idea that her son was constantly measuring himself against other people. It had taken her just a couple of pages to realise that he was keeping a record of every small failure and grievance, always blaming someone else for his angst and plotting small ways to get his own back. She could see, as she carefully turned the pages, unable to stop reading despite her growing discomfort, that his catalogue of punishment and recompense comprised taking action so subtle that no-one was ever likely to notice. In fact, much of his retaliation had simply been to write down the offences in his book, using capital letters and underlining to condemn his tormentors.

'Funny how you make yourself do those things', she thought, turning the pillow over to its cold side in another attempt to get comfy for sleep. It had been like picking a scab or biting a nail that's already down to the quick, reading on and on through pages of her son's hurt and resentment. She'd known she should just stop reading and put the notebook back where she'd found it, guarding William's damaged pride and absolving his vitriol. It had hurt to read on, but it had been completely compelling; like the cheese in the fridge and the biscuits in the cupboard.

And giving in to that compulsion had hurt her more and more as she surrendered to it. She'd felt pity for William, guilty for raising a son that had to process his emotions by itemising every blow to his ego in his small, sloping scrawl. She'd also felt angry with him for exposing her to both of their failures by committing it to the page. In her hand, every episode existed, it was real and permanent. All those fleeting disappointments and thoughtless comments that litter an existence had not been washed away by distractions or a change in mood, or the influx of tiny nice things that could have offset them. William had plotted a course of sourness, anchoring every episode in place and time, allowing her to find it.

Inevitably, Moira had found reference to herself in the notebook too. Most of the pages had been filled with school rivalries or references to teachers who'd failed to understand him, or had taken pleasure in humiliating him. But there were occasional references to how she'd snuck mushrooms into the lasagne to piss him off, or ignored him when he was explaining something because she'd been so caught up in praising the pathetic achievements of his brother James, even though it might benefit her to learn from his knowledge.

Moira shuddered with discomfort at the memory, realising that she was picking that scab once again. But she was unable to stop. As she tried to fall in with the regular rhythm of Billy's heavy nearly-snore, she carried on fretting away at the memory until it bled, her subconscious belligerently refusing to do as it was told.

Moira remembered how William and James had returned home early the day she found the notebook, because the heating system had failed, so their school had closed just after lunch.

The school where she worked had been on half term, but the boys were not breaking up until the following week, and she'd been making the most of the empty house to get ahead of jobs so they could all be free at the weekend. The boys' head teacher had sent an email, but she hadn't seen it. Funny how those random, disconnected blips in the natural order of things can send a meteor crashing into an ordinary day, she thought as she gently nudged Billy to give her more space in the bed.

She'd been surrounded by half-organised clean washing, with the contents of William's bin neatly tied in a bag by her feet when her son had walked into the bedroom to find her reading his notebook. He'd entered the room full of smiles, excited to share his news of the boiler breakdown and how he'd missed geography, but his expression had changed immediately when he recognised the notebook.

She'd protested that she hadn't been reading it, that she'd just found it when she was tidying up. Her sentence had gone on and on as she tried to justify the evidence in her hands, but he'd just stood there looking at her. So, she'd rambled about the washing and how he was old enough to put his own things away in his drawers and she could just leave it downstairs for him to bring up to his room and organise himself if he preferred. She'd done her best to plot a route out of the room with words, but every syllable had become trapped in a moment that wouldn't move forward, while all the time she'd clutched the notebook with its pages still open.

Her supplications had trickled to a stop mid-sentence. She'd found herself feeling incoherent under his gaze. He'd walked silently towards her, taking just two steps and bringing with him the familiar teenage boy base notes of stale sweat and hormones. He'd snatched the book from her then, held it up in front of her and snapped it shut so close to her face that she'd felt a draught from its pages as they closed, and flinched as though he'd slapped her.

'You can go now,' he'd said, and he'd stood so close she'd been able to feel the warmth of his breath until she moved to the door.

She'd paused there, hoping he might say something, thinking she might be able to find some words that would tip the whole thing into a chance to have a shared moment, a shared secret with her son.

'We're very proud of you,' she'd whispered without turning round to look at him.

The contents of William's bin had hit her on the shoulder with the words, 'you can take that rubbish down with you' and she'd picked up the neatly tied bag full of crisp wrappers and used tissues with the sound of her racing pulse throbbing in her head.

Moira looked up at the ceiling, searching out the swirls of the ancient Anaglypta so that she could distract herself from the memory of the day she'd found the notebook by focusing on something mundane. She knew every nuance of that ceiling; every crack, every patch where the paint hadn't quite covered the ancient tobacco stains of the house's previous owners. She'd lain there many nights, tracing her thoughts around the repeated sequence of motifs, losing herself in a trance far away from the stifling routine of raising her family and the snoring of a husband who was increasingly disinterested in her or anything she had to say.

But the maze of worries and sadness in the ceiling weren't going to help her sleep. And the rain had stopped abruptly, as though someone had turned off the tap, the sun sending fingers of light to clutch the edges of the curtains, promising a good drying day. If she pulled herself out of bed now, she could get the washing out on the line again after its soaking in yesterday's showers, and put another load in. And there was that nice marmalade she'd bought the day before, the one with the big chunks of orange in, she could have tea and toast in the peace and quiet before Billy and William interrupted the silence of the house.

A quick glance at the clock gave her permission to vacate the bed: 7.34 – nothing like a Sunday morning lie-in but not the middle of the night. She slipped from under the duvet, crept round the bed, took down her dressing gown from the hook on the back of the door, and left the room with a much-practiced silence.

The quiet followed her downstairs and filled every corner as she wandered into the kitchen to put the kettle on for a cup of tea. Every small noise she made exploded into the room like a pebble thrown into a pond. The click of the light switch, the brief whirring of the fluorescent strip and its final ping into life as the current became light. The swoosh of water from the tap and the double click clack of first the switch at the socket and then the button on the kettle as she set it to boil. The steady build-up of heat as the water began to mutter and grumble. She was transfixed by the sounds in a much more dream-like state than she'd managed while lying in bed.

She orchestrated the sounds, they were all part of her morning symphony that gently eased her into the new day.

William's voice behind her as the kettle reached its crescendo, asking her what she was doing up so early on a Sunday morning, tore through the serenity and jolted her into full wakefulness like a defibrillator, causing her heart to leap in her chest.

Turning to find him standing in the doorway, fully clothed with muddy trainers on his feet, she recoiled from the dampness and unpleasant sourness he exuded, both in his expression and his odour. she mumbled something about not being able to sleep and his dad's snoring, then volleyed the same question back at her son.

'Same', William replied, but rather than limiting the answer to his usual monosyllabic response to questions, he launched into a long-winded tale of sleeplessness and getting up in the night and deciding to go for a walk to get some air and tire himself for sleep. His narrative explained the route he'd taken and how he'd been to the park ended up near the canal. He paused, as though thinking back to his walk and reliving the experience, 'I saw a fox', he said, and he told his mother all about how the fox had stared right at him and more-or-less invited him to follow.

Moira listened without interrupting, finding it hard to connect the familiar face of her son with this chatty young man with so much to say.

6

Yvonne

Celeste didn't like bananas, but she liked banana cake. Yvonne had joked with her daughter for years about how she would only accept fruit when it was transformed into the least healthy version of itself; banana when it became a loaf, grapes when they became raisins, oranges when they were Jaffa Cakes, and apples when they were fixed to a stick and covered in chocolate and sprinkles.

If she was honest with herself, Yvonne wasn't a huge fan of bananas either. She admired them as a self-contained, healthy snack, with a natural wrapper, no pips, and built-in portion control. But their softness and smell made the reality of eating a banana in its natural state much less appealing than the idea of it. She often took a banana on a day trip to the office, only to bring it home again in the evening and leave it on the kitchen counter, where, looking less appealing than ever with its browning skin and developing mushiness, it would sit waiting until she grabbed it on her way out of the door the following day.

Yvonne dropped her keys and purse onto the kitchen table with the milk and bananas she had bought from the shop. She took off her green cardigan and hung it over the open door. It was too warm for cardigans, but not warm enough for bare arms. Too overcast to risk pegging the washing out, with the line still wet from the night before, but not cold enough to put the heating on to dry it. First world problems, she reminded herself. But annoying, she said out loud. Annoying not to have anyone to whinge to about it in the empty kitchen while Celeste slept through the morning.

She switched the radio back on and sang along to a power ballad, able to remember all the words but not the singer. She put the milk away in the fridge and took the bananas into the living room, replacing three tired brown ones, with the new bunch of five fingers of sunshine. When Celeste woke up, it would be to plenty of milk in the fridge and the smell of freshly baked banana cake. '*It's a cake not a bread*', Yvonne smiled, thinking of her daughter's regular rant. '*Why do people insist on calling it bread when it's clearly cake? Does it have yeast No. Does it have egg? Yes. Can you use it to make cheese on toast? Mop up your gravy? Have a chip butty? No. No. NO! Because it's not a bread, it's a cake!*'

As she walked back into the kitchen reminding herself to eat the new bananas before their skin warned her they were past their best, Yvonne pictured herself and Celeste laughing about all the bits of shared irritations and interests that connected ordinary days into lives lived together. She had missed her daughter with a grief that had been hard to bear when Celeste went to university. She had found it hard to cook a meal just for herself and spent the first few weeks eating the same thing two nights on the trot because there had been two portions. She'd bought plastic boxes in the end to store Celeste's dinners in the freezer and whenever she had visited her daughter in Liverpool, a plastic box of unidentified frozen meal had gone with her, slowly defrosting en route and there to feed her daughter the following day. 'Freezer surprise', they'd called it, after Celeste had messaged to say 'thanks for the freezer surprise – you are the best!!' after the first time.

But Yvonne's visits to Liverpool had been few. Celeste had been busy. And it had often just been a day trip. Celeste had

51

come home too, of course, sometimes for weekends, always for holidays, but having her visit was not the same as having her there.

Yvonne took out a large bowl, peeled the past-their-best bananas, discarded the skin in the little compost bin under the sink and began mushing. She'd been distressed for her daughter when her job applications had gained her an interview but never a job. It had been hard to see Celeste compare herself to friends since she'd returned home and watch her try to retain her confidence in the face of so much rejection. But her daughter's disappointment had been Yvonne's opportunity to wrestle back a place at the centre of Celeste's life. They had chatted, drunk wine together, ranted at the TV news, left little notes for each other, relied on each other for a shoulder to cry on and a quick cheer up, bitched about strangers' dubious fashion choices. Yvonne missed her little girl as she mashed and mashed, releasing an even stronger scent from the banana, but she was delighted with the adult woman who had replaced her. 'What a pity I can't keep both of them', she said out loud. 'Come on Yvonne, you're making cake, not pity pie.'

The DJ shared a sad tale of a devoted husband sadly lost a year ago and played Roy Orbison, adding, as the song began, that this was for everyone who had lost someone this year. Yvonne stirred as she listened to the words of the song, it was a beautiful sentiment, but bringing someone else's grief into the kitchen felt like an intrusion of both their privacy and her quiet morning. Why did people feel the need to share their most personal thoughts and feelings with a radio DJ and all the strangers listening to the radio? Why did they want to share it with any strangers? She wondered if it had been such a good idea to post the letter asking for a dedication to Celeste after all. Maybe she should just have invited her daughter to a kitchen disco and told her she loved her face to face instead?

The banana cake was more of an intuitive experiment than a recipe, it always had been. A few times Celeste had said 'that one was amazing, can you make it like that again', but Yvonne never could. There were too many variables – how many bananas, how ripe they were, what else she might add – raisins, sultanas, walnuts, pecans, yoghurt... a lot depended what was in the cupboard or the fridge on the day and how bold she was feeling about chucking in new ideas. In the big bad world, Yvonne had never had the courage or impulse to be rebellious, but in her own kitchen, where the worst that could happen was a cake that no-one wanted to eat, she could throw caution to the wind and do whatever popped into her head. Not carrot and banana though. She'd tried that once and it hadn't ended well – carrots needed to stay in their lane.

A few pecans, a dash of cinnamon and some dried cranberries dangerously close to their use-by-date later and the cake was ready to go in the oven. Yvonne took a paper loaf case out of the cupboard, used it to line the tin and poured in the mixture. She adjusted the oven shelf to sit in the centre, placed the tin inside – sideways on like her mother had taught her – and checked the time. 10.50. Time for a quick shower before the cake was baked and then she would wake Celeste. 'Don't let me sleep in past 11' Celeste had said, but Yvonne knew that what she really meant by that was, 'call me at 11 and I might be out of bed by 12'. Yvonne smiled at how well she knew her daughter and how much a girl of that age could sleep; let her enjoy it while a lackadaisical body clock and lack of responsibility would let her.

Yvonne switched on the shower to warm up, then went back to her bedroom to choose some clothes for the day to replace the old joggers and T-shirt she'd thrown on to go to the shop. She paused outside Celeste's bedroom on her way back to the bathroom to listen for signs of life. It was quiet, the only noise in the house was the whir and waterfall of the shower, and the radio downstairs, where the DJ was wrapping up the show and wishing everyone a great week ahead. Shower, Celeste, Cake, Yvonne reminded herself. In that order.

Her thoughts turned to her own life as a twenty-two-year-old as she soaped herself in the shower. She'd been working by then and living in a house share in Salford. She'd thought herself all grown up. She had been grown up. She'd had rent to pay and meals to cook; though a meal had quite often been a Pot Noodle or cheese on toast. Her Pot Noodle days were behind her but cheese on toast was a good idea – perhaps she would have that for lunch.

Yvonne got dried and dressed, reminding herself not to dawdle because Celeste's vague timetable might be flexible, but the cake would be baked when it was baked, and five minutes could make a big difference. She checked the time, it might be ready by now, she could put socks on later.

She knocked on Celeste's bedroom door. 'It's just gone 11 Celeste. You said to wake you up so you don't waste the day. Do you want a cuppa?' No answer. Banana Cake. Kettle on. Try again.

She sprinted down the stairs. The problem with baking a cake by intuition rather than by recipe was that there was no specified bake time. It could be burnt; it could be raw. There was no smell of burning though; just that comforting warm sweetness slowly spreading through the house. It could be ready.

She opened the oven. The cake was browning around the edges but was still like blancmange in the centre. She pushed the shelf back in, closed the door and turned the temperature down a little.

Tea. When she'd been in the house on her own, Yvonne would just make tea in the mug, so the brown teapot had sat largely redundant on the counter-top for weeks on end when Celeste had been at university. She remembered the row they had when Celeste had thrown the old brown teapot in a rage. The replacement Celeste had bought was both identical and a symbolic legacy of that argument. They had used it to make and share tea ever since, solving the problem of the smashed pot and salving the issues of their fractured relationship over hot tea, warm chats and an inestimable number of Jaffa Cakes.

With the tea brewing in the pot, Yvonne checked the cake again. Less wobbly but still not done. She poured a mug of tea for Celeste, leaving her own in the pot, and added a splash of milk before heading upstairs. Maybe she should have made her some toast too? She was bound to be in need of carbs after a night out, and no toast tastes as good as toast someone else has brought to you in bed. Tea first. Yvonne reminded herself not to over-do the waiting on her daughter hand and foot. It had to be a kindness, not an obligation. If tea and toast in bed was offered too freely, too often, it might be taken for granted rather than appreciated. Sharing the house with her adult daughter was a constant balancing act, with Yvonne's desire to give love on one scale, and her need to be shown love on the other.

Yvonne knocked on Celeste's bedroom door. No answer. She knocked louder. 'Rise and shine. I've got a cup of tea for you. Wakey wakey sleepy head.'

She knocked again. 'Can I come in?' She was cautious about walking in without permission, even after knocking, in case Celeste had brought someone home with her. She didn't usually have a guest in her room, but caution was better than embarrassment for both of them.

Yvonne knocked again, louder still. 'Come on Celeste, this tea will get cold, and I've got a cake in the oven. I'm surprised the smell of baking hasn't got you up already.' Knock, knock, knock. The kind of knock that Yvonne's own mother had referred to as a bailiff's knock. 'I don't really want to leave it on the landing, it'll go cold, and you'll only knock it over when you finally do get up.'

She listened. There was no noise, apart from the cheerful tones of the next DJ chatting away to an empty kitchen downstairs. If Celeste had a friend with her, they were both asleep. Yvonne opened the door slightly and peeped in. She could see the bed. She could not see Celeste. She opened the door properly. She could see the room. She could not see Celeste. 'Celeste?' Yvonne switched on the light. The room was a mess. The bed was a mess. It was the same mess it had been the day before, with Celeste's potential outfit choices still strewn across the duvet.

Yvonne put the mug of tea down next to the bed as though still delivering it to her drowsy daughter, and went to find her phone. It wasn't in the kitchen. Where had she left it? She'd not somehow left it in the shop had she? She fought against the fog of frustration and remembered she'd taken it up to the bedroom to keep an eye on the time when she was getting showered and dressed. She sprinted back upstairs, found the phone and dialled Celeste's number. She heard it ring several times and then switch to the familiar recorded message '*Hi, you've reached Celeste. Don't leave a voicemail because I never listen to them. message me. See ya.*' She did as a previous version of Celeste had instructed and sent a text message. 'Hey, it's Mum. Just checking where you are. Message me to let me know you're OK will you? Love you xx'

Yvonne paused. Celeste had been used to not having to let anyone know where she was when she'd lived away. She sent the same message to Celeste on WhatsApp. She looked at the screen to wait for the ticks. One tick. Two ticks. But the ticks didn't turn blue, they just sat there.

She called again. Again, Celeste's recorded voice told her not to leave a message. She sat on the bed and looked at Facebook. Nothing. Instagram, a story from the night before with Celeste posing and smiling by herself and with Esther. Could she message her on Instagram? She didn't know how it worked really, Celeste had tried to show her and laughed that Facebook was so Gen X. Yvonne hadn't listened and now she wished she'd paid attention. She looked at WhatsApp again, the ticks were still grey. She tried calling again, Celeste's voice was still a recording. She checked for a reply to her text, there was nothing.

Celeste had stayed out before, once or twice, a handful of times since she'd been back from university. But she'd texted every time to say not to worry. And she'd called in the morning to give Yvonne an idea what time she'd be home. Yvonne checked her phone again. There were no messages. There were no missed calls. Maybe Celeste had tried to call or ring but her phone had run out of charge? No. The phone had rung when she'd called, Celeste had just not answered. Maybe she'd lost her phone or it had been stolen? Celeste would have found a way to get in touch. She would have called from Esther's phone. She would have come home and said *'I've lost my bloody phone!'*. Yvonne ran downstairs again to the landline in the hall and dialled the voicemail. There was a message from the optician confirming an appointment for Tuesday morning, that was all. Where was Celeste?

Esther! Esther would know. Yvonne searched her contacts for Esther's number, but she didn't have it. She could go round to Esther's to ask her where Celeste was. No. She realised she didn't know where Esther lived either. Everything had changed since the girls were at school together. Esther didn't live with her parents anymore. The girls didn't tell their mums where they were going and what time they would be back. They just came and went. But they were still supposed to come back. Joanne. Esther's mum. She might not know where the girls were, but she would know Esther's number. She would put Yvonne in touch with Esther, one step closer to Celeste.

Yvonne fumbled through her contacts again and called Joanne E Mum. It rang a few times before she heard a man tell her in a Yorkshire accent that 'the person you are calling is not available.' Yvonne ended the call and almost immediately her phone rang. *'Hello Yvonne, lovely to hear from you...'*

'Joanne? Joanne. Listen. The girls were out last night. Celeste and Esther...'

'I know. I...'

'Is Esther home? Have you heard from her? I know it sounds stupid and paranoid and dramatic but Celeste isn't home. She hasn't been home since she left to go out last night I mean. And she would normally text or call or text *and* call if she was going to be out all night. But she hasn't texted, and she hasn't called. She's not here Joanne. I don't know where she is. Have you heard from Esther? Do you know where they are? Do you...'

'Yvonne. Yvonne. Just breathe for a minute. They're fine. I'm sure they're fine. Esther never texts or calls. I'm lucky if I hear from her once a fortnight. Let me ring her now and see if Celeste is with her or if she knows where Celeste is. She's probably just had one too many, crashed at Esther's and forgotten to text. The pair of them will be fast asleep blissfully unaware that you're worried.'

'You could just give me Esther's number and I'll call. Hang on, let me find a pen...'

'Yvonne. Honestly. It will be fine. I'll call Esther. You keep your phone free in case Celeste calls. I'll ring you straight back. Or Celeste will. One of us will.'

The call ended and Yvonne sat on the stairs. She checked for blue ticks on the WhatsApp message again. They were still grey. She stared at the home screen, a picture of Celeste aged about six with her face covered in chocolate. She waited for the phone to ring.

Yvonne answered as soon as the phone made a sound a moment later. 'Yvonne, don't worry. Esther didn't pick up but that doesn't mean anything's happened. It just means she hasn't answered her phone. She's a devil for screening her calls. I'll keep trying her, you keep your phone free in case Celeste calls. I'll let you know the minute I get hold of them. Then we can string them up together for worrying a decade off our lives. Speak to you in a bit.'

Yvonne found nothing to say but 'OK'. But it wasn't OK. How could it be OK? She checked for the blue ticks again. They were grey. She should keep the line free. She should wait to hear back from Joanne and Esther. But what if something had happened and she was sitting here doing nothing? What if something had happened to both of them?

She called from the landline to keep the mobile free. '*Which service do you require?*'

'Police please.'

Yvonne took a deep breath as her call was put through.

The scent of burning cake crept through the hallway unnoticed.

II

Celeste

*T*here is a coldness running through me like a river. It has taken over my veins and I am no longer a warm-blooded creature, but a cold, immobile, inanimate thing, with arctic liquid pumping inside of me.

I can feel the sun on my skin but it doesn't warm me. The wetness of the grass and the ground beneath me are seeping into my body. Or I am seeping into them? Am I keeping this patch of ground moist while the day warms everything around me and wakes it up? I am creating a new eco-system; a tiny new republic with me as its queen. I am feeding this patch of ground. How long would it take for the ground to swallow me whole? For me to sink into the soil and be gone? How long before grass grows on my belly and daisies spring up across my chest?

I can feel the sun's warmth; it teases me but offers no comfort. I focus on my hands, they are cold, but they are sentient. They remember who they are and that they belong to me. They remember who I am. They recall the mugs of tea they have made and how they've cupped the hot porcelain for heat on cold mornings. They let the memory of that sharp burning prick them, and relive the reassuring, radiating heat it becomes as the shock of the temperature wanes and the fire becomes a gentle, welcoming warmth.

My hands are comforted by memory and I test them. I communicate to each finger in turn, calling them to order like the children on the teacher's register. 'Left thumb,' 'present miss'; 'left index,' 'present miss,'; 'left middle,' 'present miss'; moving from left hand to right hand via the little fingers, the ones Esther and I used to link together for pinky promises, and back to the right thumb. After the roll call, the exercise. I bend each finger and thumb in turn at the knuckle. My nails scrape across the grass and the soil, doubling the sensation of being alive. My hands tell me 'look, we can move and we can feel the texture of the ground below us. We can disrupt the soil and make a path through the grass. We are alive, Celeste, wake up. Wake up! Move like us.'

But I cannot move the rest of me. Instead, I repeat and repeat my fingers' journey across the tiny patch of grass. That patch of grass is my territory; my connection to the world outside of this cold lump of body moulding into the earth and this brain struggling to put thoughts together in the right order. My fingers are my explorers. My dove sent from Noah's ark, my Amerigo Vespucci, my Francisco Pizarro, my Captain James Cook. I'm trying to unravel the threads of geography lessons, Sunday school colouring-in, my fingers, this cold, this damp, this noise behind me telling me 'shhhhhh, go to sleep, shhhhh' go to sleep, shhhhhhh, sleep, sleep sleep.'

But I am awake. I know I'm awake because I can feel my fingers bend and scrape across the grass. Bend and scrape, bend and scrape. I command them one at a time, then one hand at a time, then both hands together. And they listen and respond. I have control of them and they tell me I can do more, if I just keep going, just keep up the momentum of this small expedition.

I am exploring and I am excavating. Each time they take a turn to bend at the knuckle and pull back, my fingers excavate the grass and the soil to make a groove. Ten small grooves in the earth below me, one for each finger and thumb. There will be soil under my fingernails. I can feel it and I know it. I am damaging the earth with my fingers and it is punishing me for disturbing *it with dirt under my nails. My dad always said my nails were disgusting. He always told me that I was the only person on earth who could wash their hands and have dirty fingernails a minute later. He scrubbed them with the nail brush until they were squeaky clean and tingling from the hard bristles rubbed forward and back, forward and back. He was proud and pleased when my nails were clean.*

My nails are dirty now. My nails are dirty, Daddy, and I am cold and heavy, and I want to go home. Where are you now, Dad? Where are you now?

7

Esther

Esther woke up alone. She oozed into consciousness, first feeling the heaviness of her body and the pressure against her forehead, then acknowledging the light beyond her eyelids. What time was it? What day was it? She opened her eyes slowly, then shut them quickly. The light was sharp and unnecessary. She must get some thicker curtains, or some black-out blinds. Maybe she should ask her parents for black-out blinds for her birthday and get Dad to fit them for her? He would like that. And they'd probably buy her something else as well because blinds are a bit boring and Mum would probably want to take her shopping and have one of those girly days she loves, with lunch and a wander around the designer stuff in Harvey Nicks. Good plan. So that was 19th June sorted. What about today? What was today again? She interrupted herself to call to mind what she'd done yesterday to help her identify her place in the week. Sunday; no need to get up. The guy she'd come home with...

She reached out to feel the empty space next to her and, once confident of his absence, opened her eyes again to check. She was neither upset nor relieved but felt an unease somewhere in the middle, irritated that he'd decided to leave instead of allowing her to tell him it was time to go.

The fitted sheet had pinged off the edge of the bed revealing the mattress, which had lived in her rented flat longer than she had. She clumsily tried to cover the evidence of the people that had slept in her bed before her, and the boy that had been there until when? A couple of hours ago? A couple of minutes ago? But it was hard to reach the corner without sitting up and she couldn't sit up. Not yet. Her head was too heavy and the bricks of the hangover weighing it down shifted around like clothes in a tumble dryer when she tried to move. The sheet admonished her with its ping-back for the third time, and she gave up. Even if she couldn't see the mattress, it would still be there. She'd been reminded of it now, so it was too late to unthink all that grubbiness. The boy may have gone, but he had also been there. She'd not only let him come back to her flat but had insisted he see her home safe and come in for the kind of coffee that gave her aching hips and the burn of oncoming cystitis. She closed her eyes again and tried to sink into the mattress.

'I couldn't figure out the coffee machine, so I made tea.'

Esther was jolted from her attempts to go back to sleep by the boy in the doorway dressed in just his pants holding two mugs of tea; the green one she never used because the rim was chipped and the 'Greetings from Cornwall' one she never used because it was the last gift her Nanna had given her before she died. She struggled to form coherent thoughts into words and eased herself onto her elbows.

"I'm more of an instant man," the boy continued, approaching the bed and jostling the clutter on her bedside table out of the way with the Cornwall mug until he'd made a space big enough to set it down. 'Chuck in a spoonful, water, milk, done. Keep it simple.'

He walked round to the other side of the bed and put down his own mug, while he paused to draw the sheet over the corner of the mattress before getting back in the bed and reaching over to pull the duvet towards him. He sipped his tea and looked across at her, nodding in the direction of the drink he'd made for her to remind her to drink it.

So, he wasn't just here, he was making himself at home. And he was nice. He'd made tea and sorted the sheet out without being asked to do either of those things. She wondered if she looked as bad as she felt. Would she be able to drink tea without feeling more nauseous? Managing a smile, she slowly extracted herself from the bed with a polite 'excuse me', as though she were trying to get to the door when her bus reached its stop. But she wasn't on her way to work, she was awkwardly naked with a man whose name she was trying hard to remember by squeezing her throbbing brain, which growled back and refused to cooperate.

In the bathroom, Esther barely had time to flush away the contents of her bladder before turning round to face the toilet bowl, dropping to her knees and emptying the contents of her stomach. Eyes shut, she breathed deep waiting for the next wave and felt a presence behind her, as the boy gathered her hair into a makeshift ponytail to keep it out of her way. She half heard him mumble something about Tequila shots as she released another volcano of vomit into the toilet bowl and sat back on her heels to catch her breath. Without letting go of her hair, he flushed the toilet with his other hand, stroking her shoulder and waiting for her to indicate whether she would get up from her prayer position or continue.

'I think I'm done,' she uttered, remaining firmly fixed to the ground.

He waited. Let go of her hair, then let go of her shoulder.

She waited. She couldn't think of a polite way to tell him to just go and leave her to it. She didn't like asking for help. She didn't like being helped. She liked being capable, independent, in charge of her own choices.

'I'll get you some water.'

Esther closed the bathroom door behind him, brushed her teeth without looking in the mirror and sluiced out her mouth half a dozen times. The taste was still there. The smell was still there. She sniffed the ends of her hair and wished she hadn't.

Back in the bedroom she found him sitting, fully clothed on the bed.

'Maybe we can do breakfast another time?'

She forced her face into a smile and he looked at the floor while she made it across the room and under the duvet.

'Thanks for the tea.'

She sipped as they both waited for their next cue.

He stood, walked round to the other side of the bed and sat again. 'I've left my number on your whiteboard in the kitchen. We could do something with more clothes and less puke next time?'

She smiled a laugh at him, and he leaned over to kiss her, choosing her forehead in preference to her mouth.

'It's on the whiteboard. Hope you feel better after a sleep.'

She sipped and watched him leave the room, then waited to hear the click of her front door and the heavy thud of the door to the building as it closed behind him.

Feeling a new wave of nausea from the tea, Esther set it down and closed her eyes, hoping the sound of a thousand bees gently travelling from one ear to the other through her head would abate if she just lay still with her eyes closed.

She woke again after seconds? Minutes? to the sound of her phone ringing, irritated with herself for being too drunk and too occupied the night before to put it on silent. It took her a moment to figure out what the noise was. It stopped and began again. She didn't remember giving him her number. Maybe he'd sent himself a text from her phone. Would he do that? Tom, that was his name, it was pretty definitely Tom. Or Dan, could be Dan. It was a one-syllable, easy-to-remember, Tom, Dan, Ben, Nat, three-letter name that she couldn't remember.

The phone mimicked an old-fashioned landline with a piercing bell stopping then starting again before Esther picked it up and read 'Mum' on the screen, with a picture of herself and her mother, heads together as though accidentally superglued. She let it go to voicemail.

Maybe she should ring Tom, if that was his name? Apologise for being sick, for not saying goodbye. For what else? She allowed fragments of the previous evening to float into her head. Celeste, it was Celeste she needed to apologise to. Esther had promised her a girls' night out with no Casanova bullshit getting in the way. Celeste was queen of the withering put down, probably the reason she was so consistently single, and they'd agreed that she would hurl some of her big, sharp words at any would-be suitors. Esther had reneged as soon as Tom appeared with his ripped jeans and perfect hair. She'd whispered apologies for her belligerent friend, explained how she'd been stung in the past, how it made her get in with the stinging first these days. Sad really, Celeste was bitter, cynical. Quick to judge and dismiss.

Celeste had been annoyed. She'd probably still be annoyed. Perhaps it was best not to call.

Esther cautiously stepped out of bed, pulled on a jumper her earlier self had conveniently left draped on the chair, and fetched a pint glass of water and a packet of ibuprofen, getting back into bed with her new companions. She swallowed two of the pills with big gulps of water. Just because she and Tom (was it Tom?) had leapt straight forward to pass go, didn't mean they couldn't begin again at the start. He was nice. He had great hair. Maybe he was a keeper.

Esther's phone rang again. Again the screen said 'Mum'. She waited for the sound to stop and called Celeste's number; if the line was engaged her Mum would be reassured she was still alive but might take the hint to stop ringing for now. She could talk to her later, but hungover in her messy bed was not her favourite time for chatting about things to have for dinner and bargains her mum had spotted at the shops.

She put the phone on speaker so that she didn't need to hold it to her ear and listened to it ring. She listened to it ring then switch to '*Hi, you've reached Celeste. Don't leave a voicemail because I never listen to them. message me. See ya.*'

Esther hung up. Maybe Celeste was screening her calls? Maybe she was just busy? She could be asleep, or in the shower. She might have the phone in her bag and not be able to reach it in time. Esther ran through a carousel of scenarios where Celeste didn't answer the call because she couldn't get to the phone or didn't know it was ringing, or she was just busy. Anything to work around the possibility that Celeste was so pissed off she wouldn't answer. Was Celeste looking at Esther's name on the screen and just allowing the call to ring out? What time was it anyway? Just shy of twelve. Her friend might not even be up.

Perhaps a text message was better anyway, Esther thought. She could apologise without the weight of Celeste's aggressive silence interrupting her. '*I'm so sorry I bailed on you last night.*' Esther paused, deleted the words and began again. '*Where did you get to last night? I turned round and you'd gone. Hope you got home OK. Give me a shout if you fancy a coffee later.*' She re-read her words. Best not to apologise, it was Celeste that had stomped off after all. They could have had a good night, the three of them. If Celeste had hung around, Esther might have given Tom her number and not just taken him home. Celeste could have saved her from her raging hangover and dirty sheets.

She sent it. Up to Celeste whether she wanted to make an issue out of it now. Esther had other things to get on with, mostly pulling herself together and starting the day.

She left the bed again, filled the percolator with coffee and water and set it on the hob, then stripped the bed and squished the bedding into the washing machine, turning the dial to the only programme she ever used before switching it on. The coughing sound of the coffee brewing and the churn-pause-churn of the washing machine threatened to escalate her nausea once again, so Esther quickly turned off the heat, poured a coffee and returned to the bedroom. Her phone was on the bed, ringing again.

Esther snatched up the phone, an earful of Celeste's recriminations was better than a day of silent passive aggression. She noticed only as she tapped green to accept that the call was her mum again.

'Thank goodness you're OK, I was going to give it one more ring and then come round there just to check you weren't dead in a ditch.'

'Good morning to you too, Mum.'

'Listen Esther, you need to answer when I call, especially if I've rung half a dozen times. I know you're all grown up and independent and can take care of yourself....' Esther stopped half-listening to her mum's familiar script as she struggled to put her coffee down before she spilt it. She shoved the cold tea and half-drunk water out of the way to place it on the bedside table, where months of previous coffee cups had created a complex Venn diagram of arcs.

Esther tapped the screen to switch her phone to speaker, allowing the blah-di-blah-blah-blah to swish around in the background like traffic noise, while she sipped her coffee and picked fragments of purple varnish from her nails.

'Blah, blah blah,' her mum continued, 'especially when Celeste has gone AWOL.'

Esther looked up from her fingers and straight at the screen.

'What do you mean, Celeste's gone AWOL?'

'That's why I've been trying to call you, if you'd picked up the first five times, you would have known. I've had Yvonne on this morning, she hasn't got your number, so she rang me. She said Celeste went out with you last night and hasn't been home. Did I know if she was staying at yours. Could I get you to give her a ring. I've had to call her back and tell her I can't get hold of you to check. So now she's called the police and they're coming round to take a statement. The police, Esther, all because you won't pick the phone up.'

Esther pushed aside her mother's flawed reasoning and forced her heavy head to pick through what her mum had said. Celeste wasn't home. That didn't mean she'd gone missing, it just meant she hadn't gone home. She could have met someone after she'd left the bar and gone home with them. She could have gone on somewhere else and met up with other friends and stayed at theirs. She could have gone home and got up early to go out somewhere. She was always talking about starting Couch-2-5K and getting fit. Maybe she was just slightly out of breath and taking a break on a park bench?

Esther visualised each of the options to try and make them real, but she knew none of them were true. Anxiety drenched her as she struggled to think of new possibilities that would explain how everyone was getting their knickers in a twist over nothing. But the trickle of uncertainty that had started when Celeste didn't answer her phone was drowning her now, and her mother's voice was pushing her back into the flood as she gasped for air and struggled to cling to anything solid.

'So did she stay at yours last night Esther? Esther? Did she? Seriously, Yvonne is worried sick, and I know how she feels because you've taken about 10 years off my life this morning by not picking up after five million calls.'

'I'll call Yvonne,' Esther said, 'What's the number?'

8

Abi

Abi was pleased to have a reason to leave her desk when the call came through.

She usually enjoyed working Sundays. This was the one day of the week that was quieter out there; everyone needs a day off at some point, even the muggers and the robbers. The shops may open, and the churches may be struggling to get bums on seats, but Abi could still see a legacy of the Sabbath as a day of rest and staying home. Sundays had a different vibe, inside the station and outside in the not-quite-city, not-quite-suburbs corner of Manchester where she worked.

It had changed round here, no doubt, since the days when her dad had been a young copper, walking the beat and knowing half the neighbourhood by their first name, but the Sunday feeling was fading so much slower than the general pace of change. A cultural inheritance passed from one generation to the next by means of roast dinners, vegging out on the sofa, and the apathy of hangovers.

Roast dinners. An excuse to swerve the ritual of communal over-indulgence was another reason why Sundays at work appealed to her.

The quietness out there on a Sunday morning meant an opportunity to catch up on paperwork, or pause and chat when she was called out to a job; to actually be there for people when they needed someone to listen and understand. She liked the quietness in the office, too; the lack of pointless chit chat about the football or last night's telly. The absence of meandering anecdotes that had been recounted in various versions a hundred times before.

But this Sunday seemed busier. There were no more officers in the station than usual but all those with the biggest bulk and most audible personalities were gathered together in the same place at the same time. And because it was quiet out there, they were all busy with conversations that were too far away for casual eavesdropping, but close enough to irritate and distract her.

Worst of all, PC Noel Fisher, a man who liked to describe himself as built for comfort not for speed, had brought last night's leftover curry to work for his lunch. He had been heating it up in the microwave when she went into the kitchen to make a mug of black coffee. He'd talked her through how it was a melange of deliciousness; leftover lamb rogan josh and saag paneer all mixed together. 'There's plenty if you want some', he offered with a grin. Adding that a sparrow like her could do with some meat on her bones. Abi liked him, he was a kind and good-natured man who always had a smile for her. But his flabbiness repulsed her almost as much as the smell of his lunch. The thought of the mess she knew he'd leave behind - in the microwave, in the sink, on the worktop - made her feel ill. She quickly stirred boiling water into her freeze-dried coffee, muttered something about still being full from breakfast, and returned to her desk with a 'thanks anyway, enjoy!'

It was when she got back to her desk that the call came through. Low risk, missing person called in by the mother of a twenty-two-year-old white female. She remembered being twenty-two and the lectures she'd had from her dad about girls who go missing or get found dead in a ditch or raped in an alleyway. He'd told her the stories to scare her into keeping safe, but he'd mostly just scared her. And then she'd joined the force too and scared herself some more. She knew from her own experience and from her job that girls of twenty-two are mostly just too busy living to let their mums know where they are. Time behaves differently when you're young; there's fun to be had and you're the centre of your own universe. Mostly, it turned out the girls that didn't make it home as expected were just too wrapped up in themselves to think of the worry they might cause. But not always.

Noel offered to come with her through a mouthful of his curry mash-up, and Abi gave him a genuine smile for the offer but had to supress a shudder at the thought of the confined space of a car bulging with his largeness and the lingering scent of his lunch. Anyway, an anxious mum might feel more anxious to have two of them turning up. Sometimes it was better to make it just a quiet chat with someone who could relate. She downed the remains of her coffee, grabbed the keys and left the office with a wave that most of her colleagues didn't acknowledge.

Abi struggled to park near the house. It was on one of those old-fashioned streets, built for another era, when no-one had cars. She finally managed to squeeze into a space several doors down and felt the familiar scrutiny of curious eyes trying not to look at her directly while they wondered why the police had arrived. She let them wonder, and walked purposefully back up the street to number 18.

She almost fell backwards down the step when the door opened, because it was pulled back so quickly, as though an actor had been standing behind it, waiting for a cue. 'Mrs Parker?' Abi asked, and the woman, who had been waiting in the hallway, watching out for the police to arrive and hoping to see her daughter walk up the path, stumbled and nodded through a sudden snort of tears, moving backwards to allow the policewoman to step into the hall.

Abi followed her into the kitchen and took out her notebook. Her host switched off the radio and put on the kettle, fussing around finding mugs and getting milk from the fridge while the water boiled, and the tea brewed. She punctuated her busyness with thank yous for Abi's rapid arrival and apologies for the slow boiling of water as she moved around the kitchen finding things to do.

Eventually, the woman poured Abi a cup of tea that she didn't want and had already politely refused. Abi didn't like tea, and the milkiness was nauseating, but she'd been in the job long enough to understand the purpose of tea. It was both a distraction and a talisman. The process of making it was something to soothe the worried woman's restlessness. The drinking of it was a magical libation that would trigger a return to normal times. Abi shared the shadow of a hope that the sound of the mugs landing on the table would be accompanied by the rustle of a key in the door and a flood of a thousand apologies for such fuss and thoughtlessness gushing through the hallway.

The mugs made a gentle tap, tap on the table, as Mrs Parker placed each one carefully straight onto the wood with no coaster. There was a hefty silence of mutual hesitation.

'What about a biscuit? I should have had some banana bread to offer you, you know, cake. But I burnt it with all this going on. Sorry. Sorry about the smell. I did open a window, but it lingers, doesn't it. I can get you a biscuit though. Do you like biscuits? Celeste loves Jaffa Cakes. We always have Jaffa Cakes in. Unless she's eaten them all. She might have eaten them all.' Mrs Parker ignored Abi's assurances that she didn't need a biscuit and thrust her head into the cupboard to assess the Jaffa Cake situation. 'It looks like we're out of Jaffa Cakes but there are some Bourbon Creams or some cheese crackers if you prefer savoury?'

The woman turned back to Abi to search her face for an answer. Abi recognised the look of desperate parents and partners from years of forcing the start of tough conversations and delivering bad news. This woman wasn't asking which biscuit she preferred, with the words Jaffa Cake, Bourbon Cream or cheese cracker, she was asking 'will everything be all right?'

This was a woman who had made a call about her daughter being missing. She'd started a prologue to a conversation that she now wanted to avoid with tea and biscuits. If she was busy perhaps her daughter wouldn't be gone. If she behaved like Abi was a friend who'd just popped in for a brew and a catch up, perhaps her daughter might not be lost. If she didn't say the words out loud, perhaps there would be nothing to say.

Abi rose from her chair and gently took Mrs Parker by the arm. There would be no comfort in the questions she had to ask, but she could offer compassion. With a soft, 'let's forget about the biscuits, shall we?' Abi led the woman to a chair and took her own seat again, as though this were her home and Mrs Parker were her guest.

Quietly, she ran through a checklist of questions and wrote down the answers in her notebook.

Name – Celeste

Age – 22

Last seen – 8pm, Saturday 12th May

Description – white, tall, slim, long dark hair (loose)

Clothing when last seen – floral top, black skirt, black tights, brown boots, leopard fur jacket, hoop earrings, star-shaped silver pendant, red lipstick.

Abi read her notes back to Mrs Parker, who nodded her agreement that the information was correct at every pause. 'You can call me Yvonne, if you like love.' She reached out and wrapped a warm hand around Abi's tiny fingers. 'Thank you.' The gesture confused them both as they tried to process who was offering comfort and who was accepting it.

'Can I see Celeste's room?' Abi asked, easing her hand out from the cosiness of Yvonne's warm fingers and hoping to find something reassuring amongst Celeste's things. They talked as they walked upstairs, Abi asking questions about where Celeste had been the night before and who with. Her questions continued when they reached the bedroom, gentle but relentless. She asked about boyfriends and friends, colleagues and family members. About drinking habits, drug taking and whether Celeste was sexually active.

It was easier to ask questions while she walked around the girl's bedroom, looking at pictures and postcards stuck to the wall, and rummaging through a pile of clothes abandoned on a chair. She wrote notes from Yvonne's responses without making eye contact, aware of the worry trapped tight in every word. She forced herself to keep pushing for answers in the hope that they would somehow rearrange themselves like the letters of an anagram to fill in the only blank that really counted: where is Celeste?

'It's such a mess,' muttered Yvonne, and Abi was unsure whether she meant the lost daughter, the state of the bedroom, or something else. She knew it was best to pause and open up space in the room for Yvonne's thoughts to shape themselves into words.

Abi looked out of the window. It overlooked the back of the house, and Yvonne had already pegged out a wash in the yard this morning. The policewoman wondered if she'd done that earlier, before she'd realised her daughter was gone, when it was just a normal Sunday, or if it had been how she'd kept busy before there had been an excuse for making tea and hunting for Jaffa Cakes. There was no sign of the showers of the day before now, or last night's heavy downpour, just clear skies across the backs of houses and out towards the church, where a banner declared 'God is Love' to anyone who cared to look up at the tower. A woman sat in the community garden, chatting on her phone while her dog foraged to no avail in the borders.

'It's hard bringing up a child on your own.' Yvonne drew Abi from the view through the window and back into the room, where the mother was holding a large yellow jumper, cuddling it against her.

Yvonne sat down on the edge of the bed and poured out a jumbled life story, as though making her first confession after years of apostasy. Abi absorbed every detail of the room as she listened to Yvonne explain the mistakes she had made and the choices she'd got wrong. How she'd opted for the handsome one with a chip on his shoulder and a drink dependency over the modest, caring alternative. How it was a bad choice of husband and an even worse choice of father. The sorrow she felt that it was Celeste who had suffered most for those choices; an only child with first a detached, then an absent father. Celeste had suffered twice over, Yvonne explained, with no dad and a stressed-out and over-occupied mother as a result. The narrative paused, and Abi remained silent, allowing the guilt to disperse in the room and tracing with her eyes the arc of a rainbow crayoned on the wall. She reminded herself to remain at a safe emotional distance from this woman and her anticipation of sorrow.

'Do you have children?' Yvonne asked. Abi looked for an answer in the rainbow. She had been trained for this; taught how to evade personal questions kindly and keep the conversation on a professional level with a focus on the task at hand. It was a question people often asked, not so much at work, but socially. Even strangers making small talk in the queue at Costa or in the gym, it was a lazily predictable common ground people assumed they could use to connect and keep talking.

Falling back on the excuse of her career as an opt-out from a straight answer, Abi explained that the job wasn't really compatible with motherhood, and she loved the job. Both statements were a lie. She struggled to make eye contact as she uttered them, conscious of how candid Yvonne had been with her, and feeling guilty for repaying her with dishonesty and evasion.

Perhaps it would be Yvonne, with her gentleness and sensitive emotional state, who would finally catch her out. The lie was becoming harder to say, making it harder for anyone to believe. She had many colleagues, female colleagues, who juggled work and children. They looked tired and complained a lot, but they had the subconscious swagger of fitting into the central ellipse of the Venn diagram made up of 'women who work' on one side and 'mothers' on the other. They had pictures in their wallets and a reason to get off shift on time to make it home before bedtime stories. They were a club of shared experience from which she was permanently excluded so, rather than allow herself to envy their lives, she came up with an armoury full of reasons not to want what they have.

The pause lay heavy in the room for a moment as both women searched for what to say next. There had been no obvious signs of an intention to leave in the bedroom. There were no signs that Celeste had been in any kind of heightened state of distress.

Yvonne looked at Abi and opened her mouth to speak, but no sound came out. She pulled her face into a smile of sadness and shrugged her shoulders.

'These things usually play out with the young person calling us to apologise for wasting our time because their phone was out of charge or they just didn't think to call home,' Abi said, knowing that with every minute that passed, this sentence was less and less likely to be true.

Yvonne muttered something barely audible about how it wasn't like Celeste to let her worry like this. Her short sentence triggered the end of her quiet stoicism and the onset of tears, as she buried her face in the yellow jumper.

The other woman's emotion switched Abi back into the detached, efficient police officer she had been trained to be. Other people's emotions were something she could deal with; she had the defined role of an outsider and a figure of authority now. She could be nurturing but sensible. Kind but unsentimental.

Taking Yvonne by the elbow, Abi led her back to the stairs with platitudes about cups of tea and trying not to worry. Back in the kitchen, she set Yvonne the task of making another pot of tea to keep her occupied while she looked back over the notes she'd taken for any gaps or hints that more useful details could be hiding somewhere, unsaid.

As Yvonne poured the boiled water onto the tea bags in the pot, Abi asked her about the friend Celeste had been out with the night before.

'Esther?' Yvonne replied, pausing as she opened the fridge for the milk. Abi listened and jotted down single words and phrases as Yvonne explained how she'd never much liked Esther, had always found her two-faced and the kind of girl who'd pick up with Celeste when she wanted something or had nothing better to do, then drop her like a hot brick if she had a better offer or couldn't be bothered. Not as pretty as Celeste, Yvonne pointed out, but twice as confident, always talking but never with anything to say.

'I'm sure you know the type,' Yvonne sighed, placing two mugs of tea on the table.

Abi nodded without saying anything, and blew on the tea without drinking any. She watched as Yvonne sipped her own drink, holding her hands around the mug to warm them for comfort, even though it was a mild spring day. She waited to see if any more words slipped from Yvonne's thoughts into the quiet of the kitchen.

But the absence of words continued. Yvonne looked somewhere beyond the room and the day, apparently waiting for an idea about where her daughter might be.

The phone interrupted their shared silence. Not Yvonne's mobile plugged in to charge next to the kettle, nor Abi's tucked away in her pocket, but the landline in the hall. Yvonne looked at Abi for permission to answer it in the way Abi often saw people defer to her, as though she were a parent, or a teacher keeping them back in detention.

Abi tried to eavesdrop as Yvonne answered the call, but Yvonne's voice was too soft for her to make out the words. She could hear the panic though. It was the same tone she'd arrived to earlier.

She followed the conversation into the hall to find Yvonne repeating that she didn't understand. 'I just don't understand why you'd think it was OK to leave her on her own,' Yvonne repeated, looking at Abi as she poured her recrimination into the receiver.

'It's Esther,' she said turning to Abi, still holding the receiver and staying on the call. 'She says she's been trying to call Celeste to check she got home OK, but it just goes straight through to voicemail.'

9

Robert

Robert was waiting until five. Five was a reasonable time on a Sunday to open a bottle of wine and sip it slowly. It was civilised, middle-class even, to open a bottle of wine on a Sunday at five, and sit around a table with the family, enjoying a roast chicken dinner and a chat and a laugh. Passing the gravy, squabbling over the last roast potato, asking if there were any more Yorkshires going begging, just on the off chance one or two had been held back in reserve in the kitchen.

Robert couldn't remember the last time he'd had a roast chicken dinner like that. Probably when he was still married to Yvonne and used to pull the wishbone with Celeste, trying to make sure she always snapped the bigger half and earned the right to make a wish. He had a chicken roasting in the oven, there was a chicken every weekend, covered in foil at first, then taken out, brushed with olive oil and sent back in to brown for the last half hour, the way his mother had always done it. But there was no Sunday roast ritual in his flat. The chicken could be on a Saturday or Sunday, it could be in the morning or the afternoon. No-one set Robert's routine for him. No-one was expecting a roast with all the trimmings brought to the table bang on time while they paused the conversation and cleared a space. Nobody cared whether there was a chicken or not. Robert's chickens were eaten alone with boiled spuds, carrots and cauliflower when they were fresh from the oven, then eked out in sandwiches or with oven chips for the rest of the week, until, finally, when just the slimy and gnarled remnants were left on the carcass, he carefully scraped off the last bits of meat and made a stir fry. Once, he had even made a soup using stock from the boiled remains of skin and bones, inspired by an enthusiastic chef on TV. But the sight of the rib cage in the bubbling liquid and the tiny fragments of meat floating away from the bones had turned his stomach. He'd had to fish the skeleton from the liquor to throw it away, and what he'd bought as meat had suddenly become the remains of a living creature. He had eaten the first bowl of soup then flushed the rest down the toilet. He had never made soup with chicken bones again.

Robert was waiting until five. Forty-five minutes to go. He could break the rule, it was his own rule after all. He could call it an aperitif; if that's a good enough excuse for French people to crack open a bottle of something before their meal, why should it not be a good enough excuse for him. Who was watching? Who would even know? But if he opened the bottle now, before food, would he drink it quicker, without the need to alternate with forkfuls of chicken and potato? If he started early, would there be enough to last the night?

He could always pop to the off license on the corner if he got to the end of the bottle before bedtime. He didn't have to. He probably wouldn't. But it was good to know the option was there. So, if he started early, and if he did get to the end of the bottle, he could just get another and have one glass from it, just one, a small one even, and then replace the cork to drink the rest another day. That would be OK. The rule he'd given himself was no more than one bottle, but if the first glass was an aperitif, a little cultural experiment adopted from across the channel, and the second bottle was only purchased as a way of topping up that missing glass from the first, then he wasn't really breaking his rule. Just adapting it. And it was his rule. And it was Sunday. What are Sundays for if not for treats and special occasions? Roast dinners and red wine.

40 minutes to go. The scent of chicken was creeping silently from the grease-stained oven and dispersing nostalgia liberally across Robert's open plan studio apartment. Open-plan studio apartment is what they'd called it on the details when, having been politely told 'we think it's time you moved on' by the other residents of his house share, he'd looked for somewhere affordable to rent by himself. They'd called 'apartments' like these 'bedsits' back in the day, but, like so much else, the idea of a flat where you cook, eat, sit and sleep all in the same room, had been sanitized and rebranded over the years. While 'bedsit' said grubby, dingy living on a shoestring and giving up on life, 'studio apartment' said minimalist, compact, convenience of knitting together all the threads of life and lifestyle in a single space. It's not where you are that matters, but where you see yourself. Robert saw himself in the mirror, unshaven - not in a considered, fashionable way, but in an unconsidered, hadn't got round to it way. He saw the sum total of his fifty-two years added up around his eyes, across his retreating hairline, speckled white in his week-old stubble. He was here not by design but by default. He was not in a studio apartment but in a bedsit, brought here by the decisions he'd made and the choices he hadn't made.

35 minutes to go. Elgar's Cello Concerto reached the part he loved, where the refrain returns quietly, and the cello is almost alone. He paused to listen. Perhaps he should just uncork the bottle to let it breathe while waiting for the chicken to finish cooking and browning. Another small process before lighting the gas under the potatoes? The packet said *salad potatoes* but to Robert it said no peeling required. They were sitting ready in the pan, small enough to cook quickly, the water already salted for flavour and a faster boil. Robert would have preferred roast potatoes really. What's a roast dinner without the roasties? But the oven wasn't big enough for both the bird and the spuds at

once and having everything hot and ready at the same time was enough of a juggling act already.

He hunted for the corkscrew. Robert didn't believe in screw-top wine bottles; if a cork had been the best way to seal the bottle for centuries, why wouldn't it still be the best option now? It did involve laying his hands on the corkscrew though, which, after much rattling through the cutlery drawer and moving of objects to check for hiding places, he eventually remembered was by the bed, along with yesterday's empty bottle. He carried both back to the kitchenette, setting the bottle down next to the neat line waiting to be taken out for recycling. There was a familiar and comforting order to all of this. It may just be him and Jacqueline du Pré for dinner, but that didn't mean things shouldn't be done properly. He had set the table, the wine glass was ready, the plate would be warmed while he made the gravy, and the bottle would be uncorked ready for him to pour as soon as he sat down. He might even put a splash in the gravy for flavour. He removed the foil, screwed down into the cork and lifted the arms to release it from the bottle. He sniffed first the cork, then the neck of the bottle. Half an hour to go.

Routine. It's one of the things they'd advised him when he'd dabbled with AA, before stepping away from all the over-sharing, and the temptation to compare himself to the others in the group. He didn't have a drink problem, he had a drink routine, part of the structure of his week, his day. The thing that gave him a structure to his week, especially his weekends when there was no work to get up for and no Newsnight to bookend the day. Routine is what had been lacking from his life with Yvonne and Celeste. Every day had been chaos. Even when they'd made plans, they'd usually strayed from the path they'd agreed. There had been mess, food at irregular times, a third person in the bed most nights, taking up space and taking away his sleep. He couldn't live there. He couldn't watch them living there without him and doing OK. That's how he'd ended up moving so far away and being so far removed from his daughter's life.

He remembered the day it had dawned on him that he might need to have some separation between himself and his wife and daughter. A pause; a buffer zone. He thought about the rainbow that had appeared on Celeste's bedroom wall just a week after he'd spent an entire weekend decorating her room and making it nice. He'd laboured over the wall, steaming off the paper, filling the cracks in the plaster, sanding and sugar-soaping to prepare the surface, then painting two coats. Yvonne and Celeste had been delighted with the results. The girl had been giddy with excitement about her new room, kissing the walls because, she said, she loved them. Kissing her Daddy because she loved him too. Yvonne had been proud and grateful. But just a few days later, while he was just trying to take half an hour of quiet time reading, Yvonne had taken her eye off the ball. She'd taken her eye off the kid who was always up to something, and Celeste had wrecked the whole thing with brightly coloured wax crayons that stained the wall and would not wipe clean. She hadn't been remotely apologetic or contrite, quite the opposite. She had ushered him into the room enthusiastically to show him what she'd done to ruin all that time and effort he'd put in for her. That was the moment he realised she would never appreciate how much he loved her.

He brushed away the memories of how he'd shouted, how Yvonne had held Celeste behind her so that he couldn't get his point across. He replaced unwelcome recollections of the way his daughter had cried, the way his wife had scrubbed the wall to no avail, the way the yelling had continued into the evening, and the next day, and the next, by reminding himself that the gravy would not make itself.

Twenty-five minutes to go. Unable to find the oven gloves or concentrate on looking for them, Robert took two tea towels from the drawer and wrapped them around his hands. He bent with an involuntary and unacknowledged groan to take the chicken from the oven, placing the heavy roasting tray on the breadboard. Peeling back the aluminium foil, he released steam infused with a lifetime of sitting still at the table, saving the best roastie till last, reaching for the dregs of the gravy. It occurred to him that he should call his parents. Or he might call his brother, suggest going over for a visit, for a weekend even. But the comfort of home and family was always tinged with the bitterness of their disappointment and tedious conversation. He remembered the word he'd learned on University Challenge the previous week – *hiraeth*: a nostalgia for a rose-tinted version of home. Home had never been all cosy roast dinners. What he'd wanted it to be had never been there then, and it still didn't exist now. He was better off with an evening alone with Jacqueline and her cello, perhaps Ernest Hemingway could join them after dinner, and he could share the Merlot with them, while still getting to drink the whole bottle himself.

Robert took a second roasting tray from the cupboard and placed it next to the first. He stabbed the chicken with a fork behind each wing, lifting it to release the juices before placing it in the clean tray and drizzling olive oil over the top. With a paintbrush, designated for the purpose, he brushed the oil across the chicken and put the bird back in the oven to brown. Twenty minutes to go. He was behind schedule.

Images of the rainbow, and of Celeste hiding from him interrupted Robert's train of thought. A memory of the card his daughter had made for him saying 'I am very sorry about the rainbow, Daddy. I promise I will never draw on the walls again' entered his head unbidden and unwelcome, as he tried to focus on pouring the liquor from the chicken into a pan and finding a stock cube to make the gravy. The box of cornflour had fallen sideways in the cupboard and spilt its creamy powder around the surrounding tins and packets, dusting them like snow. Robert up-righted the cornflour and took it out of the cupboard, closing the door on the mess for another time when he wasn't so busy. He put a teaspoon of cornflour in the mug with a broken handle that he always used for gravy making, and rubbed the stock cube between his fingers, crumbling the brown flavour onto the magic white dust. They'd taken it in turns to crumble the stock cube, Robert and his brother, Jason, as boys. Their mum had called them into the kitchen to do it and it had been the signal that dinner was nearly ready. She had let the boys lick the salty meatiness off their fingers and Robert had developed his crumbling technique to make sure as much as possible was left on his skin as a teaser for the meal to come. It had been part of the pre-match warm up for a Sunday dinner, a tradition he'd passed onto Celeste, along with the wishbone, saved from the carcass and washed under the hot tap for snapping with little fingers to a combined chorus of 'make a wish.'

Robert lit the gas under the potatoes and took out another pan for the carrots and the broccoli - they could cook together; no point getting two pans dirty. He chopped the carrot without peeling it and put the kettle on to boil. He glanced at the wine waiting patiently with his knife and fork on the table. 15 minutes to go.

Pouring the chicken liquor into the pan and swilling the empty roasting tray with boiled water to capture the last remnants of flavour before pouring this too into the soon-to-be gravy, Robert thought about Celeste. He tried to picture her face, but it was hard to visualise what she looked like now, already an adult, because his time of fathering every day was so long ago. Pulling an image of her all cute and trusting from his memory seemed dishonest. He had an adult daughter now, one who had grown up in episodes, noticeably older each time he'd seen her. Her journey from little girl to pre-teen, then awkward teenager to young woman had jumped from one moment to the next, and he'd been shocked by the change every time. He wondered whether Yvonne had found the changes less shocking as they crept forward in tiny increments, or more alarming because they happened under her nose but without her seeing them.

With the juices and the fat from the chicken bubbling away, Robert poured a spoonful into the broken mug and stirred the mixture together, making a beige cement, which he poured back into the pan. The pale paste dispersed like heavy cloud in the liquid, and he stirred again, pleased that the watery fluid began to transform into a viscous and opaque gravy. Something he could do well every time, without fail. He flicked the switch on the kettle to bring it back to the boil and poured boiling water over the carrots, placing the lid on the top to keep the heat in. The broccoli sat on the side, waiting for its turn. 10 minutes to go.

He checked his phone. No messages, no missed calls. He wasn't expecting any. He kept the phone on silent so as not to be disturbed while he was busy, but it almost never rang. He sometimes had a text from Celeste. He sometimes texted her, or called. But there was no regular routine. She was beyond the age of a childhood timetable and had not yet settled into adult habits; somewhere happily in the middle, her life was fluid, her hours unaccounted for and flexible. Robert didn't envy her lack of routine but he envied her the lack of feeling the need for one.

He checked the chicken, took it out of the oven, turned it 180 degrees and put it back in to brown on the other side. When was someone going to invent an oven that browned everything evenly all over, without the need for the hokey-cokey? Perhaps they already had, just not for studio apartments. He could just have a little sip while he waited. Just a taster, like in a restaurant when the waiter stands over you while you take a sip from an almost empty glass, then waits for you to give him the nod that it is, indeed, wine, and you are prepared to drink the rest of the bottle. He had never rejected a bottle in a restaurant, he wondered if anyone ever did that. Time for the broccoli. Time to turn the heat down on the gravy so it didn't catch. Time to check the potatoes by stabbing one through with a knife. Ready. Heat off. Five minutes to go.

A watched pot never boils. He liked this and other idioms. He'd learned lists and lists of them at school, as though in a classroom full of aliens being taught to assimilate, tutored in the art of being an earthling that could fit in. A watched pot never boils. A rolling stone gathers no moss. A stich in time saves nine. He went out of his way to use them to keep them going. They mustn't die out, these odd concoctions of words that connect the life we have now with the generations of people who have called upon the same well-worn sentences for decades and centuries before. These were comfortable and worn in combinations of words, a little frayed around the edges, but useful. Handy for awkward pauses and small talk. A watched pot never boils, so he left the kitchenette and walked over to the table. He could just read the label on the wine. It was nearly time. If there were a waiter, the waiter would present the bottle to him and let him see the label; not long enough to read it but long enough to check that the name on the bottle matched the name on the menu. Perhaps Celeste drank wine now? What do young people drink? Beer? Vodka? Cocktails? He could invite her for dinner. Pick her up, take her to choose the wine – or tipple of her choice – on the way over, and maybe even see if she wanted to stay. It would be a squeeze, but they could manage it. He could use the sleeping bag on the floor and let her have the bed. He would get the bedding washed in the morning and put the chicken in to roast before he drove over to collect her. He sniffed the bottle, breathed in the familiar warmth of the red wine scent and put the bottle down in its place again. Less than five minutes to go, it would be foolish to cheat himself out of making it until five now.

He switched off the gas under the vegetables and the gravy, took the chicken from the oven and replaced it with an empty plate. The chicken sat resting while he strained the potatoes and then the vegetables in the colander. A funny idea the meat resting, as though it were reclining on a chaise longue with a good book and a cup of milky tea. He switched off the oven, retrieved the hot plate carefully and began to assemble the meal, with potatoes and vegetables spooned out, before slicing breast meat and pulling off a leg, then finally bathing it all in gravy.

He sat down at the table, poured a glass of wine to the brim and sipped it, then took a full, pleasing mouthful. His phone, sitting quietly next to his hand as he sliced through a potato, vibrated and then stopped. It vibrated again and he picked it up and took the call.

'Robert, it's Yvonne. Is Celeste with you?'

III

Celeste

*T*he breeze on my face makes me think of the seaside. Sea air. The otherness of walking on sand. The calm, repetitive timelessness of the waves, tumbling forward and pulling back endlessly as they have done forever.

Let's throw pebbles into the sea. Let's take our shoes and socks off and go for a paddle. Jump over the waves Celeste. Ready? Jump! Again! Jump! Tuck your skirt into your knickers. Hold on tight to your shoes and socks. Jump. Wait. Jump!

Let's go for a swim. Let's build a sandcastle. Let's bury our feet in the sand. Let me bury you up to the neck and decorate you with shells like a mermaid. Let's look out to sea and imagine who lives across the ocean. Voyages. I could swim the channel. I could go deep sea diving. Visit the Great Barrier Reef. Swim with dolphins. Rediscover the lost city of Atlantis.

'Or we could just have fish and chips,' she said. 'Fuel us up for the 199 steps.' We never had fish and chips at home and that meal, straight from the box, right by the sea, with the clouds swept lightly across the sky as though someone had rushed through with a paintbrush, was the best meal in the world. Just me and Mum and fish and chips, far from home and totally happy with grease on our fingers and the sting of salt and vinegar on our lips.

I am taking myself back there. My mum is next to me. The fish and chips are warm; warm on my fingers, warm in my mouth, *warm in my belly. They are comfort, straight from the box. This is everything I need. I am outdoors because it is where we want to be. The air is soft and cool and I can still feel sand inside my socks, inside my shoes on feet that have been washed cleaner and smoother by the salty sea.*

I am imagining every chip. I am picturing the two of us chatting. Laughing. She takes her phone out of her bag and holds it out in front of us to take a picture. 'Say 'fish!'', she says, and taps the button on the screen. 'Say 'chips!'' she says, and takes another. A woman walks up to us and offers to take a picture. We stand and move so that she can capture us with the sea and the harbour in the background. My mum puts her arm around me, and I wrap mine around her waist. We are posed there forever on the kitchen wall in an image that reminds us of what happiness looks like. The kindness of the stranger who saw a moment and recorded it for us hangs in the frame with our picture.

'Let's do the steps,' Mum said. 'I'll race you,' I laughed. And we shoved our chip wrappers in the over-full bin then stood at the bottom of the steps looking up. The sky was already going pink. The town had already emptied of people and we had the steps to ourselves. 'Are there really 199?' I asked. 'I don't know,' she said, 'why don't you count them?'

The first count was backwards for the start of the race, 'three, two, one, go!' The second count was long; out loud at first, then just in my head. We sprinted the first few, then she slowed, and I carried on, counting and climbing and looking back to see if she was still there. Stopping at each bench to wait for her to not quite catch up, repeating the number from my count over and over in my head to make sure I didn't forget it, and jumping up before she reached me, with a thumb to my nose and wiggling fingers to tease her for being so slow.

I am wiggling my fingers and pointing my thumb. I can't reach my nose, but my nose is still on my face. My fingers still wriggle. Fuck you, arsehole, I am still here, I am going to get to the top of the steps and my mum is right behind me. She is coming for me, and you can fuck right off.

I am climbing the steps. I have lost count, but I am still climbing. I got to the top that day. I waited for my mum to catch up. It took a while, but she got there. I waited and she came. I'm here Mum. I'm here. I'm waiting for you. You can make it.

10

Yvonne

Yvonne was expecting him, but she was still surprised by Robert 's presence on the doorstep. She had heard the hard metallic knock-knock of the old door knocker that she and Celeste used instead of the newer addition of the doorbell. It was mostly only Celeste who used the knocker, and Yvonne had leapt up hoping to find her daughter standing there. She'd sprinted to the door for a garbled tale of Celeste's key mislaid and phone on silent, for a rambling apology with hugs and tears and strong words tucked away for later.

But, instead of her daughter, she found her ex-husband on the doorstep. She knew from the hall it wasn't Celeste. Through the frosted door pane, the blurred outline of a person was not her slim, long-haired daughter but a dark heavy shadow, shifting from foot to foot in irritated impatience. She was not just disappointed to see him, she was angry that it was him and not Celeste, sounding his presence with an anachronism only ever used by those who had formed the habit before the doorbell was added.

It was Yvonne who had called Robert. She who had told him Celeste was missing. Her that had urged him to get there as quickly as he could.

But now that he'd arrived, she didn't want him there. She only wanted Celeste.

It seemed to her that Robert had played a nasty trick, substituting himself for the daughter she had believed, just for a few seconds, might finally be home. As she reached for the thumb turn to let him in, her disappointment turned to anger. Anger that he hadn't been there sooner. Anger that he hadn't been there at all.

She paused before opening the door; if it wasn't Celeste, there wasn't any hurry, and she needed to compose herself. She took a deep and conscious breath, exhaling the bitterness she felt that he wasn't Celeste, that he hadn't been there to prevent Celeste from going missing. She tried to arrange her face in an expression that might communicate what? Gratitude? Relief? Hope? He had arrived. She had asked him to come, and he must have left within minutes to be here so soon. She had asked him to come, so she needed to behave as though she was pleased he was here. Or at least as though she believed he had a right and a reason to be involved.

As she pulled the door open, she consciously composed her face in neutral, quickly swallowing her distaste at his shabby appearance, and casting years of resentment to one side. She was used to his crumpled greyness and the mustiness that clung to him like the smell of a night out in the pubs of their early days together, but she hadn't been expecting this level of drabness and neglect.

His face was creased and pallid, like a worn and discoloured bed sheet, and his hair, which almost touched his shoulders, was much greyer and less thick than she remembered it being when she'd last seen him. When was that? As she stepped back to let Robert into the house, Yvonne rummaged in her memory to recall when he'd last been to see Celeste. September, just after her birthday? Or October even? The weather had been on the turn, and he'd showed up with flowers and a £20 note, but no card. No, it had been Christmas. Robert had taken Celeste to the pub on Boxing Day, and the pair of them had returned giggling and stumbling. Yvonne had had no option but to let him sleep on the couch, the ghost of Christmas past come back to remind her that they would always be connected thanks to Celeste, no matter how many years or miles separated them.

The memory peeled back the lid she had worked so hard to keep tightly closed on her fury over the years. If she made sure all of that was locked away in a dark place, she was safe from it; protected from the creeping, suffocating ire that was powerless to harm him or change anything, but could cause her to crumble in a moment and keep her trapped under a blanket of regret for weeks. She had married him, it had been her choice. She had cajoled him into agreeing to have a baby, that had been her choice too. He'd reminded her of that, bluntly and frequently, any time she'd complained about having to get up early, or about the mess or the lack of a single minute for a coherent, independent thought, from the moment she woke to the moment she closed her eyes to sleep. His solution to her exhaustion had not been to offer her any respite; to change a nappy, entertain Celeste, take their daughter out to the park, occupy her for an hour when she woke up at dawn. Robert's solution had been to call it a day with just the one child. When Yvonne had suggested they might think about a little brother or sister, he had actually laughed and reminded her that she was 'always moaning' about the daughter they already had, and 'would never cope' with another. So Celeste had been promoted from the eldest child status she might have had, to the only child status she would always have. And now Yvonne's only child was missing, and she regretted inviting Robert into her torment as soon as she saw him.

'Any news?' Robert asked as Yvonne opened the door. She shook her head and glanced at the floor, afraid to speak in case her voice cracked. She had sworn, years before, never to let him see her cry again, and she knew she was in danger of breaking that resolution. Before she could look up, he walked past her without a hello, and straight through to the kitchen, leaving her to close the door behind him. She found him in the kitchen

96

doorway staring at Esther, who was sitting at the table with her eyes glued to her phone, scrolling the screen with her finger.

The two of them were like a theatrical tableau, not moving from their appointed positions. Yvonne had been thrown on stage to start the scene without any chance to prepare her lines, and she was forced to say 'excuse me' to her ex-husband to gain access to her own kitchen.

Yvonne explained Esther's presence to Robert, filling the kettle as she spoke as a way to be busy and reclaim ownership of the kitchen, the house, the situation. 'So Esther has called and messaged everyone she can think of, and she's put something on social media, Facebook and things, she's doing everything she can, aren't you Esther?'

She could feel panic fizzing through her as she fumbled with the jar of tea bags and pulled out three for the teapot. In a moment, he would begin telling her what she had done wrong, what she hadn't thought of, what she should be doing better. He wouldn't see how much she had already coped with on her own. He wouldn't see how much effort it was taking for her to stand upright in her own kitchen, with Celeste absent and him present.

Robert pulled up a chair next to Esther, too close, so that he could peer across at her phone. She showed him the montage of pictures she had put together and explained that she had posted it on her own social media accounts and tagged Celeste's name. She showed him the community group posts and the friends and friends' parents she'd asked to share it.

'I've put 'missing, please share' in caps,' Esther explained, 'and people have been sharing it with people we don't know, so that's great. And, if Celeste sees it, she'll know we're worried and get in touch. I've used a good picture of her face, and a picture of the coat and boots she was wearing, and a picture I took last night, but that's a bit grainy. I'm sure it'll help. I'm sure she's just, you know, wrapped up in whatever she's doing and hasn't even thought about how worried we'll all be.'

Yvonne registered how concerned Esther's voice became as she tried to reassure Robert that she wasn't worried. Her words and her voice didn't match, like those cognitive challenges with the names of colours spelt out as a word in a different colour where you have to name the colour you see, rather than reading the word. Esther was speaking the words, and the colours were all wrong. Her words were all yellow, but her voice was grey.

Putting the teapot and three mugs on the table, Yvonne went to sit down so they could begin a conversation about what they should do next. But, before she had even drawn back her chair, as though he had forgotten his ex-wife was in the room, Robert began questioning Esther. The picture from the night before... where had they been? Who had they been with? Where had Esther been when she last saw Celeste? Why hadn't they left together? Did Esther think it was OK to let her friend go home alone?

The girl began by telling him they had been in a bar they often went to and how it might be worth contacting the bar or going down there with a poster. But as he interrupted her with more questions and an accusatory, hostile tone, she was less and less able to include even fake hope and positivity in her responses. Their conversation became less about what she knew and how it might help them find Celeste, and more about Robert's insistence that she feel guilt and remorse.

Esther shuddered and hastily wiped a tear from her face. 'It was her decision to leave. We asked her to stay and she more-or-less stormed off in a huff. I didn't send her home, I just didn't indulge her tantrum by going with her.'

Robert banged the table then and stood up sharply, throwing his chair to the ground in the process and making Esther flinch. Yvonne could see how mortified the girl was that her choice to stay in the bar when Celeste left might have made the difference between Celeste being at home, making toast and wandering around in pyjamas half the day, and her daughter being absent. Missing. Lost.

Yvonne stepped into the pause between the sound of the chair falling and Robert's failure to acknowledge he needed to pick it up.

'This is not Esther's fault.' She hesitated, waiting for the words to register with both of them and to make sure she really believed them herself.

'This is not Esther's fault,' Yvonne repeated. Her words sounded more honest and convincing this time and Robert had begun to pay attention, like a child might when the teacher raises her voice. 'Can you pick up the chair please, Robert. We need to decide what else we can do to find Celeste. If you want to help, fine, if you don't want to help, you're in the way and you'd better go.'

Robert picked up the chair and sat down. Sitting herself and pouring the tea, Yvonne imagined how delighted Celeste would be to see her take charge. She had berated herself throughout Celeste's life for failing to be a role model of the strong woman she'd always instructed her daughter to be. The coaching should have been in her actions, not in her counsel, she realised. Perhaps only a crisis could have taught her that. Perhaps when Celeste returned, she could hold on to that as a legacy of the incident and they'd laugh, for years into the future, about how she'd changed and become a no-nonsense harridan, not to be messed with. They would refer to the whole thing as a blessing in disguise. They'd be grateful for how it would bring them closer together.

She looked up to find Robert and Esther both staring at her with her hand poised, the teapot still in it, as though someone had pressed the pause button. The tableau was set for the curtain to rise again, but the lead player, our heroine, was still missing.

Yvonne glanced at Robert and Esther. She could see they were waiting for her to say something. She didn't know where to find any words that would fit this scene, so she finished pouring the drinks and they all listened to the sound of liquid filling the mugs. They let the tea fill the silence while Yvonne hoped the right words would tumble out of the spout behind it.

'We have contacted everyone we know,' she said. 'And we've alerted the police. We've left messages and sent texts to her mobile, which is still ringing, but she's not answering.'

Robert interrupted. Theorising about why Celeste wasn't answering. Because she'd lost her phone? Because she couldn't answer? Because she was being prevented from answering? Because she and Yvonne had had a falling out and this was all about a juvenile strop that had got out of hand?

His insinuation that this was somehow Yvonne's fault was not unexpected, but it still stung her hard and pushed her resolve off balance for a moment. She had already spent the day wading through a swamp of guilt and regret. Had she been sharp with Celeste yesterday? Had she hugged her before she left the house for the evening? When was the last time she had told her daughter that she loved her?

She had never found any armour effective enough to protect her from Robert's words; whatever barrier she'd ever put up, he'd always found the vulnerable spots and prodded and poked until all her defences crumbled. A tiny drop of poison could spread so quickly, and he always choose the most innocuous route in, setting the cancer of self-doubt on a path to her subconscious before she realised what he was up to.

She glanced at the photograph of herself and Celeste on the wall opposite her. A picture taken on their first holiday together as a family of two, snapped by a stranger on the seafront at Whitby as Celeste proudly showed off her fish and chips and Yvonne proudly beamed at her daughter. She had reason to be proud. She had built a lifetime of memories with Celeste in Robert's absence. She had nurtured a girl with the confidence to leave, and given her a safe place to come back to. Her daughter was not gone because of something she had done, or not done, she was gone because of some other unknown.

She closed her eyes and pictured Celeste's face, pulling her daughter into the room, focusing on the only thing that mattered.

'Have you quite finished?'

He seemed for a moment like he might answer her with words, but instead glanced at Esther, as though looking for an ally to back up his line of questioning. Esther avoided his eyes and instead looked at Yvonne giving her permission to continue speaking.

'You can sit around wondering why Celeste isn't here and throwing blame across the table if you want, but I'm going out to find out where she is and bring her home. Come with me, or stay here, or go home, do whatever you like, but I've spent enough time talking and worrying and drinking tea; Celeste needs me to get up and do something.

'Esther, can I ask you to stay here in case Celeste does come back. You can help yourself to whatever. Just let me know if she gets in touch or if someone who's seen her gets in touch. Do you have my number?'

Before Esther could answer, Yvonne began scouring the kitchen for a paper and pen, opening drawers, cursing under her breath that there was never a pen anywhere when you need one.

'I can just put it in my phone,' Esther suggested.

But as she spoke, Yvonne was already scrawling it on the blackboard that hung by the kitchen door, under the words Celeste had written there the evening before '*Mum, don't let me sleep in past 11 tomorrow, even if I'm grumpy when you try and wake me up!*

Love ya :-)'

Esther read out the number on the blackboard and tapped it into her phone.

'Right. Are you coming?' Yvonne threw the words at Robert like a ball he needed to catch quickly before it hit him in the face. He stood up with the urgency she'd challenged him to feel and made for the door.

'Wait.' She ran upstairs to Celeste's room and returned clutching a photograph of her daughter, pulled from the pinboard on the bedroom wall, with a small tear where she had ripped it.

'Now we can go.'

Yvonne pulled her coat from the banister as she marched through the hall to the door, and waited on the doorstep for Robert to walk past her so that she could close her own front door behind him.

'We can split up or knock on doors together, what do you think?'

'Let's stick together.'

Disappointed but not surprised, she set off and allowed him to follow. Knocking first at the next-door neighbours' house, where the old man never spoke to her but often watched her struggle with heavy bags as she brought in the shopping.

'My daughter, Celeste, didn't come home last night so we're just knocking on doors to ask if anyone's seen her. This is her.'

11

Moira

Moira felt the full length of every piece of clothing as though she were frisking it for drugs, only taking it down from the line when she was convinced it was fully dry. She folded each item that passed the test and placed it neatly in her plastic basket before moving on to the next. With another couple of hours of daylight left, and a steady breeze, she was confident there was still some drying time left in the day, so anything with a hint of damp was unpegged and re-pegged in a different orientation to give it the best chance of drying all over.

She was a master at this. It was one of those skills she'd honed over years and years of practice. One of the many talents that would never win her any awards or applause. Banal, routine, but necessary. Billy and the boys would never be impressed by how efficient she was with the washing, but they couldn't do it. If she asked them to peg out a wash, it was all bunched up; thrown at the line as though a hurricane had taken it and deposited it there. So it was rare that she even asked them. Between the heavy sighs of 'I'll do it in a bit', the lingering resentment at being called upon to handle the damp fabric of their own clean garments, and the still moist, crumpled mess she got back at the end, it was easier to do it herself.

There was more than she'd hoped being given a last turn on the line this evening. Yesterday's rain and the downpour first thing had made her dither over whether to bother putting a wash on or not, and, by the time she was confident it had brightened up for the day, she'd deliberated a little more, wondering if it was too late for the washer's cycle and sufficient time on the line. There were a thousand small decisions to be made every day and it was tiring. Deciding what to buy, what to cook, which drawer to put things in, what to throw out, when it might be safe to hoover without William complaining about the noise and disruption; it all clogged up her brain. She'd thought she'd be able to save space for books and films and politics and internal debates about all of life's big questions as the boys got older and needed less hands-on looking after, but there was no space left. Working at school all week filled her head with the answers to the questions thrown at her from all quarters - teachers, parents, kids, delivery men – but at least she got thankyous and *'you're a lifesaver'* and *'brilliant, what would we do without you?'* At home, the treadmill of questions to answer, things to provide, jobs to be done was just as busy, but here there were no thanks for all she did; only complaints or sarcastic comments if something was left undone.

The last of the items to be turned on the line was William's joggers from the day before. They had been filthy with mud and damp from the rain and, as Moira turned them to peg them at the ankles, she tutted to see that they still looked a little grubby. William had put them on to wash himself - a minor miracle given that she didn't even know that he could work the machine. She couldn't be cross at him for that, but had she done it herself she would have sprayed them with stain remover first and maybe chosen a hotter wash, but it was too late now. If he was going to go on late night walks in the rain and get mud on his pants it was his own look out. At least he'd put his wet and muddy clothes in the machine, not left them festering on the bedroom floor for her to find when the wash was already mid-cycle. He'd even come and told her that he'd put his muddy stuff on to wash and muttered an apology for getting his things so dirty.

She thought back to how she'd loved seeing the boys' clothes flapping on the line when they were younger. Brightly coloured trousers with worn knees, T-shirts with dinosaurs and cars printed on them, and pyjamas with matching tops and bottoms. It had been James back then who had given her the headaches with getting stains out of things. He was the one who would climb trees and slide down hills on his bum. It was him who would spill raspberry sauce down his front every time she treated them from the ice cream van, and him who couldn't eat spaghetti without wearing as much of the tomato sauce as he actually swallowed. William had been much more careful; fastidious even. From being a toddler, he'd disliked having any dirt or food on his face, and they'd joked about his regular calls of 'wipe me,' sometimes multiple times during a single meal. While James was never happier than when he was ankle deep in mud, William had missed out on exploring and fun because he didn't like the mess. And every time, when James was delighted and filthy from the games he'd been playing, William had been envious of the fun but still unable to overcome his distaste for getting dirty.

She remembered how James had played upon his brother's idiosyncrasy to torment him, reassuring William that this bit wasn't muddy, or there was no risk of getting splashed if he ran through quickly. Then there were the practical jokes; the pockets full of sand and the Jam donut handed to him at the perfect orientation to squirt wet, sticky jam all down his chin and onto his T-shirt. William had been furious at that one. He had chased James all around the house to get his own back by rubbing his sugary hands through his brother's hair. James hadn't cared of course, a bit of sugar in his hair was no big deal to him and more than worth the satisfaction of seeing his elder brother so furious over something so ridiculous. James had laughed and laughed with the double joy of the squirting jam and the resulting fury. William had become even angrier at being laughed at, so angry that he'd picked up the trophy James had won for playing football and hit his brother over the head with it. The incident had resulted in two stained T-shirts thrown in a hot wash; one with a big splash of red jam down the front, the other with a big splash of red blood. Billy had sent both boys up to bed with no tea and a stern warning that they needed to learn to get on or they'd both be swapped for a pair of dogs that could be trained to behave. He'd made them shake hands and apologise to each other before climbing the stairs to bed at four in the afternoon.

Moira shuddered at the memory. She'd taken each of the boys a drink and a sandwich, finding James sitting up in bed making something out of Lego and William lying on the duvet, staring straight up at the ceiling as though he might burn a hole in it. She'd given both boys the same lecture about being kinder to each other and learning to get on. James had nodded, promised to try, and given her a hug; perhaps in apology, perhaps as a thank you for bringing the sandwich. William had continued staring at the ceiling and said nothing in response to her little speech, so she'd returned downstairs to her own mini-lecture from Billy about how she'd been too soft on the boys and was seeing the outcome of that now with this nasty, violent behaviour. She only had herself to blame, Bill had assured her, and taking them snacks when he'd sent them up there as punishment undermined him and made the punishment futile. He'd warned her then that he wouldn't step in to punish the boys again if she was only going to question his authority by downgrading his punishment, and he'd pretty much left her to it ever since.

She closed her eyes for a moment to try to erase the image of her two pre-teen boys, both spattered with red and blaming each other. The powerful, metallic scent of lighter fluid drifted through the fence from next door, taking her back to the days, years before, when she would stand at a safe distance holding hands with William on one side and James on the other while Billy lit the barbecue, keeping them safe despite their excitement that there would be fire and food cooked outside by Daddy.

She'd been warned that those days would not last. She'd been urged by older women to treasure every minute of them, including the tantrums and the sleepless nights. But, somehow, they'd disappeared long before she'd been ready for them to go. And the worst part was, she hadn't noticed them leave. The transition between those two trusting, sweet boys, each holding one of her hands and connected by her and their shared excitement, and the two grown men they had become had happened in moments. Time had passed with such stealth and miniscule, imperceptible change that she felt robbed of the chance to say goodbye at every stage. Who had taken those sweet boys from her and replaced them with William's moodiness and James's indifference?

She opened her eyes to see the grey smoke from next door's barbecue accompany the lighter fuel smell and frowned as she realised the washing she'd just repositioned so carefully was at risk of absorbing the scent of petrol and smoke if she didn't take it inside. But the alternative was draping it over the cold radiators and maybe even having to turn the heating on for an hour to get everything dried through.

Moira went back up the line, feeling how damp everything was one more time and deciding on balance to leave the last few things out for another hour to squeeze the last of the drying time out of the day. She wondered whether she should suggest to Billy that they might have a barbecue too. She could invite Monica and Ruth from work and see if William wanted to ask a friend over. She would check the weather forecast, there was no point in bringing the idea up if the weather was going to turn again.

As she brought the dry things into the house, William walked from the living room through the hall, heading for the stairs.

He asked her had she pegged out the things he'd put into the machine.

'Yes, thank you love, they're almost dry,' she answered smiling at him as he paused to peer into the basket she was carrying.

She thought he was going to say something else, but he just stood for a moment before moving towards the stairs.

There was a knock at the door, but William ignored it and continued towards the stairs.

'Answer that will you love, I've got my hands a bit full here.'

William sighed, taking heavy steps back down the two stairs he'd climbed and opening the door to a woman with a photograph in her hand and a man standing a few steps behind her.

'It'll be my mum you want,' he said, before the woman could open her mouth to speak. And he returned to the stairs, calling 'Mum, there's a woman at the door,' as he thudded up to his bedroom.

Moira carried the washing basket to the door with her and held it on her hip to indicate that she was busy. It was always the best way to politely cut short the evangelists and charity chuggers who arrived uninvited. She was sure she recognised the woman, but it was so hard to remember all the faces she'd seen come to the school office over the years. So many parents had been in and out of school to pay dinner money, collect for dentist appointments, drop off forgotten PE kits. She'd had to remember so many names and connect so many adult faces to their children, her memory held a whole ocean full of faces. And each parent remembered would suddenly be gone, just like that, when their child moved to high school, and she would never see them again, except at the shops, or in the street, where they would often vaguely recognise each other, but rarely say hello.

'Hello?' said Moira, trying to sound friendly and communicate 'make it quick' with her single word greeting.

The woman held up the photograph, pinching the edges with her fingers so that Moria could see the whole image clearly. She explained that this was her daughter, Celeste, missing since the night before. Last seen in town by her friend about 11.20pm when she left a bar to come home, but out of touch since. Not answering her phone, not with any of her friends. It wasn't like her, the woman said, she could be thoughtless, but she had never just stayed out all night and all day the next day without getting in touch.

The woman on the doorstep was struggling to speak without crying and the man standing behind her chipped in.

'We don't know whether Celeste actually headed home when she left the bar, so we're just asking round to ask if anyone's seen her.'

Moria looked at the photograph and the woman. She recognised the girl and her mum. An unusual name, Celeste, and she had been a delightful girl, always excited to be register monitor or be given a job to do. Always polite and good mannered. She'd seen her around the neighbourhood now and then since she'd left school, but not for a while, certainly not the night before.

Moira commented on how lovely the picture was and told the woman she remembered Celeste from her days at Redwood Road Primary. 'I work in the office there, I remember Celeste, such a lovely name, such a lovely girl.'

'Yes, but have you seen her?' The man asked.

'Not recently,' Moira said. 'I'm afraid not last night or today.'

'Well thanks anyway,' the woman said. 'If you do see her, or hear anything, can you let us know, I live just round the corner. 18 Limewood.'

Moira looked again at the photograph, which the woman was still holding, as though showing her work in assembly. The girl was laughing silently from the picture.

'We could ask my son,' she said. 'He was out last night, he might have seen her. We can ask my husband too. I doubt he'd have seen her because he's been home all weekend but let's ask him.'

She called to Billy and William. But there was no reply from either so, apologetically, she left the visitors on the doorstep and went to fetch Billy from the living room. He followed her to the hall, carrying the book he had been reading. He glanced at the photograph and shook his head.

'Lovely girl,' he said, 'hope you find her soon,' and he ambled back to his armchair to continue reading.

Moira called to William again. Still there was no response.

'I'm so sorry, noise cancelling headphones,' she smiled. 'Mum cancelling headphones I call them.'

She left the woman with the photograph on the doorstep for a second time and ran upstairs to fetch her son, calling his name as she walked across the landing to knock on his door.

William was reluctant to come downstairs, assuring Moira that he'd seen no-one when he'd gone out for a walk the previous night and pointing out he'd been at home all day.

'So just come down and tell them that, can you?'

'Why can't you tell them?'

'Because I said I'd come and get you.'

'So?'

'So, just come and look at the photo and tell the woman you haven't seen her daughter. She's worried, it's the least we can do.'

He muttered under his breath how he didn't see the point and he couldn't help it if he hadn't seen her, but sluggishly followed his mother down the stairs.

The man had retreated out of the gate and was waiting impatiently on the pavement when they arrived back at the door. The woman was looking at the photograph.

'I didn't see anyone,' William said, before she could show him the picture.

She held the image up for him to see.

'I'm sorry,' he said, and walked back upstairs, leaving the woman to sigh her 'thanks anyway' and Moira to close the door.

12

Faith

Faith could hear the kettle boiling and clicking itself off, but she couldn't summon the will or the energy to go and pour the water onto the tea bag. There hadn't been a moment all weekend when she'd been able to sit alone like this. If she moved, she might break the spell. Sophie or Laura might see her on her feet, or might hear her pull herself up to standing, no matter how silently she tried to creep into the kitchen, and then she would inevitably be pulled back into bringing something, helping with something, answering questions. Noise, and busyness and work had consumed every waking minute of her weekend. And there had been far too few sleeping minutes.

At least the girls had had their tea at Grandma's and Grandma had cajoled them into the bath on Saturday evening so she could just supervise pyjamas and bed tonight. But bed times were creeping later. Sophie had negotiated a 9pm bedtime on the basis that, at three years older than Laura, she should be entitled to more time. But more time for Sophie meant even less time for Faith, and even more whining at the injustice of an 8.30pm end to the day from Laura. She shuddered at her own thoughts of chasing them away to bed as soon as possible so that she could drink that cup of tea without conversations about TV programmes she hadn't watched or school friends she didn't know. She yearned for the peace of an uninterrupted evening, nothing special, just the kind where she might eat chocolate without sharing and watch a film on TV without explaining the plot every five minutes, or missing the ending because she was busy fetching drinks and snacks. But the minute she allowed herself the fantasy of delegating another evening to someone else while she spent some time alone, she felt guilty and ashamed. She'd missed so much time with the girls already, working to look after other people's families while her own daughters were at home with their dad or at Grandma's or at holiday club, or fobbed off on any parent she vaguely knew who was willing to take them for a few hours. Sophie was already taller than Grandma. Another year and she'd be off to high school, reinventing herself as a teenager and leaving her talkative, imaginative younger self behind. Faith found it hard to envisage. Perhaps Sophie wouldn't become a sullen, self-absorbed teenager like she had been; maybe she would just be a bigger version of the little girl who was always drawing pictures and playing hide and seek.

Sophie had presented Faith with a picture when she'd stopped off at Grandma's to pick the girls up on her way home from work. She'd finished at 4.30pm and been at the door of her mother's house, still wearing her uniform, for five as she'd promised, but the girls hadn't been ready and her mum had lured her in with the promise of a cup of tea and a slice of lemon cake that she'd baked with Sophie and Laura that afternoon. The girls had been so proud of their cake and full of tales of how they'd cracked one egg each and managed not to get a single bit of shell in the mixture. The sweetness of the cake and the luxury of having a plate of something delicious and a mug of something warm brought to her as she sat had lifted Faith. She'd enjoyed the pleasure on her children's faces as she had tasted and approved the cake, and had felt the warmth of her mother's care in the hot tea as it slipped down her throat, while she listened to the tales of what they'd done in her absence. The funny things they'd said, the way they'd entertained themselves in the church garden.

When the girls had gone off to pack up their things, checking one more time did she enjoy the cake and did she like the picture, Faith had thought she'd have a moment to exhale her exhaustion. She'd hoped that her mother would see it hanging in the air and blow it away, as she'd blown tears and bathwater from her eyes when Faith had been the little girl and Grandma had been the mum. But before she could swallow the sip of tea she had taken, her mother filled the space left by the girls to tell her about the sister of a woman whose name she couldn't quite remember at church, who had died suddenly of an ulcer she hadn't known she'd had. And wasn't it awful how death could just take you like that at any time. And she hadn't even been old this woman, or ill. No sign of it happening. Just like that.

Faith had swallowed all the tales of death that had surrounded her during her shift that day with a final gulp of her tea. Sunday shifts were always the worst for deaths on the ward, as though those with little hope for the week ahead were tidying themselves away to make space for Monday morning. As the ward sister, it was often her job to break the news to those left behind, interrupting their roast dinners and National Trust saunters.

'I'll need to be getting back,' Faith had said, standing up and taking her plate and cup to the sink. 'Mark's been texting me to ask when we'll be back, he's been chucking up half the day. It's back from ministering to the sick in hospital to ministering to the sick at home for me now.'

She'd called up the stairs to the girls, only to find them already standing at the kitchen door with their coats on. 'You'd better take the rest of this cake with you,' Grandma had told them. 'I won't eat all that and you two did make it.' Faith had waited some more while her mum wrapped the cake in foil and handed it to her.

'You make sure you take some time to look after yourself too,' her mum counselled her in the doorway.

'I will,' Faith had promised as she hugged her mum goodbye, thanking her for the cake and the babysitting. She'd watched the girls scramble into the car arguing over whose turn it was to sit in the front, and paused somewhere between aching to stay and wishing herself already home. Home was only a minute away, a short walk if she hadn't already been in the car stopping off on the way back from work. Nearly there.

Faith had been relieved to find Mark asleep when she got home. She'd taken her pyjamas from under her pillow and tiptoed into the bathroom to change out of her uniform before heading back downstairs. The kettle had boiled, and the cake was in the kitchen, still in its foil. She could hear the TV and the girls chatting in the next room and, as much as she wanted a cup of tea and something to eat, she was reluctant to do anything but sit in the quiet and solitude of the back room while that option was still available. She wasn't sure her leaden limbs were up to the job of supporting her long enough to make tea and toast anyway.

Faith was surrounded by mess and colour. The back room had always been the playroom, so its walls were crowded with the girls' artwork, some of it no more than daubs of brightly coloured paint, much of it self-portraits or primitive depictions of the four of them, with 'I love you Mummy' carefully traced in infant wobbliness over the template of neat adult writing. The pictures overlapped, with curled and torn edges, some of them mounted on brightly coloured paper at school and brought home with Sophie or Laura's name written neatly in a corner, some of them drawn on the back of an A4 envelope or the inside face of a cereal packet, capturing pieces of debris that should have escaped with the recycling to as treasured artwork. There were years of moments pinned to a wall that Faith saw every day and seldom looked at. She looked now, suspended in the calm of a moment with no job to do and no question to answer, bombarded by all the days she had raced through for a decade and the small seconds of focus they had contained when she'd stuck each of these drawings and paintings to the wall.

Her phone pinged in her pocket. It was a message from Mark. She clearly hadn't crept in and out of the bedroom as quietly as she'd thought. *'Still feeling rubbish. Could eat though. What are we doing for dinner?'* The girls had eaten. Faith had had a slice of lemon cake since the sad looking ham sandwich she'd eaten for lunch hours earlier. There was food in the fridge, but she had neither the will to cook it nor the desire to eat it. *'Cheese on toast?'* she messaged back. There had been tales of husbands cooking roast dinners and chicken curries at the handover meeting when she'd finished her shift. Faith was never envious of anyone's fancy house or posh car, but a husband that had dinner ready when she got home, that was a dream that she could only aspire to. She waited for a response, thinking about how much she didn't want to stand in the kitchen making cheese on toast, then taking it upstairs to Mark and serving it to him while he lay in bed. The girls would inevitably smell the toast and want some too, so there'd be three platefuls to dole out before she could make her own. *'Or take out?'* she messaged again. *'Chinese,'* he responded, then messaged again, *'You choose, nothing too spicy, still feeling a bit dodge xx'.* She replied with a smiley face and a bowl of noodles emoji, allowing the graphics on her phone to convey the enthusiasm she didn't feel.

She scrolled through the take-out app, looking for places with good reviews and free delivery, dithering over menus, before finally confirming her choices and paying. She smiled at the thought of how excited the girls would be because she'd added spring rolls to the order for them. Estimated delivery time: 7.45pm, what were the chances of her spending half an hour alone in this room relaxing and regrouping before the food arrived and she had to switch back into enthusiastic mum, responsible adult, person in charge?

She scrolled through Facebook, pausing to like pictures of friends' Sundays out at parks with their kids, the cakes and DIY projects they'd done, the things they'd bought and the nights out they'd had. She was drawn into a labyrinth of photographs, links to articles and things she could buy, then back to the top of her feed again, seeing some of the posts for the second time and snippets from the lives of friends of friends whose lives she could peek into because someone she knew had commented on their news.

Faith paused over a post that a friend had shared. It said 'Missing: have you seen Celeste?' There was a picture of a girl smiling, a long-haired, pretty girl with mischief in her eyes and not a care in the world.

Faith touched the screen to read the full post. *'Missing since Saturday night around 11.30pm. Last seen at McCain's bar on Empire Street, Celeste left to go home alone but did not arrive.*

'Celeste is slim and 5ft 8" with long dark hair. She was last seen wearing a leopard print jacket, a flowery top, black skirt, black tights and brown boots. Please get in touch if you have seen her, or ask her to let us know she is alright. Her mum is very worried.'

There was a phone number for the police and an email address and several more pictures, some of them of the girl wearing the outfit described with her arm around the girl who had originally written the call for help, Esther. The post had already been shared several times by people Faith knew and people she didn't. There were pictures of some of the clothes on their own, downloaded from internet shopping sites, the fur jacket and the boots.

Faith looked through the images and read the description a second time. She had thought when she'd first begun training as a nurse that she'd become desensitised to suffering, that it would become like news coverage of disasters happening in other countries; she would see it and know it was awful but feel detached from it. But the pain she saw every day weighed heavier and heavier on her shoulders because she had to absorb it and move on so quickly, never acknowledging it, never being able to pause and process it. It wasn't her pain, but it was in the room with her, she witnessed it, she inhaled it. She could never exhale. And the pain of loss was the worst pain of all because there was no cure for it, no hope or respite, no plan.

Faith used her finger and thumb to expand the pictures for a closer look on her small screen. She knew the face. She didn't know the girl, but she had seen her. At the hospital maybe? Or just round and about? She thought she remembered seeing the coat too. But not last night, she'd been in bed at 11.30 last night ready for an early start this morning.

Sophie appeared at the side of Faith's chair as though she had appeared by magic. Faith hadn't heard the door open or her daughter's footsteps across the carpet, she'd just felt the child's presence and her warm breath as she leaned over to look at the phone.

'Who is she?' Sophie asked.

'Just a girl who lives near here, her mum doesn't know where she is and they're trying to find her.'

'Do you know her?'

'No, but we can keep an eye out, can't we?' Faith looked up at her daughter and smiled. Before she could switch off the screen, Sophie stopped her.

'Can I look?' Sophie took the phone and scrolled through the pictures. 'I've seen a boot like that. This morning in the garden at church. It's a really nice boot isn't it? But there was just one. Me and Laura were playing with it.'

Faith took back the phone, trying to smile, trying to appear as though finding a boot identical to the one worn by a girl last seen the night before was nothing to worry about.

'Did you? That's a coincidence. What did you do with the boot when you'd finished playing with it?'

'We just left it there. We hid it, actually, we were taking turns to hide it and the other one had to find it. Grandma takes ages when she's talking to her friends.'

Faith smiled through a wave of nostalgia for the games she and her own sister had played while waiting for their mother to finish talking outside church.

The doorbell rang.

'That'll be the Chinese, I'll get it,' Faith said to her daughter, putting her phone into her pocket and getting up from the chair.'

'We're having Chinese? Are we having Chinese? Spring rolls? Laura, Laura, we're having Chinese! We're having spring rolls!' she shouted, waving her hands in the air like a footballer after scoring a goal.

Sophie followed her mother to the front door, with Laura joining them from the other room to greet the delivery.

But the door didn't open to a take-out delivery. The woman on the doorstep was clutching a photograph, with a man standing behind her looking dishevelled and uncomfortable.

'I'm sorry to disturb your evening,' the woman said, 'but I'm looking for my daughter and I'm just knocking on doors to see if anyone's seen her.'

IV

Celeste

*T*he words *my mum kept repeating when I fell off my bike when I was seven and hit my head keep rolling around in my brain like a ball bearing in a pinball machine. Don't go to sleep. Don't go to sleep. Stay awake. Don't go to sleep. Awake. Awake. Awake. Don't sleep.*

She told me to think of anything: times tables, what we had for tea yesterday, my favourite thing on TV, Christmas. I think of Christmas. The tree, the bauble with my picture in. It has glitter inside and when you shake it the glitter sparkles and falls like shimmering snow across my face. How old would I have been when the picture was taken? Me and Father Christmas trapped in time after a visit to the Trafford Centre. It was before the bump on the head. Before she told me not to fall asleep.

Stay awake. Think of anything. Think of being at home, of playing with your toys. Barbie dolls, Girl's World, Kerplunk. There's no place like home. Dorothy. Toto. You're not in Kansas now Celeste. Red slippers, more sparkles. Click those glittery shoes Celeste. There's no place like home. Home, with the doorbell that we never use because it used to be broken so we only ever used the knocker. Home, where we make tea in the brown teapot that was bought to replace the one I threw at the wall in a rage when Mum grounded me for whatever it was. The new brown teapot is exactly the same as the old one. We never mention it. It didn't happen. I wrap my hands around the new teapot to warm them on cold mornings just like I did with the old one. Warm hands. Cold mornings. Tea. Kitchen. Mum. Home.

Stay awake. Stay awake. It's time to get up. Rise and shine and brush your teeth Celeste. Wash your face now. Imperial Leather, the scent of home, the little gold label. Feel the smoothness of the foil fixed firmly in the centre of the soap Celeste, peel it back and run your finger over the groove cut into the soap that exactly fits the sticker with the shiny logo. Put it back and smooth it down and sniff the soap. There's no place like home, there's no place like home, there's no smell like home.

I was brave, very brave they said when I fell off my bike and hit my head. No helmet. The helmet was in the house, I didn't like it, it made my head itch. Four stitches up on the right under my hair where no-one will ever see them. You'll have a tiny wee scar there, the nurse said. Tiny and wee; two kinds of small. Just like the nurse, a small woman with child-sized hands. I remember her hands. She gave me a lollipop for being so brave. Cola. Suck on the sweet, sticky lollipop, Celeste. Remember the flavour of that? The taste of courage.

And there was a cake for me when I got home too. A big cake to say well done, you were brave. A cake to say we're more happy that you're OK than we are cross at you for not wearing the helmet. And a necklace, a star for being a star, Mum said. It suits you, she said. Celeste means heavenly you know, and the heavens are full of stars. She always told me that. You are a star from heaven, Celeste, a heavenly gift in the shape of a girl. Full of stars, the heavens. How many stars? Count the stars Celeste, don't fall asleep. There's no place like home. One, two, three, four, fifteen, twenty-nine, one hundred.

13

William

William stood just to the right of his bedroom window watching through the gap between the net curtain and the window frame as the woman made her way back up the path to the gate. He knew exactly the right spot for peering out onto the street without being visible from below. Odd, though, how many people would look around when he stood observing like that, as though they could feel his attention on them. Or perhaps people were just paranoid. If they had nothing to hide, why would they be bothered that anyone was watching?

The woman's feet crunched on the gravel as she walked with purpose towards the gate, sighing at the man as he leaned on the gatepost. The gate let out its usual groan of weariness as she opened it, complaining, as it did every time, that no-one had oiled it in years. She let it clank shut behind her, rupturing the quiet of the still Sunday evening. She said something to the man and began walking purposefully towards the next house, pausing for him to catch up. And then, there it was. As she paused, she looked around, as though trying to see a bird she'd heard or looking for a clue in the clouds. She could feel that someone was watching her, but she didn't know it was him. But when she looked up, straight at him, all she would be able to see was the lace patterns of the curtains and, perhaps, the dinosaur lampshade that had been in place above William's bed for as long as he could remember. She couldn't see him. And she didn't know what he had done.

He watched as the woman let herself into next door's garden and knocked on their door and repeated herself and showed her picture. How many more doors would she knock on before she gave up, he wondered. How many gates would clank? How many couples would wait for each other to answer the doorbell? How many meals would be interrupted? Or baths? Or TV shows? Or computer games? Nobody could tell her anything because no-one knew anything. Sure enough, there she was again, trying to hide her disappointment behind a polite 'thanks anyway' and leaving another gate to swing closed as she moved on to the next house and the next.

He watched her until she had turned the corner, and he could no longer see or hear her visiting one house after the next. He was impressed by her determination. What would his own mother do in a similar situation? Would she be out there, knocking on doors too? Would she be ringing round and getting neighbours together to have a look? Or would she be at home, making tea, trusting the police to do something? Hoping for the best?

William stepped away from the window and stood behind the door, listening. He waited for a sound on the landing; a footstep, a breath, but there was nothing. His dad would be flicking through the channels and complaining to his mum, as she ironed the clean washing, that they put the same old shit on TV every Sunday afternoon. His mum would be nodding her agreement between puffs of steam as she stood, half watching the screen, half watching the creases disappear with every purposeful sweep of the iron. His parents had spent every Sunday evening like this for as long as he could remember. They were locked into the scene as though playing to a new audience of bored onlookers every Sunday evening. If the script changed, the world might be knocked off its axis. The butterfly effect could happen right there in his own living room, with its cream wallpaper and dado rails, but his parents were not the type to rock the boat. Routine had been invented by them, they had never even considered doing anything brave or different. They wouldn't know it if they saw it. There would be no history made here.

He sat on the bed and thought about Celeste. It was unfortunate that she'd been sitting there just at that moment. If she'd just gone straight home and not stopped, things could have been so different for her. If she'd just stayed in. Or just stayed out a little longer. If she'd walked a different way home, or lived somewhere else, or been someone else, things could have been different for both of them. She was the one who'd started a butterfly effect, sitting there with her shoe off at a stupid hour of the evening. Odd behaviours lead to odd things happening, and it had all unravelled so quickly it was hard for William to remember now how it had started or how he'd ended up on the dual carriageway embankment next to the bridge. It should have ended in the trees, but she'd rolled down onto the embankment. She'd been heavy and difficult to manoeuvre for such a slim and elegant thing. Strong, but easily put in her place. And then quiet, as though she'd been expecting someone like him to come along. As though she'd been waiting for him.

He opened the drawer under his bed, where years of jigsaws and board games were still stored. Leaning down to reach between the boxes, he fished around with his thumb and his index finger to find the necklace he'd dropped into the drawer when he'd got home the night before. He panicked as he felt nothing but the hard, smooth laminated board of the drawer. Perhaps his mum had been in and found it? Maybe she wasn't downstairs ironing? Maybe she was on the phone to the police? At the police station? Waiting with an officer in their living room with the TV switched off and the iron still cold in the understairs cupboard.

He glanced out of the window. There was no sign of a police car and his mum's red Peugeot was still parked on the opposite side of the road, just where it had been all day. An ice cream van played the Match of the Day theme tune from some street nearby and one of the neighbours was trundling out the bin ready for the recycling collection in the morning. Everything was normal. People were just getting on with their Sundays. Apart from Celeste and her mum. Everyone else was just getting on with their Sunday evening and he needed to relax.

But he did also need to find the necklace, so he knelt on the floor, pulled out the drawer as far as it would go and began removing the boxes. Some of the games had never been played. Others he remembered from Christmases and the end of school terms, when they were allowed to bring a toy to school, and making the right choice of something that everyone would want to play had felt like a matter of life and death.

He piled them high on the carpet next to him, until, finally, he could see the little silver star and its delicate chain curling like a signature at the bottom of the drawer where it had worked its way under the boxes. He reached to take it out as the door opened behind him.

'The ice cream van's on its way round. Me and your dad are going to have a 99, or I might have a tub. It's the whippy one. Do you want... What's all this?'

His mum was standing in the doorway with her purse in her hand and a concerned look on her face as she spotted the pile of board games and jigsaws. As she looked at it, the tower toppled over, with some of the boxes spilling their contents across the floor.

'Now look what you've done, coming in and creating a draught, just when I was in the middle of having a clear out.'

'Here, let me help you.'

As she stepped forward and bent down to start clearing the boxes, William quickly closed the drawer in the divan, as though simply moving it out of the way. There was a jumble of dice and counters, cards, pencils, bits of plastic and jigsaw pieces on the floor, but the necklace was safely hidden away by itself in the drawer.

'This could take a while,' his mum said, stating the obvious with her patronising smile.

But her smile wasn't aimed at the mess, it was directed at a piece of paper, poking out of one of the boxes.

William reached for it, but she had already snatched it up and quickly held it in both hands. It was a piece of paper folded in two with a picture of a flower and a butterfly on the front. She opened it up and read the child's handwriting inside.

"To the best mum in the world," she read aloud, *"I love you forever and ever. Love from William."*

William tried to return her smile as she sighed 'What a lovely boy you were,' but he couldn't remember being the boy who drew that picture and wrote those words. He tried to picture himself sitting somewhere in the same house, or maybe at school, to create the thing his mother now held in her hands. But he couldn't recall it. He couldn't visualise himself doing that. It was a page taken from another time. The evidence of that boy was still around, in the games and the picture and the mum who had held his hand and read to him, baked with him, given him Calpol when he was poorly in the night. But all of those things only connected him to that boy by the flimsiest of threads.

'And you still are,' Moira added, smoothing out the paper on her leg and placing it carefully next to her on the floor. 'Why don't you let me clear all this up, I can take it to the charity shop on my lunchbreak tomorrow, or school might want some of it for wet playtimes and after-school club. You could go and get the ice creams.'

She held out her purse towards him. How could he leave her in his room by herself? What if she looked in the drawer?

What if she did look? She would only see a necklace. It could be any old necklace, she might think it belonged to one of the games. Some of them had come from the charity shop in the first place. Some of them had been to school and back more than once. The worst that could happen was that she'd find it and take it. Wear it maybe. Or decide it must belong to some girlfriend of his and leave it there. She'd probably say nothing. She probably wouldn't snoop because she knew he'd hate that. She was not so bad most of the time. She'd been the kind of mum the kid he used to be made pictures for.

'OK,' he said, reaching to take her purse from her. 'Tub or 99?'

'Tub with a flake, please. Get a 99 for your dad and whatever you want.'

He stood up to go.

'No raspberry for me,' she added. 'I always get it down my front. Thanks, love.'

William left his mother sifting through jigsaw pieces and sprinted downstairs, conscious that he had to put some shoes on and go out and find the ice cream van before it moved on too far to make it worth the effort. His trainers were not in the rack by the door and he sighed as he realised he'd have to go back upstairs to find them. But, as he made for the stairs again, he remembered he'd left them on the doorstep; they'd been muddy when he'd got home, and still sour with the scent of vomit, so he'd taken them off outside and left them on the bottom step where the rain might wash them clean. Just there, where the woman had been standing with the picture of her daughter. The picture of Celeste.

He had tried not to look at the picture. Tried not to see her face laughing at him. But there she had been, practically calling out of the photograph '*Mum, it was him, this is the one.*' He shuddered as he recalled the woman on the doorstep but reminded himself that he had given nothing away. She'd had no reason to disbelieve him when he said he hadn't seen Celeste. No reason to question why his trainers were so muddy, or why they had been left out on the step. No reason to even to notice they were there at all. If she'd seen them, she hadn't said. Why would she?

He tucked his mother's purse into his back pocket, put on the spare trainers that he never usually wore because they looked like something you'd wear for PE at school, then closed the door behind him, listening for the ice cream van to help him identify where it had moved to. He'd have to sort out the other shoes when he got back. Put them in the washing machine maybe? Or leave them in the back garden for a few days for the rain to wash away the dirt and the stink.

There it was again, the familiar melody he and his brother had sung along to as boys. Allowed to stay up on a Saturday evening to watch the match highlights, they had lolloped in pyjamas on the floor, with a chocolate milkshake and a packet of malted milk biscuits, singing along with '*Da da di da di da di da da, di da di da di da*' as though casting a spell to make the players appear on screen. William had never been that interested in the football, just in the treat of staying up and eating snacks and watching something just for the boys while his mum baked a chocolate cake for Sunday.

William walked towards the distorted tune cutting through the bird song and traffic sounds of the early evening. He found the ice cream van in the next street, its tune no longer playing. As he turned the corner, he could see there was no queue, so he braced himself to break into a run to catch it, or at least let the driver have sight of him and know not to move off for a moment.

But the driver was still standing at the counter, his engine running to keep the freezer switched on, but showing no signs of returning to his seat to drive off. He was looking out between sliding windows that displayed pictures of lollies and varying sized cones, bringing the child catcher in Chitty Chitty Bang Bang to mind for William.

As William got closer, slowing from a purposeful march to a casual stroll, he could see the ice cream man was watching something, or someone. Perhaps he'd spotted a child that might be tempted to run home and ask a parent for some money for an ice lolly. Or a parent, just on the brink of giving in to the mithering and agreeing to an ice cream just this once.

But, as William reached the van, it became clear that it was neither a hopeful child nor a pestered parent that was holding the ice cream man's attention. He was watching as the woman who had brought the picture of Celeste to the door – Celeste's mother – stood at another door, with the man – Celeste's father he presumed. The man was standing much closer this time, taking part in the exchange instead of sitting back like a member of the audience, concerned he might be roped in to taking part in a street theatre performance.

William tried to focus on the ice cream van. He was getting close enough to see the prices, written in black marker pen on stickers beneath the picture of each item on the window. What had his mum asked for again. He tried to remember: a 99 with raspberry? Or without raspberry? There was something about raspberry, but he could think whether it was a definitely do or a definitely don't. They were talking outside the house where Celeste's parents were standing, her mother with that photograph half-forgotten in her hand and the father nodding and looking around as though trying to get his bearings. The second woman, the one standing on the inside of the doorstep, was bending to fasten her shoes, calling to someone behind her. What was she saying? Who was she talking to. It couldn't be Celeste? Could it be Celeste? She had a name. That girl, that coincidence who just appeared right there on the bench just at that moment when he'd been angry and hurt, emotionally and psychologically battered by Anne, Annie, Mitch the bitch. The other girl shouldn't have been there when he was just trying to pull himself together after all that. She had a name. Celeste. She had a mum and dad, and they were looking for her.

William felt his insides lurch the way they used to when he and James had urged his dad to speed over the bumps on country roads and they'd cheered and laughed at the sensation. But he was in control of his own two feet now, and the ground was solid beneath them. He hesitated, taking his mother's purse out of his pocket and pretending to count out the correct change while he loitered as close as he could reasonably get to the house to eavesdrop. It wasn't Celeste, it was a younger girl calling back to her mother, 'I'm coming, I'm just doing my laces. I'll show you. I'll show you where we found it.'

He had to pretend he wasn't listening and just keep moving towards the ice cream van. He just needed to focus on the errand he'd been sent for. Three ice creams and home. Three ice creams and home. The words, repeated in his head beat out a rhythm for him to follow as he walked, and he reached the window of the van as though teleported from where he'd taken the purse from his pocket.

'Three 99s please, one with no raspberry,' William was talking to the ice cream man but looking at the house where the child was now taking the lead with the two women following, the man traipsing behind them, and a second man standing in the doorway with a second girl holding his hand.

The ice cream man was watching them too, right up to the point at which the child leader and her posse disappeared from view around the corner. There was the smallest of pauses; a breath, a shiver and the ice cream man stepped back into his skin. 'What can I get you, young man?'

'Three 99s please, one with no raspberry,' William repeated. He wanted to ask the ice cream man if he'd heard what they'd said, if he knew what was going on. But he didn't need to ask.

'It's a terrible business, isn't? They've not seen their daughter since last night and the police won't do anything.' He held a flake in the air as he spoke and then planted it in the first ice cream. 'Nothing.'

William took the ice cream as the man passed it through the window without replying. There was no need to hide his curiosity in casual questions, because the ice cream man had spent years driving his van round uneventful streets with nothing more dramatic to re-tell than the odd fall off a bicycle or domestic at the front gate.

'Everyone's talking about it. All over Facebook apparently, and that other one, what's it called?'

'Instagram?' William took the second 99 through the window.

'That's the one. Anyway,' he paused, waving and pointing with the flake for the third ice cream, 'it looks like the people at number six know something because when the mother knocked on, there was much more chat and they've gone off now to look at whatever it is they've gone to look at.' He punctuated his sentence by stabbing the ice cream with the flake before squirting raspberry sauce on it.

'I said one with no sauce.'

'Did you? Sorry mate. It's got me a bit distracted to be honest. I might head after them and see what they've found. That'll be £6.00 please.'

William counted out a variety of coins from his mother's purse, struggling to retrieve them one-handed while holding two cornets in the other, but determined to make the man wait and continue holding the third cone as a punishment for messing up with the raspberry sauce. The ice cream man hadn't even sounded sorry, and now William would have to apologise to his mum, who was bound to assume it was his mistake.

The delay would also, maybe, prevent the ice cream man from following the procession of Celeste's parents, the woman, her daughter and the handful of neighbours who were shameless enough to tag along behind them at a short distance. William wondered whether it was feasible for him to take a detour home and take a look at what the fuss was about. There were others nosey enough to do it, so no-one would think it odd if he were amongst them. But the ice cream was already melting, and it would be difficult to think of a reason for not going directly back home. He'd find out soon enough from his mum, who always knew everyone's business, and from social media, where everyone over-shared.

He strode home, licking the drips from all three ice creams as he went. As he lifted his hand to knock at the front door, it opened, with his mum standing there holding a pile of games and jigsaws under one arm, as though she'd just won big at the school fair tombola.

'We thought you'd got lost!' she exclaimed, standing back to let him in.

'The stupid ice cream man put raspberry on all of them, sorry,' he said, handing her one of the cones.

'Had he run out of tubs too? Well at least you've saved me the trouble of spilling it all down myself. Look at you, you look like you've murdered someone.'

William followed her gaze to his T-shirt, which was spattered down the front with a long drip of raspberry sauce. He reached instinctively to wipe it off, smudging it into a large gash in the process.

'You'd better take it off and bring it in the kitchen so I can get the stain out before it sets like that for good. Take that one in to your dad first, will you though? I need to put these down somewhere.' She nodded towards the boxes under her arm, and he noticed she was wearing the small star necklace he'd hidden in the drawer.

Moira noticed that he'd spotted it. 'I found this in the drawer when I put some of the jigsaws back – there might be grandchildren to entertain one day, mightn't there. It must have ended up in one of the boxes when you took a game to school. Nice isn't it. I might as well have it – no chance of returning it to whoever it belonged to now.'

His mother disappeared into the kitchen and, unable to do anything else, William took the two remaining 99s into the living room, where his dad greeted him with 'Ooh, a flake and everything.'

14

Orson

Orson didn`t like social media. He viewed it as a place for unhappy people to brag about how happy they are, bicker about politics or moan about things they might be able to change if they spent less time seeking solace from vague acquaintances and more time sorting their lives out.

He had an Instagram account, with pictures of himself in yoga poses or meditating, both of which he carefully composed using the timer function on his camera, or with the help of Mimi, his friend, friend-with-benefits, soulmate, sidekick, partner-in-crime, assistant. His Mimi – everyone should have one.

Orson paid close attention to the expression on his face when photographs were being taken, as well as the perfection of his pose. He had to look calm. More than calm; he had to appear transported to another level of peace and tranquillity. And handsome too, he was selling an aspiration of beautiful body and beautiful soul in perfect harmony. It wasn`t about vanity, he explained to Mimi, it was about creating the look that made people want to buy yoga from him, instead of someone else. He had to be someone they wanted to be. It wasn't about showing off; it was about business.

He didn`t count his Instagram account as social media. Building his follower numbers was building his profile, and nurturing a profile that sold his carefully crafted brand combining his skills and aesthetic was just as important as maintaining his practice and delivering classes his students enjoyed. Since graduation, yoga had transitioned from a side hustle to a career path. His evolutionary anthropology degree had been great, but it had never been about preparing for the world of work. For Orson, university had been education for the sake of learning, not earning.

Knowledge should be its own reward, he'd told his parents, just as it had been for the great scholars of the past. He'd never imagined himself in a suit, or with a nine-to-five of any kind; that sort of rigid structure seemed like a slow death to him. If his studies had taught him anything, he explained to his mum and dad, it was that life is short, so it's important to make the most of the time and gifts you have, and live your best life without the shackles of other people's routines and expectations. A wild and free life he called it, when he inducted his students into his philosophy. He talked to them about the importance of his 'why' to his yoga practice (and theirs), and challenged them to 'leave now' if they were interested only in what yoga could do for them, rather than why they were taking on this journey. He'd had the phrase printed on a sweatshirt – a green one to symbolise connection with nature – which he wore all the time since his yellow jumper had gone missing. He'd loved that yellow jumper, and he was pretty sure it had been Celeste who had taken it. But it was probably best he hadn't accused her or asked for it back. He didn't need the drama. If she wanted it, let her have it. Her karma, not his. All loss is experience, and he knew that accepting whatever hand the universe dealt him would prompt unexpected opportunities, even from things he might initially find unfair or annoying. Without the loss of his signature jumper, he wouldn't be wearing his branded sweatshirt all the time; branding that brought him enquiries, followers, customers.

It was the same with his 2:2. He'd hoped for a first and believed himself certain of at least a 2:1, so he'd been distressed when the result of three years of study had been so disappointing. He'd decided to reframe the news when he opened the envelope, told his parents that it was part of a drive by the university to give disadvantaged students a lift, while those from more prosperous homes were marked down to achieve a balance overall. He explained it so convincingly that he became convinced himself. Adopted the lie as a truth and the consequences as an inevitable twist of fate. *'Wyrd biþ ful aræd'*, as he was fond of quoting from the Anglo Saxon poem: *'fate is utterly inexorable.'* He knew now it had been a blessing in disguise. Fate taking a hand to show him what his next steps in life should be. He'd set up Wild and Free Yoga Flow and Meditation, persuaded Mimi to invest so that he could get a website built and have more sweatshirts printed, and T-shirts and water bottles too. If he could make his clients a walking ad for his business, why not?

And hadn't he been right? People loved his brand, and they loved him too. Things were going well, and there was plenty of scope for expanding his client base if he attracted the right kind of clients online. It wasn't about filling the classes in church halls and community centres anymore, it was all about tailored private lessons for people, mostly women (all women in fact), who looked after themselves and wanted to take care of their mind, body and soul. Women who loved the wild and free philosophy. Their jobs, kids and relationships might stop them from living it, but he could help them feel the possibility with a one-hour session of yoga and meditation. And he knew if he could get a new client to do one private session with him, they'd be back for more. And recommend him to their friends. Evangelise about him on their own social media even. Women eager to spend good money on the dream of freedom and fulfilment, even if it was just for an hour, once a week. Even if they never went further than their own open plan kitchen diner, and had to schedule their sessions around school pick-up, date night and the supermarket big shop. He could make them feel amazing about themselves with the right poses, encouragement and compliments. He could make them practically beg him for a regular slot. Then he'd reach into his battered rucksack, pull out his dog-eared diary with a sigh, and tell them he was very tight on availability, but he'd see what he could do to move things around and fit them in. They all loved the paper diary and the pencil. Sustainable. Old school. Personal. They all appreciated him taking the trouble to make space for them in his busy schedule.

He scrolled through his Instagram, checking for likes and comments, searching his #wildandfree hashtag to see how many times his clients were using it in their posts, and keeping a close eye on what other yoga teachers were doing. He was careful to drip-feed positive comments across posts from his followers, especially his students, and to like content from other teachers, as long as they weren't local; it was good for his brand to be magnanimous in his praise of others. It was good to gather ideas like shells off a beach and upcycle them to something new later.

Orson regularly told people he didn't like social media, but he was excited to see his follower numbers steadily rise every time he checked his account. He loved reading the comments on his posts and clicking on the little heart to send some love back. He was building a community and filling it with positivity.

And while he was walking the halls of Instagram for work, why not also take a peek behind some of the doors of his old life and check out what everyone else was up to these days? Maybe even check in on a few people. They might follow him. They might know people who would want to follow him. So many of his student friends had moved back home or off to somewhere else, but he'd chosen to stay in Liverpool after finals. He had students in Liverpool, there was a vibe and people knew him. There was money in the city too, not everywhere, but in the waterside apartments and the leafier suburbs there was an ideal mix of cash in the bank and a culture of looking good and being on trend; a perfect demographic for his services.

Orson knew his way around too. He could amble across the city from one side to the other in an hour and even head out as far as New Brighton or Chester in less than 45 minutes on the train, with all the stops on the way to either. Back 'home' (as his mum still liked to call it) for Orson was a big house with even bigger expectations for how he should behave and what he should do with his life. It was nice for a visit, for the home-made dinners and freshly laundered sheets, but it was always a relief to leave. Liverpool was home now, and his Insta gave him an armchair ride around the lives that he'd dipped in and out of since he'd first arrived in the city, fresh from his year out in Kerala, and full of ideas about how he'd make the place his own.

Orson took a deep breath and stretched, arching his back and tipping his chin towards the ceiling before re-focusing on the screen and scrolling through the accounts he followed, deciding who to visit first. As he looked down the list, his phone vibrated. Mimi's name lit up, along with a picture of the two of them, arms clutching each other's shoulders and tongues stuck out at the camera. He let the call ring out. She'd assume he was teaching. She had a knack for calling when he least wanted to talk to her. It was as though she could hear him tiptoeing around other people's lives and wanted to join in.

He checked Celeste's account first. Was she with someone new or still holding a torch for him? She'd been fun but naïve. Clingy. Keen to make more of their thing than it actually was. Not very good at taking the hint. She looked good though. There was a picture of her in a bar from a couple of days earlier, he clicked the like button. Why not? She looked cute, pouting like that with her arm around another girl and that defiant look in her eye. He smiled as he remembered that look, and reached inside his pants where the memory was physical.

His phone vibrated and lit up with Mimi's name again. She definitely had a sixth sense. He took his hand out of his pants and clicked on a different face, ignoring the call again. This girl had only been to his class once or twice. She'd been in the year below him and he couldn't remember her name, but they'd always ended up at the same parties and he liked her Vintage Fashion Junkie account, with all its carefully curated boho looks. Her content was usually her latest crocheted top or her face peeping out from under a wide-brimmed hat, but not this time, it was Celeste again, the same picture as before, but this time without the other girl. He clicked on the picture and read 'Missing. Last seen on Friday night in the Northern Quarter at about 11.15pm. Please share. Please keep an eye out. Let's find Celeste.' There were three heart emojis and a praying hands emoji and a long thread of comments.

A WhatsApp without punctuation from Mimi interrupted the flow of comments; '*A girl is missing looks like whatshername the drippy one who was always hanging around and making out like she was the love of your life.*' Followed by a second message: '*Check your Insta SHE HAS GONE MISSING and everyone's losing their minds over it have a look she might be on your doorstep she was the stalkerish type.*'

He looked again at the pictures and clicked from account to account. Celeste was all over the internet. He checked X and Facebook, and found more pictures with descriptions of what she'd been wearing, her boots, her little star that she'd always worn around her neck. He remembered how sweet she'd been. How she'd bought croissants for breakfasts he'd never hung around to eat and waxed lyrical about picnic spots they should try, but never did.

Somewhere halfway between guilt and nostalgia, he paused to think what to do. Everyone was looking for Celeste, talking about her, sharing her picture to help her be found. He had to help. He clicked on the picture of Celeste and downloaded it, then used it to create his own post on Instagram and X. 'Vigil for Celeste. This extraordinary person is as beautiful on the inside as she is on the outside. Let's come together in love to send hope out into the universe for her safe return.' He glanced at the clock on his computer: 6.22. He calculated how quickly he could get what he needed together and enlist some support. He continued typing to complete the post, but his phone pinged again with another message from Mimi.

'*OMG they have found some clothes or something near where she lives!!!!*'

He paused. Could he find out where she lived? He knew it was Manchester, he could get to Manchester less than an hour but where exactly? The posts said Northern Quarter but that didn't narrow it down much. If they'd found something somewhere, that's where he needed to do the vigil. He jumped from one Instagram account to the next looking for more detail on what had been found and where, but he couldn't find what he was looking for. He messaged Mimi. 'I'm heading to Manchester to start a vigil for Celeste. See if you can find out what's been found and where. Join me if you like – getting a cab to Lime Street in 10.'

Orson ordered an Uber and filled his rucksack with candles, tealights, and water bottle and grabbed a yoga mat. He could keep checking for more information on what they'd found and where on the train, then post the location to invite others to join him. He pictured Celeste, getting out of bed and putting on his yellow jumper to make them both a cup of tea. She needed him. Perhaps he could get her name and face on the TV news with his vigil. He could, at the very least, help her go viral online. He'd make sure everyone was looking for her and sending love out to find her.

A picture pinged through from Mimi, showing a garden with a few people in it. '*They've found a boot here,*' the caption said. '*See you at the station we can find the postcode for the place on the way.*'

15

Abi

A bi glanced at the clock on the wall as she refilled her water bottle. It was time she was gone, but she preferred to write up her log while things were fresh in her mind rather than waiting for tomorrow. There wasn't much of a reason to hurry home anyway. Sunday night TV was invariably a cop drama with a not very credible twist and a caricatured tortured detective. She might as well be in work doing real policing, instead of at home frowning at the TV for reducing her job to sanitised layers of unpalatable grit and saccharin sentimentality.

Nobody ever sat there logging incidents on TV. TV policing had plenty of gore and psychopaths, but it skipped the vomit and snot, the kids who pissed their pants when they were caught, and the turds left on the carpet from thieves who couldn't control their adrenalin. It never included the waiting around; the form filling, the back covering, the crime numbers. Fair enough, admin might not make good drama, but she knew real police work to be all about evidence and detail, not hunches and lucky breaks. The TV cop dramas she'd seen always fell short of real because they were full of detectives walking alone and unarmed into danger, then striding out again having survived the jeopardy and cracked the case.

Abi's day had been punctuated by a mugging, an elderly corpse and a dispute between neighbours. The neighbours' argument over the replacement of some fence panels on the border between their houses had escalated until two middle aged men had been locked in separate cells while they considered how much the old fence or new fence really mattered to them. She had called the wife of one and the mother of the other to come and collect them. The mother had turned up, irritated but relieved that the matter would be taken no further. The wife had told Abi that a walk home would do her husband no harm.

She'd been busy, and her focus had been pulled in different directions all day, but at every pause, the face of the woman making tea and offering biscuits to delay saying out loud that her daughter was missing pulled her back to that anxious kitchen. It was like something she'd forgotten to buy at the supermarket, or a message she kept neglecting to pass on; a niggle of something overlooked. Was there a question she hadn't asked? A detail she hadn't noticed? Or was it just the cocktail of hope and despair on the woman's face - a look Abi had seen so many times before. She knew the impulse to feed the woman's hope and dispel her despair would have been a false kindness. She could have offered solace to the mother, reassured her with statistics, but if something had happened to the girl, no amount of faith in probability would manifest a happy ever after. Some things could be fixed, like the neighbours' fence, but Abi knew she couldn't fix everything. Most things she couldn't fix, especially when process didn't even give her permission to rummage around any further for now.

Abi sipped from the bottle as she walked back to her desk and thought about the rainbow on Celeste's bedroom wall and the mess on the floor; evidence of a real life being lived minute to minute from childhood into adulthood with memories and clutter accumulated down the years. Not a case, but a person.

In her first weeks in the job, a colleague had told Abi to try to avoid connecting with people. 'Just treat them as cases; a name, age and description,' he'd told her, 'otherwise, the job can get to you. Let emotion in once, and it will grow on you like mould until you can't function at home or at work. It's not the things you'll see in this job that will get to you, it's the things you'll feel. So, try not to feel love, trust me, it'll make you a better copper.'

She'd taken the advice on board, but struggled to follow it. Empathy was what made her good at her job, and she couldn't separate empathy from emotion. The woman hunting for Jaffa Cakes in the cupboard knew her daughter wouldn't disappear off without a word. Plenty of girls that age did, and then turned up three days later wondering what all the fuss was about, but Abi knew that wasn't what was happening here. The mother knew. The friend knew. Both of them were trying not to believe that bad news was inevitable, but it had hung in the air of Celeste's house like a plate about to smash after being knocked off the table. They could avoid looking to see where it landed, but they couldn't stop it from falling. It was the bad news already in motion that kept the faces and the kitchen and the rainbow on the wall popping into Abi's head. She hadn't forgotten anything, she'd just let the mould start to form, and it was growing.

Abi glanced at the clock again, 6.16; over six hours since she'd visited the house and still no word from the mother. But still less than 24 hours since Celeste had last been seen. And she was an adult, however much Yvonne might still see her as her child. In theory, it was too soon to assume Celeste was missing. And perhaps she wasn't. Abi reminded herself to be guided by the facts and not by the feelings of those involved. Celeste had lived away and had all the freedom and autonomy to stay out as long as she liked without telling anyone, or worrying anyone, while she'd been at uni. It was only because her mum knew she'd not come home that she was worried. Perhaps Celeste had gone AWOL before when she'd been at uni. Abi made a mental note to ask Esther about that. But would Esther know? Who would know if Celeste had a habit of staying out?

Abi tapped the space bar to wake up her screen and resolved to complete today's paperwork before heading home. She could give Yvonne a quick call to check in with her before she left, and follow up in the morning. Everything was logged on the system, so if anything happened in the meantime, someone else would pick it up.

'Are you OK?'

Abi was just re-reading the paragraph she'd been writing to pick up where she'd paused. She looked up to find PC Fisher standing next to her desk.

'You look done in? Busy day? Did you forget to eat again?'

She wondered if it was just police officers that followed every question with another, as though they had a quota for the day and needed to use them all up.

'I...'

'Don't worry, I'm not going to frog march you to the vending machine. I've got an apple.' He placed it on her desk next to the keyboard. 'My wife always sends me with healthy snacks. You'll be doing me a favour if you take it, I hate apples, they give me heartburn, but she always checks my bag, says I'll die of scurvy if I don't get some fruit in me.'

Abi looked at the apple. PC Fisher looked at her, then at the apple, then back at her again.

'You actually get more vitamin C from a kiwi fruit,' Abi told him. 'More than an orange even.'

'Yeah, but who in their right mind wants to eat something that looks like a giant hairy bollock!'

She could see he was delighted to have made her laugh.

'Go on then' he smiled. 'It's clean. Pink Lady – apparently, they are the queen of apples.'

Abi picked up the apple and took a bite. It was sweet and delicious. Fisher nodded and grinned until she took another bite.

He was not that much older than her, but with two young daughters at home, it was clear that he genuinely wanted to look after her and be a friend, rather than using pseudo concern and fruit banter as a preamble to a chat up.

Fisher nodded towards the apple again to encourage Abi to take another bite, just as her phone rang. She tried to chew the apple faster so that she could answer, but he motioned at her to slow down and picked up the receiver.

'OK. I see. Yes, she's here, she's just away from her desk at the moment. I'll let her know right away. Yes. Don't worry, we're on our way.'

'What?'

'Sorry, I should have asked you first if you're OK to stay on after shift. No worries if not, I can just pick this up...'

'What?' She was concerned her voice sounded sharp, but Fisher didn't seem to notice.

'That missing person report you went out to earlier, that young girl, they've found one of her shoes, in the little church garden round the corner from her house. That was the mother on the phone, the kids that found it are going to show her where it is.'

'Shit, you should have told them not to touch it.'

'It's OK, she said to me she won't touch it, she just wants to get there to make sure no-one else moves it. Do you want me to drive?'

They drove in silence, Fisher keeping his eyes on the road and Abi thinking of all the times she'd seen a random single shoe on the pavement or the playing fields and wondered if its owner had hopped or hobbled home. OK. It didn't mean that something sinister had happened, but it didn't give much reassurance either.

There was a small group standing by a bush in the garden when Abi and Fisher arrived. Abi recognised Yvonne. There was a woman and a girl with them, and a man standing uncomfortably as part of the group, like a wedding guest who knows no-one at the do but is sticking with the people he sat next to at the ceremony. There was a handful of others too, some trying to look as though they just happened to be there, relaxing by a wall. Too intrigued to stay away, but too embarrassed by their morbid interest to own up to it.

'I'll go and talk to the mother,' Abi said, 'she knows me. Can you get the nosey parkers away and put a cordon up.'

'On it.'

Abi took in a long breath of resilience as she stepped through the little gate into the garden. It was a pretty space, a part of the church grounds that had been made into a place to sit, for those who wanted to be close to God, or whatever they believed in, but not in the church. Abi remembered when they had made it, between pandemic lockdowns, just at that time when everyone hoped it would be over, and then it wasn't. A way for the community to get together outdoors, after so much time holed up at home with only their TV or the same tiny circle of other humans. Funny how things changed from one kind of normal, to another and back again.

Yvonne looked at Abi with a new kind of sorrow. There was no rapid jumble of words to fill the gap between fear and hope this time. She was holding things together by holding it in.

'I'm Robert,' the man said, stepping towards Abi and holding his hand out for her to awkwardly shake it. 'I'm Celeste's dad. Why didn't you do something sooner? Yvonne told you she was missing hours ago and here we are with all this time lost when you should have been looking for her.'

Anger was much easier to deal with than sorrow, despair, or pessimism. Anger was a tool for getting things done.

'Could you go and introduce yourself to my colleague over there, his name's PC Fisher,' Abi said calmly. 'He'll need to speak to those people to see if any of them have seen anything. Have seen Celeste. It will be useful for him to have you there to describe her. And an extra pair of ears. That would be really useful. Helpful. Thank you.'

She looked across to Noel Fisher as Robert agreed and began to walk towards him. It was hard to communicate *please, thank you, occupy this guy for me* in a single look. But Noel Fisher would get on with it.

'Let's see this boot then.'

Yvonne pointed to where the boot was still mostly hidden. 'This is Sophie, who found it..'

'With my sister Laura, we both found it. But it was me actually. But we both played hide the boot with it. And I tried it on. But there was only one. Laura didn't try it on because it would be much too big for her. This is my mum.'

'Faith,' said the girl's mother. 'I wasn't with the girls at the time. They were with my mum. I can give you her number. I can tell you where she lives, if you need to speak to her?'

Abi noticed Yvonne watching the faces of the mother and daughter as they spoke. She was completely focused on them. She stared at their hands knotted together as Faith kept hold of her daughter while she told her tale of waiting around for Grandma after church.

There was nothing Abi could do for Yvonne except get on with doing her job. She asked the girl some questions. Got a rough time from the mother's knowledge of when the church service had ended. When the girls had found the boot, where they'd found it, how much they'd handled it. Whether it was still in the same place they'd left it.

'Is it OK if we go now,' Faith asked, once Abi had finished her questions and taken contact details for her and the girls' grandmother. 'We've got take-out arriving, my husband's got man flu, and I need to get the girls to bed at some point. School in the morning, missy,' she added, turning to Sophie.

'Of course, thank you so much for finding the boot and telling me all about it, Sophie. You've been a super star.'

'Thank you' echoed Yvonne. And the girl and her mother walked away, the girl still holding her mother's hand and swinging their arms forward and back, asking her would there be any spring rolls left.

'What happens now?' Yvonne asked.

Abi nodded towards a bench and the two women sat down. She explained that, now the boot had been found, she could action an investigation. They'd send the boot to the lab, have a look around the garden for any further clues as to what might have happened, try and get a location on Celeste's phone, appeal for witnesses locally. She nodded towards Noel Fisher, 'my colleague is already talking to the local residents that were here when we arrived.'

Yvonne watched Noel Fisher as he chatted to the loiterers, notebook out, Robert standing behind him, interrupting with questions of his own.

'How do these things usually play out?' Yvonne asked.

Abi was ready for this question. Every missing person report threw up a version of the same 'will you find him/her?'

'Yvonne,' she said, reaching out to take hold of the woman's hand. '87% of adults reported missing are found within two days of the call coming in. That's good odds. You did the right thing. You called us as soon as you thought something might be wrong....'

'But the boot...?'

It was hard to foist hope on someone when it was clear that something was amiss. But the statistics were real, and a boot was just a boot; not blood or a body.

'I think we need to get you back to the house.' Abi smiled at Yvonne and began to gently guide her away from the boot and towards Noel Fisher and the ex-husband. 'Let's get you a cup of tea, it's better for you to be at the house in case Celeste comes home.'

Choosing the right words was easier for Abi these days than it had been when she first started in the job. But she knew Yvonne would interpret every sentence based on her own understanding of the situation. Some people might interpret '*in case Celeste comes home*' as a clear indication it could happen any minute. Others would be convinced that '*in case*' meant it was unlikely. Abi couldn't control any of that. All she could do was make sure that her words didn't give false hope, and didn't indicate all hope was lost either. The statistics, with their lack of context or detail might be misleading, but they were all she had to comfort Yvonne because the figures, the boot and the absence of the girl were the only things she could be certain of.

Noel Fisher was talking to a young man in a football shirt as Abi and Yvonne approached.

'Yeah, well I was at home,' he said, 'so I didn't see anyone, I've got this new game, man, it's like lit, so I stayed in to play that, me and my mates. We play online, you know, they weren't in the house, but I was kind of with them. But it's not really me you want to talk to, or my mates. You want to talk to my sister, Annie, she rang me, like, really late. She works at the little Tesco down there, you know, on the main road, and she walks home with this other girl after work but the other girl lives... I don't know where she lives, but anyway they only walk part of the way together and Annie like walks the rest on her own, and it's always like, fine. There's streetlights and houses, innit. But last night she called me because some guy was following her, and she proper roasted him while she was on the phone to me and then she made me talk to her the rest of the way home, which is only a couple of minutes, but it's hard to think of things to say when you were in the middle of something else. I mean, it could be any old weirdo just coming on to my sister, she's a bit of a weirdo magnet to be honest but...'

'What's her name?' Yvonne interrupted. 'What's your sister's name? Maybe she knows Celeste? Maybe she saw Celeste.'

Abi nodded towards Noel Fisher. 'Can I just take down a few details, please, what's your name?'

'Adam. Adam Mitchell. My sister is Annie Mitchell.'

'Is your sister at home now?' Yvonne interrupted again. 'We could go round and talk to her now...'

Abi could see Yvonne transitioning from numb and detached to frightened and angry, as though someone had pressed a button that switched her from one mode to another. She put one hand on Yvonne's elbow and the other on her shoulder to begin moving her away.

'Let's just leave the police to do their job Yvonne.' It was what Abi had wanted to say, but she heard the words come out of the ex-husband's mouth.

'Robert's right Yvonne. We'll make sure we speak to Annie. It was Annie, wasn't it?'

The boy in the football shirt nodded.

'Let's get you back to the house, because if Celeste comes home, or there's any news, that's where she'll need you to be.'

V

Celeste

I can sense him looking at me, but I can't really see him, I just know he's there. He's watching me breathe. He's controlling my breathing. He's telling me to think about my breath and slow it down, to breathe gradually in through my nose, to imagine the journey of my breath as it travels down through my body. He tells me to control the pace and let my body absorb energy from the universe as I inhale.

I can't see him, but he is here, in his big yellow jumper, with his dishevelled hair and his arrogance, telling me what to do and how to behave, urging me to comply to win his approval. And I want to. I want to please Orson as much as I ever did. I want him to be impressed by me. To be happy with me. To love me. But he is impossibly handsome and cool, just as always, and brutally critical and dismissive, true to form.

'Celeste, you're not listening' he says. He is smiling, encouraging not angry, and his tone is coaching and light-hearted, but I still feel like I will never be good enough. I pause my breath, purposefully defiant, ready to sleep and shut him out. Didn't he drop me without a word? Didn't he cut me loose like a fish on the line that's too small to bother with? Didn't he hurt me? The hurt is a pain in my head. A fever all over my body. A nausea that consumes me. But he's not here to hurt me now; he's here to help me. His yellow jumper is a beacon. It's a comfort: a sandy

beach, a bowl of custard, a bunch of daffodils. He is life and he's here to show me what to do.

Now is not the time to be angry with him and bite back. It would be futile; it would not touch him. Attempts to punish him have only punished me, and this would be the same. When I took his yellow jumper to get him back for hurting me, it did him no harm. He simply switched from yellow to green, just as easily as he'd switched from me to Mimi and on to the next adoring, naïve girl. I was left with a saggy item of clothing that was too big and frayed at the cuffs. I couldn't wear it because it reminded me of him. I couldn't throw it away because it was all I had left of him. So, I left it in a heap on the chair in my bedroom; a sharp hard punch of recurring pain every time I caught sight of it, every time I forced myself not to notice it was there.

How can the jumper be lying on a chair in my room, but also here now, with Orson wearing it, standing over me? But he is here, and he is wearing it. I can't see him with my eyes, but I know he's here, standing over me, urging me to do as he says and take that long, slow breath. 'Take it,' he says, 'breathe slowly in through your nose. Do it now.'

And I imagine myself back on his bedroom floor, eyes closed like I am now, feeling the grubbiness of his unhoovered carpet under my flat palms and identifying a discarded cigarette paper with my little finger. He counts slowly.

One.

Two.

Three.

I visualise the breath as a golden smoke coming into my body through my nose. It sparkles with energy, with warmth and light. It fills my head and I feel lighter; less cluttered.

Four.

Five.

Six.

The breath travels down through my throat and my lungs, waking me up from the inside, communicating with my arms, my hands my fingers.

Seven.

Eight.

Nine.

It reaches my belly and radiates through my back, my legs, my feet. It has gathered heat and radiance as it has travelled through me.

Ten.

I keep it in my belly for a moment. The pause is all about control, Orson used to tell me. 'Your breath is life, and you can control it. Focus on your breath.'

Ten feels like it lasts for an age. It's the drawn out wait of a Christmas eve, or a delay at the train station. I am waiting for him to give me permission to exhale.

Finally, I hear the word, from the image of his yellow jumper, from inside my own head. 'Exhale.' And I allow the breath to travel back up through my body and out of my mouth, with the glow of the inhale, pushing the thick grey smoke that was clogging up my body out into the day.

16

Esther

It had been a long and lonely afternoon for Esther. That nice policewoman she'd spoken to on the phone had told her she mustn't blame herself. She'd said that nine times out of ten, people who went missing were found. But what if Celeste was the tenth? What if she had let Celeste walk home alone and Celeste never came home again?

Yvonne had not told her not to blame herself. She hadn't said *'this is your fault'* in words, but she might as well have plastered it on a billboard in the garden. *'Celeste is missing and it's all Esther's fault.'* She could have done one thing differently and it might have changed everything. Cancelled their plans. Given Whatshisname the cold shoulder. Made Celeste promise to get a cab. Ordered an Uber for her. Told Celeste to message her to let her know she was safe as soon as she got home.

Esther remembered the feminist soap box Celeste was fond of standing on. 'Why should I be concerned about walking from the bus stop to my house. What man is concerned about that? Why should I text to say I'm home safe. What man does that? That should be a given. And yet here we all are, still constantly accepting an implicit level of risk and without ever acknowledging it. Just normalising that sense that we might be vulnerable, and we should protect ourselves. And because we accept that, we're inherently accepting that the threat can't be challenged and will never be changed. It's wrong.'

She was right, of course, Esther thought. But also wrong. What if it was Celeste's own stubborn resistance to prioritising her personal safety over her principles that was really to blame here? What if there was one thing Celeste could have done differently that would have changed everything? Of course there was. That was science. The exact things have to happen in the correct order for the specific result to happen.

Perhaps Celeste was OK and the unspoken events they were all thinking about were just a jump to conclusions. A leap from not home to dead in a ditch, with no evidence to power the trampoline from the fact to the assumption. There was no evidence, Esther comforted herself. But not home was not normal. Not for Celeste, the girl who always talked about the responsibility of being the moon and the stars to her mum. Esther felt nauseous at the thought of Yvonne's passively accusatory face. Yvonne had not accused her of anything. If Celeste wasn't found, or was found but was not OK, the silent blame would definitely be broadcast loud and clear, amplified by other voices and displayed in lights for all to see.

Esther had wanted to join Yvonne knocking on doors. Robert could have stayed. He barely knew Celeste. If people had questions, he wouldn't be able to answer them. He should have stayed, and she should have gone. She should have pointed that out. She should have insisted. She needed to think of the right thing to do at the right time. Not five minutes later. Not the next day. She could ring Yvonne now and suggest she and Robert could do a swap. She and Yvonne could split up and do twice as many houses. She had pictures of Celeste on her phone. Pictures from last night. She could be out there, knocking on doors, showing people pictures of exactly what Celeste looked like before she disappeared. Disappeared. Esther shuddered at the word. Celeste hadn't disappeared, she just hadn't come home. And there must be someone who knew where she was.

Esther picked up her phone to call Yvonne, and suggest she and Robert swap places. But before she had time to realise that she only had the landline number, not Yvonne's mobile, she saw she had 18 notifications, 19, 20, 30, 45. Instagram and Facebook were both spitting notifications at her faster than she could register them.

'They've found Celeste's boot.'

'OMG' they've found something'

'Police are at the church garden. Something going on.'

'Pray they find her'

' 'Not looking good for lovely Celeste'

All these people were strangers. They didn't even know Celeste. But they seemed personally invested in her story, as though they'd known her all their lives and she was the best person they'd ever known. They didn't know she could be moody, sullen, bitchy. They had no idea she could be dull, or whiney. Maybe they liked being part of the drama, instead of just watching it on TV. Who could be the first to solve the murder and bring Celeste home? Who could save the day and make the local news? They were responding to Esther's posts on social media as though they knew did know Celeste. Sharing information. Sharing their opinions. Some of them even sharing pictures of the police and the small gathering of people at the church garden. Esther expanded the pictures on the screen with her fingers. She could see Yvonne with the policewoman from earlier, and Robert standing on the other side of the garden with another police officer. There had been news while she had been sitting in the house waiting. But news isn't always a good thing.

Her phone rang.

'Hi Mum.'

'They've found Celeste's shoe. This has got serious Esther. It's really serious now. It could have been you, that. I've told you again and again about getting taxis and not walking. Is there anywhere she might be? Think, Esther. Any boy's house she might have gone back to? Any friend's house? But why would she leave one shoe behind? Do you think it's hers or just a coincidence that it's similar to the one she was wearing. What do you think Esther? Esther? Esther I'm asking you, what do you think?'

Esther heard the words and her mum's voice but they were all a jumble. The subtitles she read underneath said *'this is your fault Esther. This is your fault.'* over and over again on a continuous loop.

'Esther. Esther? Are you there?'

'I have to go, Mum. I need to keep the line free in case anyone calls. In case Celeste calls.'

She tapped the red icon and cut off her mother mid-sentence. She had no room for that conversation in her busy brain at the moment. If Celeste was fine, there would be too much relief for any recriminations. If Celeste wasn't fine, no words in the world would fix it.

She turned back to the social media feeds. There was now a #findceleste hashtag on almost every post including a new Instagram story from @WildandFreeYoga and @IamOrson. *'Vigil for Celeste at the church garden. Let's #findceleste.'* There was a montage of images of Celeste, including the one Esther had shared of the two of them, and others from Celeste's own social media accounts. They were interspersed with an image of a flickering candle. The same accounts also had posts with a picture of Celeste, edited to include the words #vigilforCeleste #findceleste. There were full details in the caption. The address for the garden, instructions to bring a candle and something to sit on. A plea to channel your energies into locating Celeste, and manifest Celeste being found safe and well. *'Join us,'* it said *'and let's bring our energy together to bring Celeste home safe and well. If you can't come down in person, please light a candle for Celeste and share our vigil virtually. More updates to come.'*

Celeste had told Esther about Orson and Esther felt a pang of guilt that she hadn't believed her. That yellow jumper could have been any old jumper, a charity shop find, or snaffled from the end of year lost property. And there'd been no pictures of the two of them together. Celeste's excuse that Orson didn't like having his picture taken seemed like a very convenient get out. And the fact that she didn't know his surname was a red flag too. Esther had assumed he was some guy she'd fixated on and claimed was her boyfriend because she would have liked it to be true. One more thing to feel guilty about.

Esther filled the kettle and switched it on. Not because she wanted tea, but because she needed to stand up, step away from her phone, and do something that would distract her from the continuous loop of 'Where's Celeste? This is your fault.' circling in her head like cars on a racing track. She had already washed the pots in the sink. Wiped down all the kitchen cupboards, and lined up all the tins and packets inside the shelves as though they were being displayed neatly for customers to select their groceries in a supermarket. She'd been to the toilet more times in the day than she would usually go in a week, just for something to do. She'd folded the tub of clean washing into neat piles. She'd watered the plants. She'd kept busy, but busy hadn't worked. Those Where's-Celeste?-This-is-your- fault cars just kept racing round and round, gathering speed as the day dragged on.

The noise of the kettle boiling disguised the sound of a key in the lock and Esther jumped when Yvonne entered the kitchen, followed by a policewoman. The policewoman started to explain that they hadn't found Celeste, but some little girls had found a boot.

'I know', Esther hurried to reply. 'I know, because it's all over here.' She picked up her phone and waved it in the air. 'Everyone wants a piece of the drama. Most exciting thing to happen in their sad little lives since that woman on Milner Avenue won the lottery and threw a street party. But it could be any old boot. It doesn't have to be Celeste's boot.'

'It's Celeste's boot,' Yvonne said. She sat at the table and held one hand in the other, as though saying grace before a meal.

Looking straight ahead at the cupboards, with their neatened provisions tidied inside.

'I'm afraid it is almost certainly Celeste's boot,' the policewoman confirmed. She paused and looked from Esther's face to the back of Yvonne's motionless head. 'We will be sending it for forensics. We'll bring dogs in to see if there is anything else to find in that location, and there will be officers going door to door, so if anyone has seen anything or knows anything, we'll be talking to them.'

The end of her sentence fell like a sharp knife cutting the kitchen away from the normal world of conversation and interaction and casting it off to the otherness of three women silently locked in their own thoughts, unwilling to say anything else in case it was the wrong thing.

'If that kettle's just boiled, perhaps you could make some tea?' The policewoman suggested, and Esther dutifully switched the kettle on again to bring the water back to the boil, and put tea bags in the pot.

'Not for me though.' the policewoman added. She explained that she needed to get back to the church garden. Explained that Esther would need to give a full statement and that an officer would be in touch to go through the details of what happened when Celeste left the bar and who they'd been with while they were out.

The policewoman apologised that she couldn't do that right now. There was something she needed to follow up as soon as possible. Probably not related, she said, but as someone had come forward and it could be relevant it was part of her job to make sure everything was considered. She explained that Robert had stayed with the officer in the garden, and he was talking to all the passers-by that had gathered there.

'There'll be more,' Esther said.

'More what?'

'More so-called passers-by. Some boyfriend, ex-boyfriend, friends-with-benefits guy from when Celeste was at uni is organising a vigil. He's on his way there with fucking candles and positive fucking energy and asking people to come along and make some kind of cosmic party out of it all. You'd best be quick with the dogs because there'll be a five million hippies chanting and activating their chakras to bring Celeste home in a bit.'

'I need to go.' The policewoman put her hand on Yvonne's shoulder and squeezed it gently. 'A family liaison officer will be coming round, just to keep you in touch with what we're doing and let you know if there's any news.'

'Thank you,' Yvonne said, without moving.

'I'll see myself out,' the policewoman said, nodded at Esther and left.

Silence returned to the kitchen even heavier than before. It reminded Esther of solitary walks to school in the winter on days when the cold air was trapped under a thick layer of cloud, and both the quiet and any noise were amplified. The silence was extra silent. Any sound was sharp and pronounced. Like the end of the two minutes on Remembrance Sunday. Like the gap before the applause as everyone waits to be certain that the ballet has finished.

'This is your fault Esther,' Yvonne said without moving.

At first Esther wasn't sure whether Yvonne had actually said the words out loud, or if she'd just thought them. She might have imagined the thoughts that had been looping round in her own head all afternoon as real words spoken out loud.

'This is your fault Esther,' Yvonne repeated. 'This is your fault. You.' Yvonne rose from her chair and turned to face Esther.

'You are the wrong girl in my kitchen,' she continued. 'I don't want you here, I want Celeste. But where is Celeste? You can't tell me because you abandoned her. You sent her off to walk home on her own. You put her in harm's way and harm has come to her...'

'We don't know that.' Esther tried to reassure herself and her accuser.

'We do know that, Esther. We know. I know. You've done your bit to help. You've tried to clean up your own mess, but you should go now.'

Esther wanted to ask her own mum what she should do. Should she leave as Yvonne had asked, or stay to make sure Yvonne was OK? Didn't Yvonne need someone there?

'I'm just going to ring my mum,' Esther muttered, reaching for her phone.

'Ring her when you get home. Go now. Leave please, Esther. Just go.'

They could have waited together. Supported each other. Tried to come up with more ideas. But Celeste clearly got her black and white, judgy side from her mum.

Esther left the kitchen, pausing at the door to say sorry to Yvonne without saying it.

Yvonne's hostile face locked the apology in Esther's throat, and she strode to the front door and closed it behind her harder than she really needed to. If Yvonne wanted to be all alone waiting for news of Celeste, let her. Other people would be glad of Esther's company. Other people would empathise with how she was feeling and reassure her that Celeste's disappearance was not her fault. They would know it wasn't her fault.

Walking to the church garden, Esther called her mum and tried to explain how Yvonne had turned on her, blamed her for everything. And she was only trying to help. But the words all tumbled out too fast, and her mum kept telling her to slow down and repeat what she'd just said. All she wanted her mum to say was 'it's not your fault Esther', but instead of just saying it, her mum kept asking her to repeat herself.

'I'm going to the vigil,' Esther said quietly. 'I'll call you when I'm home.'

Her mum tried to respond but Esther ended the call. She'd done enough explaining. Enough apologising. All she'd done was not leave the bar when Celeste decided to go home early. If they'd left together, Celeste would probably still have walked from the bus stop to the house on her own. It would have been even later. That might have made a difference. It might not have made a difference. She might be sitting in a taxi right now, on her way home from the best 24 hours of her life.

That would be brilliant.

But that would not be something Celeste would do.

The church garden looked busy as Esther approached. There was no sign of the policewoman from earlier. But Robert was still there with a police officer, and there was another couple of officers, one with a dog walking around the area they'd cordoned off, sniffing the ground.

She walked towards Robert and the policeman. The officer was talking to a tall man with curly hair, wearing a sweatshirt that said 'Wild & Free' on the back. Orson. He really did exist.

As she got closer, Esther, could hear their voices raised.

'This is a live investigation,' the police officer said. 'There could be evidence here that you could put at risk of being destroyed by trampling all over it and encouraging your friends to do the same. Is that what you want? Do you want us to find Celeste, or are you trying to actively get in the way of letting us get on with our job and find your friend?'

Esther stopped walking. She watched and listened as Orson took a step back, waved his long arms in the air and responded.

'You think that the only way to bring Celeste back is to find some shred of fabric, a bit of sweat or hair, and test it and see if it belongs to some lowlife you've already got on a database? Maybe you'll get lucky and there's a big chunk of DNA from your most wanted right there. Maybe. But what if there isn't? There's a hundred different reasons why Celeste might not have come home. And the universe knows all of them. What we send out comes back to us. You might not understand the power of a vigil, but its power still exists. We can connect with Celeste in a way that you just can't get your head around. That's OK. We're all different. But I can bring people together here, and we can make a difference in our own way. And you can't stop us.'

'Actually, I can,' the police officer replied calmly.

Esther saw straight away that this was her chance to contribute to making things better. She strode across to the police officer and into the pause he had laid down between himself and Orson, challenging Orson to make the next move.

'Excuse me officer. Excuse me,' she said. 'I'm Esther, the friend that was with Celeste last night. I'm the one that put the appeals on Instagram and Facebook and everything. So, it's my fault he's here really. But look, maybe a vigil's not such a bad thing. It draws attention, doesn't it? It means that more people will hear about Celeste and be on the lookout. It will keep people sharing online. We could even get in touch with the TV and see if they want to send someone to cover the vigil. It's something for them to film isn't it?'

Orson's nodding and punctuating 'yep' every time she paused for breath had kept Esther talking, finding ways to justify the idea of a vigil. It was something to cling to. A small thing she could do to channel remorse into action. Staying up all night and keeping a candle lit could be an act of penance and a contribution to making the search for Celeste as visible as possible.

'I think she's right, actually,' said Robert. 'Look, we've already had one person tell us their sister might know something. If there's a vigil here, people are bound to stop and ask why, or they might see it online and remember that they were here and they might have seen something.'

'And all the cranks and weirdos will be straight on the phone with tenuous theories and false confessions,' the police officer snapped back.

'Perish the thought that we should make work for you officer,' Orson said calmly. 'And what if any of the cranks and weirdos actually have information that could help you find Celeste?'

With three pairs of eyes on him for an answer to Orson's question, the officer looked back at his colleague and over at the dwindling gathering of people still watching as the dog sniffed the flower beds for evidence.

'We have a job to do,' he answered, finally. 'And if you care about Celeste, really care about us finding her and bringing her home safe and well, you'll let us get on with it. But I appreciate your point about drawing attention to the search.'

The officer made a deal with Orson, that, provided they stayed the right side of the police cordon, allowed officers to do their job and reported anything they heard, the vigil could go ahead.

'The minute there's any sign of trouble, or I get any indication that you're making nuisances of yourselves, or getting in my colleagues' way, you'll be moved on. Is that clear?'

Esther nodded along with Orson and Robert.

'Legend,' said Orson, throwing out his hand for the officer to shake.

'Seriously, you sit here quietly, light your candles, bother no-one. Least of all the officers doing their jobs.' The officer looked at all three of them in turn..

'You'll join our vigil, won't you?' said Orson to a woman crossing the road with her shopping. 'Did you bring any candles? Don't worry if you haven't, I've got loads.'

17

Annie

Annie hated being interrupted when she was in the shower. The bathroom ought to be the one place in the house where you could lock the door and lock yourself away with only the thoughts in your own head. But it never worked like that. In a house with five people and only one bathroom, which contained the only toilet, the minute you closed the door you were on borrowed time.

It had been worse since Grandma had moved in. Annie loved her grandma, they were namesakes. When she was little, it had been Grandma who had plaited her hair, Grandma who'd played shop with her, Grandma who'd spent hours doing jigsaws with her and teaching her to play draughts. But the grandma she'd adored as a child was locked somewhere in the past. The energetic older lady she had loved and spent so many happy hours with was tired of life. Grumpy. Stubborn. Entitled. The grandma Annie knew now had reluctantly moved in with Annie's parents when she was struggling to cope at home and had been given the choice of moving in with her daughter or into a residential home where there would be carers on hand to make sure she was eating and came to no harm. She'd refused the idea of being thrown on the scrap heap with all the dodderers and loonies, who can't remember their own name and don't care if they've pissed their pants, even if they're still with it enough to know they've peed. 'You can forget that,' she'd said, 'it's only my body that's on strike, not my brain. While the old grey matter is working, I'll not be going to God's waiting room.'

She'd been right about her old grey matter. Annie was only too well aware that there was nothing stopping her opinions either, nor her ability to state them loud and clear. Grandma refused to use the commode that the council had provided in the front living room, which had been converted into a bedroom for her so that she didn't have to tackle the stairs. She was happily using it to hang her clothes from and insisted on climbing the stairs to the toilet several times a day, with the determination of Hillary tackling the death zone of Everest. Annie admired her grandma's belligerence and unequivocal insistence on being more able than her body allowed. But not when she was in the bathroom. Grandma's achievement in reaching the top of the stairs was inevitably matched by an urgency to go to the loo right now, brought on by a combination of the delay of the long haul of clinging to the banister, and the effort it had taken.

So, when there was a knock at the door, just as Annie was rinsing her hair, there was no question of delaying long enough for conditioner. She squeezed some water out to avoid drips, wrapped a towel around herself and unlocked the bathroom door.

But it wasn't Grandma standing breathless and agitated on the landing, it was Adam.

'You need to come downstairs, there's a policewoman waiting. Mum's a bit freaked out. Luckily Grandma's asleep.'

It took Annie a moment to process what her brother had said.

'What for, what's happened? Is it Dad?'

'No, Dad's fine. I assume he's fine. He's at work. You know he's at work. It's about that creepy guy who followed you home last night. I've just been...never mind. Just get some clothes on and come down. We're not in trouble, she just wants to talk to you. I'm going back downstairs. Mum's properly flapping about as though there's a serial killer coming to murder us all. Be quick!'

Annie considered getting back in the shower to put conditioner in her hair, regretting not doing it before she'd responded to the knock now that she knew the interruption wasn't Grandma's urgent need to go. How did the police even know about the creepy guy? She'd handled it. It was fine. The world was full of creepy guys, if she let herself be bothered by all of them, she'd never go anywhere.

She quickly rifled through the tub of clean washing in her bedroom that had been waiting to be put away all week, digging out underwear, jeans, T-shirt, hoody, and taking the towel with her downstairs to continue soaking up the moisture from her sodden hair.

'Thank God!' Annie's mum declared when she walked into the living room, as though her daughter had only just now returned from certain danger.

'I was only in the shower, Mum. I'm fine. You know I'm fine.'

'Perhaps we'll have that cup of tea now, Mrs Mitchell,' the policewoman suggested, 'then I can have a chat with Annie, while you brew up?'

Taking his cue, Adam told his mother that he'd give her a hand and held the door open for her to walk through, evicting her from her own living room.

Their mother paused in the doorway, 'Just tell her everything you know Annie,' she said. 'You know, if there's something you haven't told me, it doesn't matter, just tell Abi – her name is Abi – just tell her, OK Annie? OK? I'll be just in the kitchen. Call me if you need me. OK?'

Adam pulled his mother through the door as though pulling a verbose celebrity off the stage at the Oscars. He closed the door behind them both, and Annie sat down, apologising for the delay in coming downstairs.

'My hair just drips everywhere if I don't keep squeezing it with the towel, you see.'

'Don't worry, Annie, it's not a problem, I'm the one who arrived unannounced,' Abi reassured her. 'I'm sorry to interrupt your evening. Your bother mentioned to us that someone followed you home last night, and I just wondered if you could give me some details. Anything you can remember about what happened or the person who followed you. Anything you can tell us might be helpful.

'And also anything you can remember about anything or anyone else you might have seen on your way home too. You may be aware that a young woman about your age has still not returned home from a night out last night so, anything you can tell us about anyone or anything you saw on your way home could be useful.'

'But why have you even spoken to Adam?' Annie was confused. How had an incident that was hardly anything, that she hadn't reported or even mentioned to her mum, ended up with a police officer in the living room and her mum practically having a nervous breakdown in the kitchen? 'Adam wasn't even there. I mean why has he told you about it? Did he ring you? Nothing happened really. I'm fine. You can see I'm fine. The world is full of creeps and sometimes you just have to put your big girl pants on and tell them to fuck off, don't you?'

Abi smiled and explained that Adam had mentioned that she'd been followed home to officers investigating the missing young woman. Annie felt her heartbeat quicken. She had walked home alone and arrived safely; just as she always did, just as she always assumed she would. Here was a policewoman in her house reminding her that she shouldn't assume her safety was a given.

'It's probably not related,' said Abi, 'but we need to rule out a connection between what happened to you last night and the young woman not returning home. And we're keen to hear from anyone who was around at the time. Just in case you can remember anything, anything at all that could help with our inquiries. Can we start with what time you left work and the route you took?'

Annie retraced her steps for Abi, beginning with how she'd left work a little later than usual because they'd had cake and a quick glass of prosecco in the back to celebrate Jess's birthday because the manager had refused to give her the night off. It was probably about twenty to twelve when they left, maybe quarter to. She explained that she and Jess had walked home together as usual, but that Jess lives nearer so they'd done what they always do, walked at far as Jess's street together. She'd given Jess a hug and wished her happy birthday one more time, then she'd waited at the end of Jess's road until she saw Jess get to her house, and carried on walking the rest of the way home.

'It's only a couple of minutes further. Five at the most,' Annie continued. 'And I always just text her to say I'm home when I get in to tell her I'm back safe. Mad that we do that really. How many blokes do that do you think? It never really occurs to me that anything could happen, we just do it without ever actually saying out loud why.'

'So when did you notice there was someone following you,' Abi prompted.

'As soon as Jess was gone, really.' Annie thought back to her walk home. She explained how she and Jess had been busy talking and the streets had been quiet, just the occasional car passing and a dog that always barks when you walk past the house, barking when they walked past, as usual.

'It was only after she'd gone that I heard footsteps behind me. And I did that thing that you always see in spy films when someone's being followed. You know, I slowed down to see if his steps would slow down, and then walked quicker to see if he walked quicker. It was only because it was so quiet that I could hear him really, because he was wearing trainers. Actually, I'm not even sure I heard him, it was more of a feeling. I kind of sensed him. Does that sound stupid? I mean, I just knew there was someone there.'

167

Abi was writing notes and Annie was conscious that she needed to remember the details and make sure that everything she said was a true account of how she'd behaved and what she'd thought at the time. She told the policewoman how she had stopped under a streetlight next to the community garden at the church. How she'd dug her phone out of her bag and got ready to call her brother.

'I mean he's useless. I knew he'd be on his stupid games console because that's literally his life, but my dad works nights so there's no point ringing him. And it wasn't really about ringing for help, it was more about just knowing that I could have someone there with me. That I could talk to someone for the rest of the way. I mean, I don't know if I was scared. I don't really get scared. But it was creepy. I should have just walked home as fast as I could and got in. But because I'd walked slower, then faster and knew there was someone behind me, walking faster and slower when I did, because of that, I suppose I was a bit scared. But I was kind of determined not to be, if you see what I mean. I just wanted to call him out and embarrass him. I wanted him to see that I wasn't scared, but he should be. Or that he should at least be ashamed. I was half expecting him to be a flasher, to be honest. I saw a flasher when I was at university, and he was just a sad guy standing there wanting someone to look at him.'

'So, last night, what happened next, after you stopped walking and got your phone out?' Abi asked.

Annie pictured how the interaction had happened. She explained that she had turned round to find him standing right behind her.

'William, his name is. I think it's William. I remember him from school. He was always creepy. And he'd kind of sneaked up right behind me. It was like when you play what time is it Mr Wolf? Did you ever play that, when someone has to turn their back and the others have to creep up behind them? He thought he was the wolf but I was the one with the fucking sharp teeth.'

Annie explained how she had shown William her phone, with her brother's contact on the screen ready for her to call him with one tap. She recounted how she'd threatened to report him. Told him that her brother could be there in seconds and how he wouldn't want to mess with her brother.

'You've met Adam,' Annie smiled, 'he's actually a total wimp. He can massacre a whole civilisation in minutes on a computer screen, but I've got soft toys that would make a better bodyguard.'

'You say you know him?' Abi asked.

'I don't really know him,' Annie replied. 'But I do remember him from school. He was in my year in primary school, in the other class. He was a bit weird then and he's still weird now. He comes into the Tesco where I work all the time and just wanders around for ages, and then buys hardly anything. So that's what I was threatening him with, getting him banned from the shop. We can do that, you know, put people on a list if they're like shoplifters. I mean, I don't know if I could really get him barred, or if he'd even care, but he doesn't know that does he? I just wanted him to know that I recognised him, and I wasn't going to take any shit.'

'Can you describe what he looks like?' Abi asked.

Annie described the tall boy, with his dark curly hair and grey sweatshirt and joggers, like a prison uniform. His not-beard-not-stubble face fuzz and broad shoulders.

Abi made more notes and Annie wondered if she'd included the bit about her not taking any shit. Probably not, she thought. Hopefully not.

'And what happened then?' Abi prompted.

'Well then he stepped back and I actually did ring my brother and amazingly he did pick up and kept talking to me until I got in. And I didn't look back. I just walked home talking to Adam.'

'So you don't know where this William went after you carried on walking?'

'No. But I'm pretty sure he didn't follow me. And actually, Adam was really good. You know I always think he's tuned out and just like, constantly in the game and not in the real world and doesn't give a shit about anyone. But he made me a cup of tea when I got home and walked round the house just to check the guy hadn't followed me all the way here. And that woke Grandma up and then we had to get her back to bed.'

Annie remembered how they'd had to tell Grandma that it was just the milkman come early, and how she'd accepted the lie, even though it was the wrong day for milk, because the anachronisms their household clung to were more comforting to her than any words they could find to express that there was nothing to worry about.

'Adam promised we weren't going to tell Mum and Dad,' Annie added, 'because Mum already worries about me walking home from work. That plan's gone a bit pear-shaped now, hasn't it?'

Abi apologised for getting in the way of Annie keeping the incident a secret from her parents.

'You know, it's not right that your parents should have to worry,' she said, 'but it's natural that they do. And how do you feel about the incident now?'

Annie repeated the question inside her own head and challenged herself to give a true answer to herself and the police officer.

'I don't know,' she began.

Abi waited, laying out a quiet space that Annie felt she had to fill.

'I feel like I was brave and stupid. I think trying to brush it off was probably a stupid idea because, even if you'd not come round, this would have come back to bite me, wouldn't it? Just like that stupid flasher guy at university. I didn't report that because I was fine and I just felt sorry for him really. But it's still there, in the back of my brain. I think that's why I thought there was someone following me. I think that's why I stopped and confronted him. None of it can unhappen now, can it? There can't be a walk home from work from now on where I don't think about what if someone is following me. There can't be a time now where I don't wonder what would have happened if he'd grabbed my phone, or if Adam hadn't answered, or if I hadn't noticed he'd been following me. Do you think he'd followed me before? Do you think he'd been coming into the shop because I was there? Do you think he has something to do with this girl going missing?'

'Honestly,' Abi answered. 'I don't know. But we need to follow it up and the information you've given me has been very useful. So, thank you. Do you know his surname at all? His address?'

'Oh God. I can't think. I know his brother was called James and his mum worked at the school. She was in the office. I can't remember. I think it began with a C or a K. Kenny or Kennedy or something like that. But it's not that, it's just something like that. I don't know. Mum might know.'

As if the mention of her name had summoned her to the room, there was a knock on the door and Adam opened it to allow his mother through with two cups of tea.

'I wasn't sure about sugar, so I guessed not, looking at how slim you are,' Annie's mother said, setting a mug down on the coaster next to where Abi was sitting.

Adam looked at Annie, who smiled back at him.

'Mum, do you remember the name of that woman who worked in the office at school? The one with the dark hair in a ponytail and all that eyeliner. She had two boys in the school, do you remember?'

'I remember her,' said a voice from the door, as Grandma walked into the room. 'What are the police doing here? Keaveney, it was Keaveney. You always called her Mrs key-for-knee, and she was always chasing me up for dinner money when I picked you up from school. Nice enough though.'

'That's brilliant, thank you so much,' Abi smiled, writing down the name. 'Annie, would you have time to come with me now, just to walk me through what happened and where, would that be OK?'

Abi looked from the girl, to the mother, to the grandmother, aware that she was really asking permission of all three women.

'I'll just have to get some shoes on,' Annie answered before the other two women could object.

Abi got up to leave, apologising for not drinking the tea and explaining that she would be able to request the CCTV from Tesco.

'But what are you even doing here?' asked Grandma.

'I'll wait for you outside, Annie,' Abi smiled, nodding her goodbyes.

Annie turned to her grandmother. 'Why don't you drink this tea, Grandma? She hasn't touched it and it's a shame to let a brew go to waste. It's still hot. I'll be back in a bit to watch that programme you like with you.'

18

Moira

Moira took the last of the clean washing in off the line. The heavy jeans and sweatshirts had done little with the extra time she'd given them, but with an iron, she might just get away with calling them dry. She sniffed them. They smelled of lotus blossom fabric conditioner, rather than barbeque burgers, so at least she'd broken even. Folding each item carefully as she took it off the line, she placed it neatly in the plastic basket she'd brought out into the garden and placed by her feet. Who needed a gym when you had all the bending, lifting and stretching of housework to do? Who needed a TV when you had keeping on top of the washing to keep you busy? And there was still the ironing to come.

Moira smiled as she remembered the advice her mother had given her years earlier, when she'd complained that the work around the house was too much on top of her job and her boys. *'Learn to love it,'* her mother had said. *'learn to take pride in it and love it like it's a hobby. Because there'll be plenty of it.'* Moira had pointed out that there were two adults in the house and only one of them doing any cleaning, cooking, washing, or ironing. *'Did he do any of that before you married him?'* her mother had asked, and Moira had been forced to admit that he hadn't. *'So why would you expect him to do it now? You might as well assume that he'd go from having two left feet to dancing like he was Fred Astaire. He was sold as seen, my love, and you can ask him to take those dance lessons, but if he doesn't want to, he won't. And if you try and force him, you'll end up treading on each other's feet and getting on each other's nerves. Talk to him about it if you like, but I've been where you are and, trust me, all you'll do is create arguments you can't win, and you'll still end up knee deep in washing up and laundry. The only way round it is to enjoy it. Treat it as a way to spend time with your own thoughts.'*

Moira had ignored the advice at first, but it had turned out her mother had been right. Her attempts to ask for a more even distribution of effort in keeping things clean and tidy at home had been met with either empty promises of help, with the caveat of *'you need to tell me what needs doing and I'll do it,'* inevitably followed by a *'I'll do it later I'm just..',* or a counter argument she couldn't reason with. *'Why does the house need to be perfect? Are we expecting a royal visit? There are no prizes for cleanest bathroom or emptiest linen basket, you know. Perhaps if you spent more time focusing on me and the boys and less time trying to make the house ready in case the Queen pops in for tea, we'll be happier.'* Faced with a one-or-the-other choice between doing all the housework against a backdrop of conflict and resentment, or doing all the housework and taking pleasure in how much she could achieve in the day, Moira had developed a love of bringing in the clean washing and ironing it as her family sat watching TV. She could keep up with the programme as she de-creased the laundry. There might be no medals, but there were bragging rights, even if she only had herself to brag to.

As she folded the last items and laid them in the basket, Moira looked forward to watching the TV as she ironed. To the comfort of routine and certainty. They may sometimes change the schedule, but Sunday evening was cosy TV, there was a scenic backdrop and a comic tone to any murders, and the person who got done in always deserved their fate to one extent or another, or, at least, had had a good innings before becoming the victim.

She picked up the full basket to walk inside, remembering the raspberry sauce down William's front as she did so. More washing. No chance of getting it dry tonight, but best to get the machine on before the spill had the chance to become a permanent stain. She might even take a shower and put her PJs on before she started on the ironing, then she could slip off straight to bed with her book once she was done, and have the bed all to herself for a while before sleep.

Happy with her plan, Moira walked back towards the house, pausing to admire the blossom on the rowan trees on the way. One slightly larger than the other, both planted by Billy to mark their arrival of each of their sons. 'We can watch the tree grow as the baby grows up,' he'd said, 'and then when our boy is big and flies the nest, we'll have a strong, healthy tree to remind us that we've raised something from tiny to fully grown.' Moira had counted through the years with the blossom on those trees, its bursts of cream pompoms marking the beginning of the warmer weather and the countdown to the summer holiday each year. There were photos of the boys, each standing next to their own tree, which she'd intended to take in the same spot each year so that she could measure them, and the passage of time, as they grew up. But some years she'd forgotten, and the blossom wouldn't wait for her to remember, it would just silently take is leave, to be replaced by berries with their red warning that another year was passing faster than she'd thought. Perhaps the blossom would still be there the next time James came home for a visit. Maybe the boys would agree to stand there while she took a picture. She reminded herself to remember, picturing making toast for James to log a visual mnemonic.

Moira set the basket of washing down on the kitchen table and checked whether William had put his sauce-stained T-shirt in the machine. It wasn't in the machine, but screwed up on top of it, lying next to two empty milk bottles that hadn't been rinsed. She swilled them with water and took them to the front doorstep ready for the milkman to replace them with fresh ones in the morning.

As she placed the bottles on the step, Moira spotted William's trainers, not under the cover of the porch, but on the bottom step, where they would get wet if it rained. She bent down to pick up the shoes, letting out an involuntary 'ouff' as she reached for them.

The shoes were wet and muddy. They must have been there all day, but Moira hadn't noticed them earlier. She lifted them hesitantly to her nose to check whether William had left them out because he'd trodden in dog poo. Before the shoes were even close to her face for her to sniff them, she discovered they didn't smell of dog poo; they smelt of sick. She gagged a little, regretting her impulse to smell the dirty shoes. More washing. Why had William not mentioned it? Maybe he'd been embarrassed. Maybe when he said he'd been for a walk, it had been a lie and he'd been out drinking, then not wanted to admit that he'd drunk so much he'd been sick. But wasn't that a normal thing for a kid his age? Wasn't it better for him to be out drinking too much every once in a while, than at home, all the time, wasting his youth on his own?

Moira left the milk bottles on the step and brought the trainers into the house, putting them straight in the washing machine. Should she wash William's T-shirt with the vomit-ridden shoes? For a moment, she considered putting the shoes in the bin, but they'd been a Christmas present just a few months ago. And a pricey one. William had been quite specific about the ones he'd wanted, and when she'd offered him money to spend in the sales instead, he'd reminded her that the sales were just a way of shifting the stuff that no-one had wanted at full price.

Best to wash the trainers on their own, and soak the T-shirt to stop the stain from getting too comfortable, then she could bob it in with some other stuff and have everything ready to peg out first thing in the morning. She threw the trainers into the machine as though trying to lob them to the back of the garden, and checked the dial. There was a programme just for shoes. It didn't specify muddy, vomit-scented shoes, but it was probably her best bet. She poured fabric softener into the drawer, with a bit extra, to boost the scent, and sniffed the open bottle before she screwed the lid on. She loved the scent of it more than any perfume she'd ever had. That would be a brilliant idea for the fabric softener companies to make a perfume to match their range. Why had no-one ever thought of that? They'd make a fortune.

Putting the bottle of softener back in the cupboard, she reached for the box of detergent tabs, only to find it empty. She'd been sure there were a couple left. She checked behind the box in case one had fallen out, rummaging in the cupboard in case there was an old box of non-bio in there. No joy. Perhaps if she just started the machine the fabric softener would lift the smell and the water would wash away the mud? But it wouldn't lift the smell, would it, she chided herself, it would only mask it. The trainers would still be riddled with bacteria, ready to spring back to life as a rank stink as soon as William put his warm feet in his shoes.

Moira sighed, why did even the simplest of jobs have to become such a chore. So much for putting on her pyjamas before she started on the ironing, she'd have to go to the shop. She put the plug in the sink and set the hot tap running. There was a stain remover spray in the cupboard, and she used it to spray the gash of red on the T-shirt, turning it inside out to attack the stain from both sides, and squeezing it gently to make sure the chemicals soaked in. She was careful not to rub the stain – these things could be fixed, but one wrong decision and it would be a rag for wiping down the garden furniture.

She turned off the tap, put the T-shirt in the water, and reached for her handbag, which was hanging from the back of a kitchen chair. Checking that her keys and purse were inside, she left the house, calling to Billy and William that she was heading to the round-the-corner shop to get some washing detergent because there was none left. She waited briefly on the doorstep for a reply to acknowledge one of them had heard her. There was none, and she closed the door without calling again – no-one would even notice she was gone for five minutes. She checked her watch – 7.49 - ten minutes until they closed. Just in the nick of time.

The street was busy as Moira walked the short distance to the shop, with a gathering of people near the church and a police car and van parked up. They must be looking for that girl, she thought, and walked a little faster, making a conscious effort not to rubberneck – someone's trauma should never be anyone else's entertainment.

The shop was busier than she'd expected too. There were people queuing with cartons of milk and loaves of bread, ready for the start of a new week the next morning. The face of the woman on the doorstep, holding up a picture of her daughter flashed into Moira's mind, followed by the face of the daughter, laughing and looking into the future as though it held nothing but fun and possibility. That woman wouldn't be planning breakfasts and packed lunches for the week ahead. Nipping out for washing machine detergent would be the last thing on her mind. Moira felt a discomfort she couldn't identify. Empathy? Relief? Guilt? Why would she feel guilty? Because that woman's child was missing, and here she was feeling nothing but irritation for her own child just because she was having to stand in a queue buying over-priced, cheap-and-nasty detergent that would probably bring them all out in a rash.

The familiar face at the till smiled at her. 'Good evening, is that all today?' Moira nodded and tapped her card. 'Terrible business about that girl who's gone missing isn't it' the man continued as the transaction failed. 'You need to put your card in love. Terrible. Really terrible. What a thing to happen. We know that girl. She comes in here all the time. We've put a poster up, look.'

Moira struggled to concentrate on putting her pin number into the reader while the man was talking. She pressed enter and looked up to see where he was pointing to – a homemade poster with a black and white picture, different from the one the woman had shown on the doorstep, and brightly coloured felt-tip writing. The writing made it look more like a poster for a jumble sale than a notice to appeal for help tracking down a missing girl.

'My daughter made it,' he said proudly. 'She thought if she used as many bright colours as she could people would see it. It's great isn't it. She's only nine. Nine.'

Moira smiled and nodded her thanks. What was there to say to that? Leaving the shop, she paused to take a closer look at the poster and turned to smile back at the man on the till, who was busy now with another customer. Perhaps he would direct that customer to look at the poster too. Perhaps this father's pride in his own daughter would help Celeste's parents to find their girl. Someone must have seen something. She wondered whose idea the poster had been. Had the little girl decided to make it of her own volition, or had her father suggested that she do it? Would a girl of that age really have heard that there was a young woman missing? Perhaps they had also had a visit from Celeste's parents and the girl had wanted to do something, in the way that all children assume they have the ability to do something that will matter?

The face of Celeste's mother returned to Moira's mind again. Perhaps she too should think of something, anything she could do to help that poor woman find her daughter. To help that young woman be found.

Moira couldn't think what the something could be, but instead of walking straight home to rescue the smelly trainers and stained T-shirt, she crossed the road to where people had gathered and the police cars were still parked. As she got closer, she could see that Celeste's dad was there with the police officer. They were talking animatedly with a tall man in a green sweatshirt and another girl that looked vaguely familiar to Moira.

'The thing is,' the girl was saying, 'they can stay outside of the garden, just on the pavement here, they won't contaminate anything, but they could jog someone's memory, or get Celeste on the news, which could prompt someone to come forward. Surely the more people who know that we're looking for Celeste, the better. More people keeping an eye out has got to be a good thing.'

The man in the sweatshirt was nodding enthusiastically. 'Exactly,' he proclaimed with a theatrical flailing of his arms.

'You'd join our vigil and help us spread the word about the search for Celeste wouldn't you?'

It took Moira a moment to realise the young man was talking to her.

'We have candles,' he said. 'We even have some cushions if you want to sit on the wall or whatever. We just need people. People who care.'

Before Moira had the chance to answer him, or the police officer had the opportunity to protest, another young woman in a floor-length dress had handed her a candle, then rummaged in a bag to pull out a turquoise cushion with flowers on it, proffering it with the words, 'this is a nice one, how about this one?'

'Thanks Mimi', the young man smiled. 'And thank you for joining us...I'm sorry, I didn't catch your name.'

'Moira.'

'Moira,' he repeated. 'Lovely name.' And he took a box of matches from his pocket and lit the candle Moira was holding, gesturing to where Mimi had placed the cushion on the wall.

Moira sat, cautiously, looking at the police officer for approval and placing her washing detergent by her feet, before sitting upright and holding her candle with both hands as though getting ready to join a procession in a church. What did a person do at a vigil? And how long would she be expected to stay?

Both of the young women sat on the wall either side of Moira, with the one who had handed out the cushion and the candle lighting more candles for each of them.

'I'm Esther, Celeste's friend,' explained the first girl.

'I'm Mimi,' smiled the second.

Moira recalled leaving the house and the lack of reply when she'd called to let Billy and William know where she was going. Would they be worried if she was more than a few minutes? If they had heard her, they might be concerned. If they hadn't heard her, they might not even notice she'd gone out. For how long? Half an hour? An hour? All evening?

She regretted leaving her phone at home. She regretted crossing the road and landing herself in a situation where she felt trapped. How could she leave now, without appearing heartless and uncaring. She wasn't heartless. She did care. Perhaps she could go home and put the washing machine on and let them know about the vigil and then come back? Maybe William would even come with her? Billy wouldn't, that was for sure, but maybe William?

Celeste's father reached across her to place the photograph of Celeste on the wall. As he stepped back, he pointed at her.

'That necklace looks like Celeste's necklace,' he held his accusatory finger still as though it had been secured in place like a hook on a wall.

Moira put her hand to her throat, reminding herself which necklace she was wearing, and remembering finding it in amongst the games and jigsaws under William's bed while he was out buying the ice creams.

'What's that?' asked the police officer.

'The necklace,' Celeste's father repeated. 'The necklace she's wearing,' He looked from the police officer to Moira to Esther and back again. 'If you move your hand,' he said to Moira, 'if you move your hand so he can see.'

She moved her hand.

'Yes, that's exactly the same as the one Celeste always wears,' agreed the young man, leaning right in to take a closer look, so that Moira leaned back and almost fell off the wall.

Esther took her turn to peer in close at Moira's neck too, declaring it to be just like Celeste's necklace.

Moira felt her skin burn, with the sensation rising from her neck. She was sure her face must be bright red and radiating heat. She ran her fingers across the necklace again. 'Oh, it's an old one this,' she said. 'I just found it again today actually, when I was having a clear out of some old stuff. It must have been in the back of a drawer for about a decade.'

'Yeah, there must be lots of star necklaces,' Mimi chipped in. 'Nice that. I remember. She did always wear something like that.'

Moira and Mimi both saw Celeste's father flinch.

Mimi quickly clarified. 'I mean, I haven't seen Celeste in a while, that's why I say I remember her wearing a necklace like that. I wasn't trying to imply. You know. She always wore it. Wears it. Doesn't she?' Mimi looked towards Orson to back her up, but he was busy taking pictures. 'I don't think I ever saw her...I've ever seen...I ever see her without it.'

'Yes,' Esther confirmed. 'She hasn't taken it off since she first got it years ago. She was definitely wearing it last night.'

Moira thought of the little girl she had known at primary school, politely returning the register to the office, and tried to recall whether Celeste wore a necklace like the one currently sitting on her own neck. She touched the little star again. She couldn't remember the girl in that kind of detail. Just her smile and her neatly plaited hair. Perhaps she wouldn't have worn a necklace to school anyway, in case it got lost or got her into trouble. Perhaps she had taken it off or lost it in a game or a jigsaw that William or James had brought home on toy day at the end of term. But that couldn't be the case if they'd all seen adult Celeste wearing her necklace recently.

'Do you live nearby?' asked the police officer.

'Yes. I...' Moira pointed in the direction of home, relieved to be changing the subject. 'Just over there. In fact, I only just nipped out to the shop, my husband and my son will be wondering where I've got to. They'll think I've got lost. Maybe I could come back?' She looked at Orson, who was busy with his phone. 'Maybe I could come back and join the vigil a little bit later when I've let them know where I am and just finished off the jobs I was doing before I nipped out to get this.' She bent down to pick up the detergent and held it up to show the police officer as though showing him a note to be excused from PE.

'Yes, we saw you and your son earlier, didn't we, when we were knocking on doors?' Celeste's father nodded.

'Then we'll probably be knocking on your door again, I'm afraid' said the police officer, visibly pleased that Orson's first recruit to the vigil was already bailing out. 'You get back to your family, we're taking all the practical steps to find Celeste, you're probably best at home unless there's anything you've seen or anything you think you can tell us?'

Moira tried hard not to think about the necklace or how much of a coincidence it was that she had found it just as a girl with something the same – similar – had disappeared.

'Thanks.' She nodded to the police officer and Celeste's father and handed her candle to Esther. 'I hope you find her soon,' she added. And, clutching the detergent in the crook of her arm like a baby, she quickly crossed the road and walked home.

As Moira stepped into the hall, Billy walked out of the living room and it made her jump.

'Oh, have you been out love? Fancy a cuppa?'

She had stepped away from a world where the police were hunting for a missing girl, back into a Sunday evening of ironing and Antiques Roadshow where no-one had noticed she'd been gone.

'I'll make it,' she said, holding up the detergent to show him. 'I nipped out for this because we'd run out, so I can get the kettle and the washer on at the same time.'

'Perfect,' he smiled, and disappeared back into the living room.

Moira lifted the kettle to check for the weight of water, topping it up from the tap before switching it on. She checked the T-shirt in the sink. The stain was barely visible now, so she pulled it out of the water, wringing it enough to stop it dripping as she transferred it to the washing machine. It might as well go in with the trainers. Then she added detergent and switched on the machine.

By the time she pushed open the living room door with her elbow, carrying two mugs of tea, the washing machine was full of soapy water, tipping Wiliam's shoes from side to side as though they were fighting the waves to sail the ocean in a storm.

'Anything good on?' she asked, as she set Billy's tea down on a coaster where he could reach it from his chair. She sat down with her own tea in the armchair that had been silently designated hers over the years.

'You've missed it,' Billy smiled, reaching for his tea. 'There was a guy on. He was convinced that this vase he had was worth a fortune because he'd looked it up on the internet and everything, but it was a fake. A good fake, the expert said, looked just the same but could have been made last week! You should have seen the guy's face.'

As a young woman on the screen explained how the bracelet had been a gift from her grandmother who was no longer with us, and how she would never dream of parting with it, Moira sipped her tea, then placed her mug on the coffee table next to her and took off the necklace she'd been so delighted to find earlier. She held it for a moment, feeling each point of the star with her finger without looking at the object in her hand. She put the necklace in the pocket of her jeans.

'Yes,' said Moira, picking up her tea and sipping it again. 'Just because something looks like something, doesn't mean it's the same, does it?'

VI

Celeste

*F*ather Christmas. Chicken dinners. Watching Dr Who wearing clean pyjamas. Jaffa Cakes. Being under the duvet on a cold morning. Chip butties. Seeing a fox. Waking up with Orson. Not Orson. Waking up with someone. Being kissed. Swimming in the sea. Ice cream. Hot chocolate with marshmallows. Some Like it Hot. Edward Scissorhands. The Wizard of Oz. There's no place like home. Drinking tea with Mum. Drinking tea. Mum. Home. Where is Mum? Mum, where are you? Mum. Mum?

I can see her. She's looking for me. Under the table. Behind the curtain. In the linen basket. Don't hide in the linen basket Celeste, it's dirty. Behind the door. Under the bed. On the back doorstep. Round the corner in the church garden. Don't leave the house when we're playing hide and seek Celeste. I was worried sick. That was stupid. You worried me sick Celeste disappearing like that. Stay where I can see you. Stay with me Celeste. Celeste. Celeste! CELESTE!

She will find me. She always finds me. Even when I left the house and hid round the corner. She was cross and something else. Concerned? Relieved? What would the word be? She was cross. There was no pudding and no more hide and seek for a week. There was a reminder every time, hiding places in the house and the garden only. Where is the house? Where is the

185

garden? She is looking for me. Is she looking for me? I'm over here Mum. I'm here. I'm sorry. Come and find me, Mum, I'm here.

If I think really hard, if I try to connect my brain with hers, will she know? Will she hear me if I talk to her inside my own head. Will she hear me like I'm in the room? Or in her head? Or in her own thoughts? What do I need to say?

Start with the good news first. She always says, start with the good news first. I'm OK, Mum. I'm here, I can move my fingers. I can feel the dampness of the ground under my skin. I'm tired. I've been sleeping. I think I've been sleeping. But I'm awake. I'm awake. I'm alive.

I don't know where I am. Mum, can you come and find me? Are you looking for me? I was home. Almost home and then. My foot hurt and I sat down and then I... Then I....Then I don't remember why I didn't come home.

I am connected to the earth here. I am sending you a message through the ground. Mother Earth to Mother, so that you can track me back. Can you feel that, Mum? Can you feel me talking to you through the earth? Can you see what I can see? I'm sending pictures from my eyes to your brain by thinking them to you.

How will I know if it's working? Can you just come and get me, Mum? Can you send me a message back to let me know you're listening? Can you send me a sign that you can hear me?

I'm waiting. I'm emptying my mind, like Orson taught me. Focus on the breath. Exhale all negative thought. One. Two. Three. Four. Inhale positive energy. One. Two. Three. Four. Hold it. One. Two. Three. Four. You are your breath. There is only the breath.

I need more than breath. I need my mum. I need to show her where I am. I can bring her here. I am closing my eyes and thinking of the detail. That pale blue dress with the wrap over and the fancy sleeves that she bought at the charity shop. The one everyone tells her looks lovely. The one she tells everyone she got for £5.50 from the charity shop. Her hair is half-up-half-down, like she's worn it forever. Like she did my hair sometimes when

I was a kid. We were twins. We both love blue. I can see her. Can she see me yet?

I can see her standing next to me with that 'what have you done now Celeste?' look on her face. But she is smiling at me. Go on Mum, tell me it will all be OK.

'It will all be OK, Celeste. I am here now.'

I'm waiting for her to pick me up. Help me up. But she just stands there. She doesn't even have a cardigan for me. Or a blanket. That's not my real mum. My real mum would have a cardigan and a cup of tea. My real mum would be kneeling next to me, never mind if her nice dress got dirty, and people were looking, she would help me sit up, wrap me up in something warm and get some tea down me. My imaginary mum is rubbish. She's just standing there. But at least she is there. At least she exists. And perhaps she is communicating with my real mum. Maybe my real mum is getting a flask ready and then she'll be on her way.

Don't worry about the tea, Mum. Don't bother about the cardigan. Just get here.

19

Abi

Abi paused outside Annie and Adam's house. A practised, conscious pause with a controlled breath to clear her mind and help her focus on what to do next. Realistically, she ought to go back to the station, brief colleagues, and go home. It had been a long day and she needed to be sharp. Celeste needed someone sharp enough to make the right choices in the right order. She needed someone who could choose their questions carefully and hear everything that was unsaid, as well as the words spoken. If Abi continued to follow the breadcrumbs personally, she'd have to find the right way to ask difficult things.

The air she inhaled was soft and comforting. Still moist from the rain hours earlier, with the freshness of spring. But deep breaths were not a replacement for actual nutrition, Abi reminded herself. She'd had water and coffee and that apple that Noel had given her, but she ought to try and eat something else.

'Are we going then?'

Annie closed the front door behind them, bringing Abi back into the moment with a reminder that she had already asked the girl to come to the Tesco with her so that they could take the same route and see exactly where she had confronted the boy and called her brother.

'Sorry to keep you waiting. I just needed a jumper, you know, with having wet hair. You get cold quick don't you? And my mum always freaks about me going out of the house with wet hair, says I'll get consumption, whatever that is. Anyway, I'm ready now, shall we go?'

Abi turned to smile at the girl, who'd apparently also needed to protect herself from catching her death with mascara and lip liner.

'Thanks Annie, it's good of you to give up your evening to come with me, we do appreciate it.'

'No worries, washing my hair was the most exciting thing I had planned, so walking to work with you like we're in some real-life CSI episode is already far more exciting that I thought my Sunday was going to be,' Annie joked. 'But can you call me Mitch, please. Everyone except my family call me Mitch, half the people I work with probably don't even know my first name.'

'Mitch,' Abi repeated. She smiled, thinking about how she herself was always Abigail with her family but Abi everywhere else.

Annie chatted as they walked, her words were like water pouring out of her and changing direction effortlessly from one topic to the next. Abi wanted to ask her to just shut up for a minute and concentrate on retracing her steps exactly and remembering anything she could. But the girl might say something of interest. Chatting might help her remember. Or at least relax her enough that she would remember. Abi tried to listen and filter what she said, discarding the waffle as background noise and tuning in for words that might actually matter.

As they approached the community garden, Annie declared them nearly there and remarked on how busy it was with police and people.

'You must be really worried about this girl. You think it was him, don't you, the guy that followed me, you think he's done something to this girl that's gone missing?'

Annie stopped. Movement and words ceasing at once, as though someone had removed the batteries. She stared deep into Abi's eyes. 'It could have been me, couldn't it?'

Abi had seen the switch from excited to frightened before. She'd felt it before. It had taken a while for Annie. Perhaps it was the police cars. Or being back in the place where she had confronted the bogeyman – not just the person, but the fear, the back of the mind, tip of the tongue threat that accompanies any lone walk home.

Annie had been brave. For a moment, the two women stood silently acknowledging that her bravery might have saved her from something, and that it had been a risk, which could have gone either way. This time, maybe it had saved her. In another moment, another identical scenario, it could have triggered escalation rather than escape.

'*The fate of all of us is determined by a million split-second decisions*,' Abi remembered her dad telling her before her first day on the job. '*Most of them we don't even think about. Most of them don't matter. But sometimes they do. Sometimes a single, seemingly innocuous decision can change everything – for better or worse. So choose carefully. Always choose carefully.*' At the time, she'd thought he was being dramatic. Over-protective. He was always trying to be Winston Churchill with his big speeches and dramatic pauses. He loved a metaphor. He loved bite-sized, thought-for-the-day, Post-It note wisdom, and, annoyingly, his advice often popped up like little pink or yellow squares; reminders stuck inside her brain. And when she checked them, the notes his words had scrawled in her head always confirmed he'd been right as usual.

'So, tell me again, now that we're here where it happened. Tell me what happened, Mitch.'

Abi took out her notebook again and wrote everything down. As they walked first a little further down the street to see the spot where Annie's friend Jess had turned off to go home and

Annie recalled again that she had stopped to watch her go, like she always did, until the other girl was out of sight.

'Normally, I would put my headphones on for the rest of the way, listen to music so that it doesn't feel so lonely walking the last bit on my own,' Annie paused. 'But I'd left my Air Pods in the pocket of my other coat, so I didn't have them. I only heard him because I didn't have my Air Pods on me.'

Abi could see Annie getting stuck in her own story, focusing less on what happened and more on what could have happened. She brought the girl back into the narrative she needed her to follow.

'So let's start from where you started to walk home by yourself. Exactly where were you when Jess left you to walk the rest of the way by herself?'

They walked to a spot on a corner a beyond the community garden and on the opposite side of the road. Annie explained that she always stopped and waited on the corner for the right-hand side of the street, even though Jess lives on the left-hand side, because she could see her friend for longer from there.

'I get a kind of diagonal line of sight, right up until she goes past that house with the giant row of trees. I can't see her past the trees, but she's pretty much home by then anyway. Like two doors down.'

'And then what did you do?'

'I went to get my Air Pods out of my pocket but they weren't there, so I just started walking home.'

'Did you see anyone?'

'No. I hardly ever do. It's boring as hell around here. There's literally nothing but a couple of shops, a chippy, the church and all these houses. That's why I can't wait to get out. I'm planning on travelling you see. Planning on seeing a world a bit bigger than these dull little streets.'

As Annie wrapped words around her anxiety to distract herself, Abi noted the position of the streetlights and gauged the distance between where they were standing and the community garden where the boot had been found. She glanced across to where Noel and Robert were standing and wondered for a moment why Esther was with them, sitting on the wall, instead of back at the house with Yvonne. The three of them had been joined by a tall man in a green top, a slender woman with dark hair, and an older woman wearing grey, who stood up from her seat on the wall, bent to pick something up, and then walked away from them, past the church and round the corner.

'OK,' said Abi. 'Let's retrace your steps, where did you walk then? Let's walk it together. And you can tell me when you started to think there was someone following you.'

They began walking and Annie stopped almost immediately.

'It was here, almost straight away after I'd started walking again,' she explained, 'but I'm only stopping to show you. I didn't stop then because I wanted to check without turning round.'

'That's right, you walked slower then faster to see if the footsteps you could hear changed pace. Smart thinking.'

Annie smiled and nodded. 'Yes, but they weren't really footsteps. It was the quietest of sounds, but because there was literally no other noise, I could hear it. Or feel it. I just knew there was someone there.'

'So you said you stopped under a streetlight to confront him. Which streetlight was that?'

Annie quickened her pace to walk to the right spot.

'Here. It was definitely this one, because when I turned I could see the garden over there and, you see this house,' she said, pointing, 'I used to have a friend who lived here. They moved away but I still always look at the house when I walk past and I stopped here because it felt like a safe place, even though they haven't lived here for ages, it still feels like kind of home ground.'

Abi moved to stand in the same position as Annie, looking back at the street they'd just walked up, and the small gathering of people and colleagues she could see at the garden. She asked Annie to recount again what she had said, how the man had behaved, how long she had paused there, whether she had turned round to look back at him.

'No!' said Annie. 'I walked backwards away from him at first so that I could check he was staying put, but once I turned round, there was no way I was going to look back. I didn't want him to think I was scared. I mean, I suppose I was scared, a bit. Angry more than scared. Irritated, you know. but I wasn't going to let him see that, was I?'

'So you didn't see where he went or what he did after you'd gone?'

'No,' Annie confirmed. 'But it felt like he carried on standing there watching me walk away. I didn't hear him move. I could kind of sense him standing there. And then I turned the corner over there, you know, to get back to my house, and Adam just stayed on the phone with me until I got back. He's a pain in the arse most of the time but he was actually an OK brother last night.'

Abi smiled back at Annie, envious of her ability to look on the bright side. The girl had clearly done her best to shake off the incident as nothing until she'd been asked to recount it. Until she'd learned about Celeste's disappearance.

'I just need to speak to my colleague over there for a moment,' said Abi. 'If you want to go home now, you can, or you can come with me to the Tesco if you'd like. It's up to you. My colleague can drive you home if you'd like to just get back to your family now?'

'It's literally a five-minute walk from here,' Annie replied, gesturing in the direction of home. 'I walk it pretty much every day of my life.'

'But it's been a quite unusual couple of days though, hasn't it?'

'Unusual, yeah. That's one word for it. I'd rather come with you if you don't mind. Then perhaps you can take me home and just let my mum know I'm not in imminent danger of death, and you lot are on it.'

'OK.' Abi nodded her consent to the plan, and they walked across to Noel Fisher.

'This is the vigil, is it?'

'There's more coming,' the tall man in the green hoody replied. Then responding to the cynicism Abi couldn't hide from her face, he added. 'You might not believe in the power of the universe, but it exists. And the more we send love out to it, the more the universe will return it. You look for Celeste in your own way, and we'll ask the universe to send her home.'

Abi looked at Noel Fisher.

'It can't do any harm, I suppose,' he said. 'And at least while they're all here lighting candles, they're not over there contaminating evidence or at home spouting conspiracy theories on the internet.'

'They have the internet on their phones,' Abi pointed out.

'Yeah, but we're only using our phones to spread the word and invite people to the vigil. We're not tin-hatted nutters. We're just concerned about Celeste. If you knew her, you'd understand.' Green hoody sat on the pavement with his legs crossed and asked the tall woman to pass him a candle, which he placed on the pavement in front of him. He stared at it and said nothing more.

'Do you want a candle?' the tall woman asked Annie.

'Nah. Thanks.'

'She's with me,' Abi replied.

Feeling a little disoriented, Abi took a deep breath to focus and asked Noel Fisher to step to one side so that she could talk to him out of earshot of everyone else.

They asked each other a question at the same time, like Hollywood cowboys drawing their guns at each other in unison.

Abi's question 'Why is Esther here?'

Noel's question 'Are you OK?'

Both answered 'I don't know.'

'You need to eat something,' Noel Fisher told her. 'And you need to go home. We can go back to the station, get this briefed in, and pick up the threads in the morning.'

'Yeah, I know, you're right,' she said. 'I know. And I will. I just want to follow up with this thing with Annie, I mean Mitch, she likes to be called Mitch. The girl there. Annie Mitchell, she likes to be called Mitch.'

Abi explained that she had a name for the guy who'd followed Annie the night before. 'It could be something and nothing,' she said, 'But the timings add up. The locations match. I'm going to go and see if I can get the CCTV footage from the Tesco. Maybe you could go and talk to this guy, his name is William Keaveney. Would you mind? I know you probably want to get back, but I just want to see if this is a red flag or a dead end.' She looked across to the officers putting the dog back in the van. 'Have they found anything?'

'There's some vomit. We'll send a sample to the lab but it's unlikely we'll get anything useful from that. There are footprints, but there are loads of footprints. About half a tonne of litter. Nothing useful so far.'

Abi looked around. These were ordinary streets. Streets where people led routine lives week after week. People might not know their neighbours in the clichéd, soap opera tradition of wandering in and out of each other's houses and knowing each other's business, but they came across the same faces here and there through the years. There were collision spaces built into this community - the church, the garden, the bus stop, the shop, the park, the Tesco; all places where people saw faces they'd seen dozens of times before. Hundreds of times before. Adults they'd seen as babies, toddlers, teenagers. Changes they'd not noticed because they happened in tiny increments while everything else stayed the same.

'Someone here must have seen something,' Abi said. 'I'll get a team out knocking on doors. Let's see if anyone's got CCTV or those camera doorbells. There's got to be someone who was letting the cat in or putting the recycling out. Is there any CCTV on the street?'

'I've put in a request for that already,' Fisher replied. 'There's nothing that covers this bit of the street, there's one just up past the shop that way, and then the next one is near the entrance to the park over there, but it should give us something of what happened before and after Celeste was here. Assuming Celeste was actually here, not just her boot.'

'Let's not assume anything. Annie's coming with me to the Tesco, you find out where this Keaveney guy lives and go and talk to him. Have family liaison gone round to Yvonne?'

Fisher nodded.

'Is there anything else I'm not seeing?'

'What about these jokers?' Fisher asked.

'Leave them, as long as they're not breaching the cordon, they're not doing any harm. They might even bring some witnesses out of the woodwork.'

Fisher told her how, so far, they'd accosted one woman on her way back from the shop and pretty much adopted a cat . 'They reckon there are more coming.'

'Cats or women?' Abi joked. 'Well if the power of the universe can find Celeste, let's plug it in. But let's also see what's on that CCTV and what this stalker character has to say for himself.'

'Get a sandwich while you're at the shop.'

'Yes officer,' Abi laughed as she gave Fisher a fake salute and then turned to see Robert glaring at her. She and Fisher had a job to do, Yvonne was at home waiting with the family liaison officer, and there was Robert, lost. He couldn't help the investigation. He couldn't sit at home waiting for Celeste because that wasn't his home.

Abi walked towards Celeste's father and offered him the only kindness she could think of.

'Thanks Robert, for keeping an eye on the vigil here. PC Fisher and I both have leads to follow up now and there are more officers on their way to do some door to door. Would you mind staying here with the vigil? There'll be an officer here, but just in case anyone comes along who's seen something or knows anything. It's useful to have someone there who knows Celeste.' Abi nodded at Esther too, conscious that the girl was also hanging around at the vigil because there was nothing else for her to do except wait for news.

'Here's my number,' she said to both of them, handing her card just to Robert. 'I'll be coming back this way shortly to bring Mitch, you know, Annie, home anyway. But if there is anything, just call me.'

'Did he tell you about the necklace?' Robert asked. 'There was a woman here, wearing a necklace, just like Celeste's necklace. I mean, she was just an ordinary woman on her way back from the shop and there might be hundreds of necklaces like that. It's a bit weird though, isn't it? Don't you think it's weird? Nobody else seemed to think that a massive coincidence like that is a bit odd.'

'And where is the woman now?' Abi asked.

'She just went home. But she said she might come back with her son.'

'Well, if she comes back, call me. Or if there is anything else, call me. Thank you, Robert.' Abi turned to Annie. 'Let's go.'

20

William

William opened and closed his bedroom door, looking at it critically as he considered the best, or rather, easiest, way to put a lock on it. It wasn't right that someone of his age should have to even consider the best ways of keeping his mother out of his room. Surely, any mother should see his age, height and deep voice as the equivalent of a 'keep out!' sign on the door. He didn't want to be rude about it. He didn't want to offend anyone. She was only coming in for helpful things like putting away clean washing and tidying up dirty cups, but she just couldn't help herself snooping while she was there. He had a right to privacy, surely?

The trouble was, he couldn't see a way of doing it that didn't involve serious DIY skills. He might be able to fit a bolt by himself, at a push. But a bolt inside the room would only prevent her from coming in when he was already in there, and she wasn't going to snoop around when he was there. A bolt outside the room could be opened just as easily by her as it could by him. Unless he padlocked it? But that would look like he seriously had something to hide, which would probably encourage her to snoop even more, in case he was a drug dealer or something.

The only thing he could do, was have a word. It would be awkward, and it might not even change anything, but it was the best option.

William sat on the bed, a little defeated by his circuitous meander around the question of securing his bedroom, only to find himself back where he'd started, forced into accepting there would be an unpalatable conversation with his mum, which might not change anything anyway. Perhaps if he spoke to his parents both together, then it might seem less like he was accusing her and more like he just wanted to keep his private space private. He might even wrap it up in wanting to help her, by clearing away his own pots, hoovering his own carpet, sorting his own laundry. He'd put the washing machine on this morning, and it was actually dead simple. A five-minute job. Two minutes. His mother made such a fuss about having to do the washing, and there was really nothing to it. He would do that. He would talk to them both about how he wanted to take more responsibility for his space and his things. How he wanted to contribute more to the household, and just throw in how there would no longer be any need to come into his room as a kind of side-effect of stepping up to be more helpful. More of an adult. It might actually work better than a lock on the door. She would be keen not to discourage him. She'd be pleased he was being so thoughtful.

He pictured his mother, sitting downstairs watching the Antiques Roadshow with his Dad. He thought about the necklace round her neck. And about the necklace round Celeste's neck. Why had he taken it? What on earth had made him take that and hide it? He knew why. He knew he'd taken the necklace because he couldn't take the girl. She'd been his for a few minutes, but he couldn't keep her. He could only keep part of her. But that part of Celeste was now sitting on his mother's neck, where anyone could see it. He needed to get the necklace back and stop any more intrusions into his space, even if it meant having a clear out of his room and bagging up stuff for the charity shop, just to prove he was serious. He had a plan. He had half a plan. The part about getting the necklace back would come to him. Perhaps he could accidentally break it? Or wait until she took it off and just take it, then convince her she'd lost it. A plan would come to him. Sometimes a plan wasn't even necessary, sometimes you just had to be ready.

Celeste's face came back into his head. It thumped in his chest like a memory of something stupid he'd done by accident. Something he couldn't put right. He thought about Anne. What a bitch. It was her fault. If she had just been a bit kinder. If she'd given him a chance, things might have been so different. What a toxic little cow. What an evil little bitch.

William stood and looked in the mirror for a moment. He practised smiling. He couldn't go downstairs with all that anger and resentment on his face. His mum would notice. She was always quick to see on his face when he was in a bad mood. '*She's a witch, your mum*', his dad had always joked, and he could believe it. Maybe it was a super power all mums had. Maybe it was because she'd worked in a school for so many years, or perhaps it was just her, but she had a knack for knowing what you were thinking, so he needed to do a quick clean-up of his brain's browsing history before he went downstairs and delighted her with his plan to help out more.

As expected, William's parents were watching TV when he walked into the living room, each of them sitting in the armchairs that were allocated as Mum's chair and Dad's chair without the need for any instruction or labelling, just from years of habit. If you sat in Dad's chair, he would tell you to 'move it'. If you sat in Mum's chair, she would sit somewhere else, but William never sat there unless he wanted to wind her up, and the discomfort for him of doing something they both knew he'd only done to upset her, while she sat somewhere else and said nothing, was more acute than any annoyance he could cause her.

'Shhhh,' said his dad as William entered the room, before he'd had chance to utter a single word. 'They're at the bit where she has to rank the things in order of how much they cost by guessing. I reckon, it's that ordinary-looking vase that's the best one, they always try to throw a red herring into the mix. What do you think, love, how would you rank them?'

William glanced at his mother, her eyes were on the screen, but her attention was not on the programme they were watching.

'Love? Moira? Which one do you think is the best – you need to be quick, otherwise you'll just be copying Fiona, or the expert will have told us.'

'Yeah,' she said. 'I think you're right. You're usually right. What do you think William?'

His mother turned towards him as she asked him the question. Just to be different, he chose another option.

'I think the blue one,' he said.

He stood in the doorway as they waited to find out the answer. The presenter chose the same vase as his parents as the 'best' option, and the one he'd selected as the 'basic' choice.

'*Well*,' said the expert. '*You were right about the better choice, but you've got basic and best the wrong way round!*'

'I knew it!' Billy exclaimed. 'Red herring. Red bloody herring! I should have known. You've got hidden talents William! Maybe you've got a future as an antiques dealer. We should send you off to the charity shop with a tenner tomorrow morning and see if you can trade it up to a hundred quid! What do you think Moira?'

He turned to look at his wife as the presenter began to explain which stately home the programme would be visiting the following week, and she seemed absorbed in taking in the information.

'Shall I make us all a cup of tea?' said William. 'I've been thinking about how I need to do more in the house. More to look after my own things and my own room. Did you notice I put a wash on this morning, Mum? You know, with me not working and you both working all week, I'm thinking you could give me a jobs list, even?'

Moira looked at him with a face he found hard to decipher. And her words gave him no clues about what she was thinking.

'Tea. Lovely,' she said. She reached for her empty mug on the coffee table and held out her other hand to request Billy's cup without asking for it. 'I'll bring these in, you put the kettle on.'

William walked into the kitchen as his mother followed him, putting the mugs on the counter top while her son filled the kettle. The washing machine was in the final throes of its cycle, sending its contents into an orbit that was making the whole machine shake.

'That's your trainers in there,' said Moira.

'Yer what?' William couldn't hear her over the noise of the washing machine and the kettle.

She turned to face him and repeated herself, pointing at the machine, doubling the volume of her words and mouthing them exaggeratedly as though talking through a window.

He looked towards where his mother was pointing, just in time to see the homogenous blur drop from its centrifuge, and propel a trainer towards its glass door.

The kettle clicked off as it boiled, and Moira repeated the sentence one more time, adding 'I found them, on the doorstep. They were all muddy and they stank of vomit so I washed them. They were filthy and they stank.'

'Yeah, that's why I left them on the doorstep,' he turned to pour the boiling water in the mugs, grateful to have a reason to face away from her.

But he had to turn back around to get the milk and she was right there, standing looking at him. 'So? what exactly did you do last night to get your trainers so full of mud and stinking of vomit?'

'Can you pass me the milk?'

It was a small kitchen. Moira and Billy had talked about extending more than once, but it had never been a good time to stretch themselves financially when the kids were younger, and now they were used to being able to reach one side of the room from the other in three steps.

Moira turned to open the fridge, passed the milk to her son and held the door open, waiting for him to hand it back so that she could replace it.

'So?' she asked again as she put the milk away and turned to face William. 'How did your trainers end up in that state?'

He told her a story, a detailed story, about how he'd gone for a walk, just as he'd said. He carefully mentioned that his walk had been in the park, a location in the opposite direction from the house than the wood-lined path next to the dual carriageway where he'd actually been. He loaded his story with realistic uncertainty. What was it called that park? No, not that one, the one with the cherry blossom trees, that's the one, the blossom was gone now off the trees but there was still some rotting on the grass. It had started raining so he'd tried to shelter under the trees but he'd still got wet and walking off the path had taken him through muddy patches. Unavoidable mud that had covered his trainers. There had been a drunk, lying on a bench under one of the trees with a sleeping bag and one of those two-litre bottles of cheap cider that you could probably use to clear the drains. The drunk had sat up as he approached and first offered him a swig of cider, then asked him for money, and then – William was sorry he hadn't been sharp enough to see it coming – the drunk guy had thrown up and it had splattered all over his trainers. In his revulsion, William had sprung back and lost his footing, ending up lying on the muddy ground and getting even dirtier as he hauled himself up.

'The guy just laughed,' said William, finishing his story. 'I think he might even have done it on purpose because I didn't want to sit there being his mate and I didn't have any money to give him.'

Moira waited, looking at her son. He wasn't sure what else she wanted him to say.

'I'm sorry, Mum. I came home after that, and I wasn't sure what to do with my trainers, so I just left them outside to sort later and kind of forgot what I'd done with them. I was going to ask you what to do about them. Thanks for getting them washed. I can hang them up and get them dry. I didn't know you could put shoes in the washing machine.'

Moira nodded but said nothing.

William filled the quiet. 'In fact, I came down to say that I want to do more around the house. Thanks for sorting all those old games and jigsaws out earlier, it's great to clear some space, but I know it should be me doing that sort of thing. It should be me tidying my own room, doing my own washing and putting it away. So, I'm going to do that from now on. I'll look after my own room and my own things, and you can even give me a list of other jobs if you like. Washing up and hoovering and that. I put a wash on this morning because my clothes from last night were all damp and muddy as well. I hope it was just mud. It smelt a bit rank. People don't clean up after their dogs, do they?'

'Yes,' Moira replied. 'I got those things dry for you, they're over there if you want to put them away.' She pointed to where his sweatshirt, pants and underwear were neatly folded in the plastic basket. 'Why don't you do that now, and then come and watch telly with me and your dad for a bit while I finish the ironing? I can take the drinks in.'

He smiled at her, picked up the basket of clothes and made for the door.

'Just one other thing,' his mother said, forcing him to pause on his way out of the kitchen. 'That necklace I found amongst all that old stuff under your bed. Did you know it was there?'

'No, I've never seen it before. I haven't played with any of that stuff for years.'

'Only - apparently – it's just the same as the one that girl wears. Celeste. You know, the one that's gone missing?'

William looked at the cups of tea, sitting on the kitchen counter waiting to be taken into another room where this conversation hadn't happened.

'Yeah,' he said, 'I think she had the same one as a kid. Maybe she lost it at school and her parents replaced it with another one the same. Must have been here all these years. I'll be back in a minute, you'd best get in there with the teas before Dad makes us watch some boring documentary about the war.'

He moved swiftly towards the door, noticing for the first time that his mother was no longer wearing the necklace and feeling her eyes on him as he went.

21

Ed

The tone of voice on the phone hadn't matched his wife's words when Ed had called to ask if she'd mind if the girls got home a little later than usual.

He'd prefaced the request with all the apologies he could think of to justify the extra hour. He knew they had school in the morning. He knew routine was important. He knew she'd be worried if they weren't home on time. That's why he was calling.

'It's fine, it's no problem. As long as they're home for half past eight,' Lisa had said.

But something in the way she'd said it had made him leave the room to continue the call. He'd taken the phone into the garden and piled excuses on top of his apologies. That's where he'd gone wrong.

His mum hadn't realised they would need to go so early, what with it being her birthday. They'd eaten later than planned. It *was* his mum's birthday. And the kids had loved being there. And his mum loved having the grandchildren there. His mum missed the days when they were all there together. 'She misses you too,' he'd said.

Asking for an extra hour of the girls' time had been fine. Wrapping the request in a tissue of nostalgia and remorse had tipped the conversation in a different direction. Blaming his mother, rather than himself, had derailed his apology and Lisa's polite acquiescence.

'You're asking me now?' Lisa had said, finally. 'You're asking me five minutes before they're due back, when it takes half an hour to get here from your mum's? You're trying to guilt trip me into being fine with it by telling me how much your mum misses seeing them? Misses seeing me? Well perhaps we would all be there together for your mum's birthday if you'd been able to keep it in your pants? Maybe you should have thought about how much your mum would miss the kids before you decided the grass was greener, eh? But you weren't thinking about your mum, were you? You weren't thinking about the kids. You certainly weren't thinking about me. It's always about you, and your agenda, isn't it? And here I am again, having to accept it, because I have no fucking choice. You're not asking my permission. You're just telling me what's happening, as per fucking usual. Have them back by half past eight.'

She'd ended the call and Ed had pulled the vape from his pocket, taking a long drag on the plastic device and releasing a cloud of thick fruitiness into the garden.

'Everything all right, Dad?' Ivy asked, walking up behind him.

'Everything's fine. We just need to do cake with Grandma and get going. Your mum just wants to make sure you get to bed so you're bright eyed and bushy tailed for school in the morning. One piece of cake only! No. Crazy. Sugar. Rush. Before. Bed.' He punctuated the sentence with little taps of his index finger on her nose after each word. Something he'd done since she was a baby, that still made her smile.

'And is Mum OK?'

'Of course she is' he replied. He put the vape back in his pocket and said, 'come on, let's get CAKE! I'll race you!' He threw off all the words left unsaid with the challenge he often laid down for his daughter, noticing as she beat him as usual that allowing her to win involved less and less fake losing as Ivy grew older.

Ed sang happy birthday in a theatrical baritone, enjoying the practised joke of embarrassing the children with the volume of his singing. Ivy and Lucas covered their ears as they sang along, and their grandma let the two of them blow out the candles on her behalf.

'I don't have enough puff to do it myself now that I'm so old,' Grandma smiled.

Lucas counted the candles. 'There are only 20.'

'21,' Ed corrected. 'Because Grandma is 21 every birthday. Has been for years!'

He followed his mother into the kitchen with the cake.

'You cut it,' she said, handing him a knife. 'I always give them too much.'

'How about we give them a small slice to eat now,' he said, cutting into the cake, 'and another wrapped up to take home. They can take one for Lisa too, might sweeten her up a little.'

'Lisa is a sweet girl,' Ed's mother replied.

'She's not pleased about me being late back with the kids. I'm not her favourite person at the best of times.' He placed slices of cake on plates his mother held out for him. 'I know I've messed everything up...'

'I didn't say a word.'

'You don't need to. It's a mess. I know. Not just tonight, but every day. I've messed life up for those kids, for you, for everyone.' He put the plates down on the counter.

'I'll get some foil and wrap some up for them to take home,' his mother replied, avoiding the topic with a practical response to getting things done, just as she always did.

Cake eaten and coats on, the children stood by the car as their father hugged their grandmother and shook hands awkwardly with her husband.

'You could still make things right,' she whispered, clasping him in the hug so that he had to listen. 'Change can happen at any time, but sometimes you have to help it along. If you want your family back, you need to work at getting it back.'

When she let go, Ed felt both relief and loss. A nostalgia for the days when his mother could make everything better with cakes and hugs. For a time when she knew what to do and he didn't have to worry about it. He needed to worry now. The clock was ticking.

More hugs, thank-yous, love-yous and see-you-soons later, they drove away from Grandma's and towards the house he'd called home until only a few months earlier.

The route was familiar. The chatter of the kids in the back, comparing the size of their pieces of cake, was familiar too. The space in the front seat next to him still felt odd. He kept his eyes focused on the road but he could feel the gap. He was the odd one out in his own car. Alone.

He'd forgotten that the low fuel light had come on during their journey to his mother's house, and as he drove, it began flashing. Not just low, but critically low.

But he was not just late, he was critically late. Stopping for fuel would mean a detour and a delay. According to the GPS, he would arrive home – at the kids' home he corrected himself – at two minutes past nine. Near enough for him to call it nine o'clock. If he stopped for fuel, it would be at least ten past. Near enough for Lisa to call it quarter past. Of if there was a queue with people filling up ready for work on Monday morning, it might take even longer. Long enough for Lisa to call it half past.

He knew people who'd been prevented from seeing their kids for not taking them home on time. A friend who'd been accused in court of trying to abduct his own son because he'd been an hour late taking the boy back to his mother. He needed to get them home. He could fuel up as soon as he'd dropped them. It wasn't that far.

The car was full of questions. How old was Grandma really? Why did she say she was twenty-one? What's so special about twenty-one? Why is it twenty-one that's special and not twenty or twenty-five? How old had Grandad been when he died? Did Grandad die before Lucas was born? What about Ivy? How old was Nanna? What about Grandad Paul? How old are people usually when they die? What did Grandad David die of?

The children had fallen easily into a tag team of alternate questions, barely giving Ed time to answer one, before he was interrupted by the next, as though he were being interrogated by the Gestapo. And it was hard for him to answer, because his ears were on the questions, but his eyes and his concentration were on his speed and the estimated arrival time on the GPS. If he went just a couple of miles over the speed limit, he might shave a minute or two off their arrival time. A little more over the limit on the dual carriageway, away from the houses and pedestrians, and he could maybe even cut five minutes off the journey.

He put his foot down as he drove onto the dual carriageway. The car speeded up, and then, almost immediately, it slowed down. Right down.

'Why are we going so slowly, Dad?' asked Ivy. He had no choice but to steer towards the edge of the road, pull the handbrake, switch on the hazard lights and take the key out of the ignition.

'Listen kids,' he said, turning to face them. 'It's all fine, but we've broken down, so we just need to get out of the car and stand up there away from the road and call your mum and let her know what's happened and then we'll get some help and get you home.'

'Will we get a tow truck to take us back?' asked Ivy.

'Just get out of the car please.'

'Will the police come?' Lucas asked.

'Will you just get out of the car, please? Get out on Ivy's side please Lucas, not near the traffic.'

'But there's hardly any traffic,' Lucas pointed out.

'It only takes one car to run you over, Lucas. Will you just do as you're told and get out of the car on Ivy's side and up onto the grass.' Ed's tone sounded sharper than he'd intended, and he sighed, reminding himself not to let stress get to him, because then it would get to the children, and this was not their fault.

His stern words did the trick, though, and once he'd cajoled the children out of the car and up the embankment, Ed called Lisa again.

He didn't tell Lisa the car had stopped because it was out of fuel. There was no need to tell her that the problem was caused by his own carelessness and lack of forethought. Her tone quickly went from eager for news to loud and furious and Ed glanced at the children's faces. Their worried looks revealed that, even if they couldn't hear every word, they could definitely hear the tone of the conversation from both ends.

A lorry passed them, drowning out the sound of Lisa's voice for a moment and creating a draught of air that made the road seem dangerously close. Ed gestured to the children to move further up the embankment, but they misunderstood him, looking behind them instead of moving towards the space he was indicating.

'Hang on a minute, Lisa. Move up there kids, further away from the road. Take my coat.' He awkwardly took his coat off passing his phone from hand to hand as he released his arms from the sleeves. 'You can sit on that up there, over there.'

Ivy took the coat and moved away with Lucas.

'They can hear every word, you know.' Ed said to Lisa. 'I know I've fucked up, you don't need to tell me. If you want to rant at me, that's fine, I deserve it. But not in front of the kids, eh? They don't deserve it do they? They're dealing with enough with everything changing, don't you think, without seeing their parents argue as well. None of this is their fault and they shouldn't have to deal with it.'

The line went quiet at the other end, and Ed glanced up the embankment to see Ivy laying his coat on the ground, and Lucas wandering even further up, towards the line of trees that separated the embankment from a footpath.

'Dad,' called Lucas. Ed held up a 'one minute' index finger to Lucas.

'OK,' said Lisa. 'You need to do better though. Send me a pin of where you are, and I'll come and get them.'

'Dad!'

'I've got to go, Lucas is calling me.' Ed looked up to see that Ivy had followed Lucas up the embankment, leaving his coat behind on the ground.

'Right,' said Lisa. 'Keep them away from the road, and don't forget to send me that pin, I'm putting my shoes on now.'

'Dad, come on, we need you,' called Ivy.

'OK, thanks,' Ed said, holding his one-minute finger up to the children again. 'I really am sorry,' he added, with an apology that referred to both his current situation and the wider context of everything. There was silence at the other end of the phone. 'See you in a bit,' he added.

Ending the call, Ed opened Google maps and marked a pin at around the correct area. Lisa would have to go up to the roundabout and double back on herself, so she would see them. Or at least the car.

'Seriously Dad, we need you NOW!,' called Ivy, walking back down the embankment to collect him.

Ed jogged towards her.

'What's so serious?' he asked, pulling a face and trying to bring a mood of fun back into his last few minutes with the children.

'There's a leopard. Or maybe a cheetah,' said Lucas. 'It's over there, don't worry, I've been keeping an eye on it. It's not moving. I think it's asleep. But you know, it could wake up. I think we should get back in the car.'

'We can't get back in the car, it's not safe.'

'Leopards are not safe, Dad,' Ivy pointed out.

'It's not a leopard.'

'Could be a cheetah?!' Lucas replied.

'It's not a leopard or a cheetah, we don't get leopards or cheetahs round here.'

'What about the zoo?' asked Lucas.

'We're at least thirty miles away from the zoo.'

'But cheetahs can run really fast!' Lucas moved both his hands round like wheels to demonstrate speed. 'It could have escaped from the zoo and run all this way, and that's why it's asleep at the moment because it's tired from running for thirty miles, but once it's had a rest...!' He held his hands up like claws and gnashed his teeth.

'It is not a cheetah, or a leopard!'

'Then what is it?' asked Ivy.

Ed looked again at where the children were pointing. In the waning light, he could see the fur on the ground. It did look like a sleeping animal. A dead cat maybe?

'Listen,' he said, turning back to face both children. 'Your mum will be here soon to collect you, I'm sorry you're late home and we've broken down and everything. You must be tired and fed up of standing out here in the cold...'

'It's not even cold,' said Ivy.

'Fed up of standing out here, then. But what we need to be doing is looking out for your mum arriving so that you can be ready to jump in her car when she gets here, and I need to call Brian and see if he can come and help me sort the car out.'

'And what about the leopard?' asked Ivy.

'Or maybe cheetah?' added Lucas. 'If you don't go and see what it is before Mum gets here, we'll never know what it is.'

'And then someone else will find it, and they will be on the news for finding a leopard,' Ivy pre-empted her brother's interruption, '- or cheetah - and we won't. And we actually found it.'

'And. And, and,' added Lucas, 'if we turn our back on it, it might just pounce on us and kill us right in front of Mum and then we'll be too dead to even know what it was. And we'll be the ones on the news, but we won't be able to tell our friends

213

we're on the telly because we'll be dead. I bet it's got one eye open keeping watch on us right now, just waiting for us to turn our backs and walk down the hill so that it can pounce on us and eat us for dinner. Because it will have missed its dinner at the zoo.'

It was clear that walking over to the dead cat and proclaiming it to be a sleeping cat was going to be the only way for Ed to get past his children's curiosity.

'Right. I will go and have a look. You two are not to move, OK? I want to see you glued to the spot, is that clear.'

Ivy and Lucas nodded their consent and Ed walked towards the animal, turning to glance back at them to check they hadn't moved. As he got closer, he could see their find was too big for a cat. As he got closer still, it he could see it wasn't an animal at all.

'It's a coat,' he called back to the children. It's just a coat. 'He lifted it in the air to show them, like a hunter raising his kill for his companions to see.

The children ran over to him, giggling.

'I can't believe you thought it was a leopard,' Lucas laughed.

'You did too,' said Ivy. 'You did too, and you thought it could be a cheetah.'

Ed braced himself for a squabble about whose fault the false alarm had been, but Lucas wasn't listening. He was looking beyond both of them, towards something a little closer to the trees.

'But what's that?' Lucas asked.

Ed turned to see what looked like a person, lying in the grass, close to the trees. He walked across, still carrying the coat, holding a hand out behind him as he called to the children. 'Stay where you are, glued to the spot again. Superglued please. Stay right there.'

Ed walked purposefully towards the figure in the grass and knelt beside her, using the coat to cover her mostly naked body.

He bent down close and put his fingers on her neck to feel for a pulse.

She opened her eyes.

'Help me,' she said.

VII

Celeste

I think some of my thoughts as feelings and I hear some as voices. Some are my own voice, 'come on Celeste, pick your bones up and make them move. Get your sad, sorry bones away from here. Try harder. Get on with it.'

But some of the thoughts I'm thinking are other voices. My Mum. My Dad. Esther. Orson. That man from the shop who always says 'good-morning-how-are-you', that bitch from the job centre who enjoys telling me that there is work out there for those who want it, but I must remember I'm not in a position to be picky. I'm not. I can't choose anything. I'd love for Bitch-face to be here now, forcing me to my feet, giving me a uniform for some shit, minimum wage, nightmare of a job in the arse-end of nowhere and making me catch 16 buses to get there. I could be there, wherever there is, and not here.

But now there are new voices. Voices I can hear, but I can't hear them. Voices outside and inside my own head. I can hear them on the outside, on the edge of my brain, but I can't make them say the words clearly enough for me to understand them as thoughts. They are near but far away, submerged in a puddle, behind the wardrobe, at the other end of a beach, on the other side of a door. I need subtitles. I need the remote control to turn the sound up. I need to sleep. Maybe they will be clearer if I am sleeping?

But I'm awake. I know I'm awake because I can hear the sound of the road; the music of the cars passing. I'd thought was water moving, but it's not nature, it's machine. So I am not all alone, I am alone with people. I am on the edge of alone, but still close enough to be part of sharing this space with other people.

I try words. I can see words. I can read them aloud as though off a page. But no sound comes out. I am keeping it to simple words. 'I am here. Come and find me. Help me.' But I'm on mute and I can't find the button to unmute myself.

I can feel where the voices are coming from. These are not voices in my head. These voices belong to the road, the grass, the air. These voices belong to the world. If I could turn my head, I could see them. If I could see them, maybe they could see me. I can't try to find words and turn my head at the same time. I have to do just one thing. Just one thing at a time.

I am turning my head. Slowly. Eyes closed. I have done it.

I am opening my eyes. Slowly. Motionless. I have done it. I can see feet and legs. There are people. I need them to know I am here. I need them to help me. This is the part of the story where I get rescued.

I look for my words and try to connect them with my voice. I know I have a voice. Mum says I have a lovely voice. The guy who interviewed me for a job in that call centre said I had a lovely voice. I just need to find where I lost it. I just need to close my eyes and remember where it might be.

I can feel the feet getting nearer. I can hear a voice turning from sound to words 'stay right there,' it says. I am staying right here. If I could move, I would have moved. There is a weight laid onto me and a warmth next to me. It bends, it puts its fingers on my neck and this has to be the button pressed to switch on all my functions.

Eyes first. Open.

Words next. 'Help me.'

22

NOEL

Noel didn't notice the doorbell until after he'd thumped loudly on the door. It was an old wooden door, probably original to the house, and as solid as the bricks either side. Thudding on it hadn't been a great idea, Noel concluded, as he rubbed the side of his hand, but he wasn't in the best of moods. He was hangry. He was irritated by the entitled little prick orchestrating the vigil, and wishing he'd got home early enough to see the kids before bed. By now, he should be relaxed on the sofa, with his wife snuggled up to him, sleep-watching her Sunday night TV drama while he kept an eye on the plot so that he could fill her in on what she'd missed.

But Abi looked done in. And there was a girl missing. And it looked like there was a slimeball in the neighbourhood who thought it was OK to follow women home from work late at night. Noel lifted his hand to ring the doorbell, but heard rustling behind the door. He waited, hand still poised ready to press the button, pausing to see if the rustling signalled someone about to open the door. He checked the number again, in case he'd accidentally knocked at the house of a harmless old lady minding her own business, rather than the lad Annie had recognised.

The door opened slowly, and the woman on the other side greeted him with the words 'sorry, these drinks are burning my knuckles!' Noel reached forward to take two of the mugs from her, saying, 'hello again,' as he recognised her as the woman who had briefly joined the vigil, then escaped.

'I'm so sorry. Thank you,' she said as she first deposited the mug she was still holding on a bookshelf near the door, then relieved Noel of the two he'd taken from her.

'Moira wasn't it?' he asked.

'Yes, it was, and still is,' she smiled. 'What can I do for you? I expect you're still looking for Celeste aren't you? No news yet? Her parents came round here earlier, and we told them we didn't know anything, my heart goes out to them though. How awful. I wish we could help. I knew her as a kid, Celeste. Have I already told you that? Anyway, I'm not sure what else I can tell you, but I know you've got to keep checking. I love a police drama, you see. I sometimes feel like I could be a detective, I've watched so many. But it's not entertainment when it happens on your doorstep, is it? It's awful, just awful.'

Noel waited until she paused for breath, then spoke without acknowledging anything of what she had said. 'Actually, I'm here on another matter, Moira. You mentioned your son earlier. Is that William? I'm looking for William. Is he home?'

Before Moira could answer, William appeared at the top of the stairs and Billy opened the living room door, as though the two actions had been choreographed to happen on the same cue.

'I thought I heard the door.' said William.

'Where's that brew, I'm close to dying of thirst,' said Billy.

The two of them spoke in unison and Noel looked from one to the other, half hearing and half missing what each of them had said.

'Are you William?' Noel Fisher said to the boy on the stairs. 'Would you mind just coming downstairs for a bit, so that we can have a chat? Do you think there might be one more in the pot for me, Moira?'

'We brew up in the mug actually,' William answered before his mother could speak. He walked down the stairs with a deliberate slowness, like the chief mourner at a funeral.

'I can make you a drink,' said Moira, turning to look from her son to Noel Fisher. 'Tea or coffee? Milk? Sugar?'

'A coffee with milk and two sugars would be brilliant, Moira, thank you. Is there somewhere William and I can sit while I ask him a few questions?'

'In here, if you like?' said Billy. He led the way into the living room, switching off the TV. 'Sit anywhere you like,' he added, as the police officer sat on one of the armchairs. William sat on the other, and Billy continued to stand in the middle of the room as though he'd forgotten what he'd walked in there for.

There was a pause. 'Perhaps you could help Moira with that cuppa, while William and I have a chat?'

Noel Fisher smiled and uttered a polite thank you as Billy left the room, turning to look at William. The boy looked ordinary. Ordinary jeans and sweatshirt. Clean-shaven. Short hair. He had a look of his mother and his father's broad shoulders and height. The three of them looked like they came as a set.

The police officer paused before he said anything further. It was a technique he'd seen a sergeant use early in his career and had adopted ever since. Amazing how often people's discomfort caused them to fidget and brought their discomfort to the surface in the form of words they hadn't intended to say. Often the person he'd come to question would start providing answers before he'd asked them anything at all.

He took in the room. There were Mother's Day cards still on the mantelpiece. School photographs of two boys at various stages of childhood and adolescence. A vase of wilting flowers placed on an electric heater designed to look like a wood burner. But the TV was the centrepiece of the room and William kept glancing at it, even though it was switched off.

'It's a serious TV that one, isn't it?' Noel began.

'My parents aren't much for going out,' William answered. 'The TV is their nights out, their cinema, their pub, why shouldn't they have a nice piece of kit?'

'I agree, I agree,' Noel Fisher could hear the defensive tone in William's voice. He could prod him a little more before beginning the real questions. 'What about you? Do you watch it much? What kind of things do you watch? Do you go out much?'

William's answers came back short and punchy like a ball being shot from one side of the net to the other in a tennis game where both players are competent, but neither is making the effort to win just yet.

There was a quiet knock on the door, and Billy opened it so that Moira could come through with two drinks, one of which had a plate of biscuits balanced on top.

'Milk, two sugars,' she said, placing one of the mugs down on a coaster next to where Noel Fisher was sitting, along the biscuits. 'And some biscuits, I bet you don't get much time for a proper meal in your job, do you?'

'Thank you so much, Moira, you're a lifesaver!' As she bent forward, Noel noticed that she was no longer wearing the necklace he'd seen earlier.

'I've made you a fresh one love,' she said to William, 'the other one had gone a bit lukewarm.'

'No biscuits for me then?' William asked.

Moira didn't answer him. she placed the second cup down and waited. 'Shall I just leave you to it?'

'Yes. Thanks Moira.'

Noel slurped loudly from his too-hot drink, then dunked a biscuit and ate it quickly as they waited for Moira to leave the room.

'Where were we?'

'You tell me,' replied William.

Noel disliked him. He wasn't allowed to have an opinion, but how could he not. The boy was like a cactus.

'Why don't you tell me about what you did last night, from say, ten o'clock onwards.'

William paused as though trying to remember, then told Noel Fisher how he'd gone for a walk in the park. How he'd sheltered from the rain under the trees and then had the encounter with the man who'd vomited on his trainers.

'My mum's had to wash them and everything. They were caked in mud with an added layer of vomit. Nice.' He pulled a face to indicate his disgust as he finished speaking.

'So where are your trainers now?'

'Still in the washing machine. Damp. I was supposed to be hanging them up to dry, but then you turned up. My mum's probably done it by now – that's Brownie points you've robbed me of there.' William gave a half laugh.

Noel smiled. 'OK, well I may need to take those.' He watched William's face as he explained that there may be evidence on the trainers, searching for a reaction that might tell him if the boy was lying. 'Even after a wash there may be trace particles on your shoes that can verify you were where you've said you were, you see.'

The boy's face was completely neutral.

'And what did you do after that?'

'I came home.'

'Straight home?'

'Yes, I just walked home. I don't know if you know it around here officer, but there's not much else to do. It's completely dead, once all the shops have shut.'

'But not all the shops had shut, had they? The little Tesco was still open till 11.30'

'Was it?'

'Yes, open till 11.30 on a Saturday. Did you go there at all?'

'I don't think so.'

'You don't think so?' Noel paused again to study the boy's body language for signs that he was nervous. It wasn't usually the words used that gave a lie away, but the face of the person speaking them.

'Just mentally go back and retrace your steps and tell me if you can remember going to the Tesco before you came home.'

'No, I definitely didn't.'

'You definitely didn't? OK.' Noel Fisher wrote in his notebook.

'What exactly is this about?' William asked. 'Has the Tesco been robbed or something?'

Noel smiled at William. 'No, I'm not here about shoplifting. We've had a report from someone that she was followed home last night, and the person in question has identified you as the individual who followed her.'

'What person? Who's said that? Why would I follow anyone. I was here, you can ask my mum. Shall we ask her? I can get her.' William began to stand from the chair.

'I'll talk to your mum afterwards, don't worry William, can you stay there for a moment please. The person who's identified you tells us that you followed her and that she stopped to confront you and recognised you from when you were at school together. She gave us your name William.'

There was a pause as Noel watched the boy enact a frown to suggest he was wracking his brain for something so trivial he might have forgotten it.

'Oh, that, yes. I remember that now. But I wasn't following her. I didn't. I was just walking home, and she freaked out at me. I mean, I was literally just walking down the street minding my own business and she turned and freaked and started calling her brother and being all weird. I mean, if she can't deal with other people walking on the same pavement minding their own business when she's walking home from work late at night, perhaps she shouldn't walk home late at night. I mean, it's a free country, right? I have just as much right to walk on that pavement as she does. If she feels nervous or paranoid or something, that's not my problem is it? That's her problem.'

'You're right of course, William, you're completely right. Everyone is entitled to walk home at night without feeling like they're doing anything wrong,' Noel smiled with practised fake reassurance, before continuing. 'Tell me, William, what makes you think she was walking home from work?'

Noel was pleased with the hesitation from William before he answered the question. He loved the game of poker that involved asking the right questions at the right time. Not giving your hand away too soon, while all the time chipping away at their nerve.

'Well, she stopped and freaked out at me, didn't she? I told you, she freaked out at me, and I could see she was wearing a Tesco uniform. You don't wear that for fun do you? You don't wear that for fashion. Anyway, I know her from the Tesco, I recognised her from there...'

'But you weren't there last night?'

'I've told you that. I recognise her from the Tesco and from school. She calls herself Mitch, but her real name is Anne. She's a nutcase with a fake name. What kind of nutter just turns around and starts yelling at someone in the street at that time of night. I bet there are lots of people who looked out of the window to see who was shrieking like a banshee last night who could tell you that I did nothing wrong...'

'I see...'

'It should be me reporting her, not the other way around. I'm the one who's traumatised from having someone verbally attack me in the street when I was minding my own business, just walking home. They talk about women not feeling safe when they're walking home alone at night, but what about men? You know, I didn't enjoy being screamed at. I felt really stressed about it when I got home. My mum will tell you, I couldn't go to bed because I was so shocked, she found me dozing in the chair this morning. But you lot are so woke and so quick to take a woman's side in anything that you'll believe I was following her home, next you'll be telling me how I threatened her with a knife, or raped her on her own doorstep.'

'Did you?' The question was only half tongue in cheek. William's defensive tirade was like an alternative confession.

The boy shifted in his chair and took a large slurp of tea, looking over the top of the mug at Noel as he did so. He put the mug down.

'No. No! Do I even have to say that?'

Responding to agitation with calm was a technique Noel had practised to a fine art.

'I just need clear answers, William. My job is to find out the truth, and understand what happened. So let's recap, shall we? You went for a walk in the park. You left the path to shelter from the rain and a man vomited, which splattered on your shoes. Then you walked home, and at some point, when you were walking behind Annie Mitchell, she turned round and accused you of following her?'

'Yes, that's right.'

'And the park we're talking about is Johnston Park? Is that right?'

'Yes, John*stone* Park,' William corrected him.

'John*stone* Park, which is in that direction,' Noel pointed to his left. 'But the location where Annie Mitchell says the two of you had your interaction in the street was near the church, which is in that direction,' Noel stated, pointing to his right.

'Well, I didn't say I walked straight home, did I? It can be confusing. These streets all look the same and some of them are dead ends, so you think you're taking a short cut, and you end up not where you thought you'd be.'

'I see,' said Noel, continuing to write in his notebook. 'And how long have you lived here William?'

'Since my brother was a baby. Since I was two.'

'I see,' Noel repeated.

'But it is easy to get confused, even though I've lived here all my life. It is confusing. It is.'

'Yes, I see that. There are a lot of interconnecting streets round here. But you definitely didn't go to the Tesco? You're not confused about that?'

'I've told you,' William let the words out with an exasperated sigh, as though losing patience with a grandparent who couldn't remember the thread of their conversation.

'Yes, you have, you've been very clear about that. I just needed you to confirm before my colleague looks at the CCTV from last night, because she's there now, you see requesting that. We'll get the CCTV from the park too, and then we can check what time you left the park and figure out which route you took home.'

'Look,' said William, his voice getting louder as he leaned forward in his chair to make his point. He punctuated his sentences with his hands, 'I've told you, I went to the park, I walked home with muddy clothes and sick on my shoes, Anne Mitchell yelled at me in the street for no reason, and then I spent most of the night awake in this chair because I was so shaken up by the way she'd behaved.'

'Yes, and we can verify all of that against what you have told me and what Annie has said. And her brother of course, he was on the phone to her, so he heard what was said too.'

'I'd like to put in my own complaint, actually, about the verbal abuse I've suffered. Can you log that please. You like writing things down, don't you, why don't you write that down?'

Noel wrote *'Keaveney became agitated when informed CCTV would be checked. Asked for a counter complaint of verbal abuse to be logged.'*

'Well, I think that's everything for now, William, thanks for taking time out of your evening to speak to me. We may be back in touch when we've viewed the CCTV footage. And thanks for the tea and the biscuits. Life saver those, it's been a long day.'

'That was my mum who brought you the tea, you'd best thank her. She'll be all upset by all of this and she's missing her favourite night of telly with you in here.'

'Well it's very kind of her,' Noel said, hoisting himself out of the soft armchair by pushing down hard on the arms for leverage. William got up to follow him and Noel paused, turning to the boy, hand firmly on the door handle, body blocking William's exit.

'Just before I go William, you've probably heard about the girl – young woman – who has been missing since last night? Last seen when she left a bar in town sometime after 11pm, and we believe she would usually have walked home from the bus stop taking a route near to where you and Annie had your, let's call it, altercation. Probably at a similar time.'

'Yeah, Celeste, I know, her parents came round earlier. What? Are you going to accuse me of following her home too now?'

Noel looked straight into the boy's eyes, 'I'm just asking if you saw anything William. Celeste's boot has been found in the garden next to the church...'

'Yeah, I know, the ice cream man told me...'

'Right. The ice cream man?'

Yeah, it's not a nickname, it's a guy in a van that sells ice creams.'

'Right, yeah. So, last night when you were out for your walk it was late and most people will have been in bed or at least inside with the curtains closed, you and Annie are probably the only people who were around in the vicinity at the time.'

'What about dog walkers? People always walk their dog so that it can have a pee before bed. It's always a dog walker that finds the body.'

Noel smiled, feeling increasingly repulsed by the boy and trying hard not to show it in his tone of voice. 'What makes you think there'll be a body William?'

'I didn't say that. I mean, they're always around. Anyway, that's the way it always ends in films, isn't it? That's the way it always ends up on the news?'

Noel paused. In the small space, with both of them waiting to leave the room, he could see that the tension was getting to William. He waited for the boy to say more.

'So have you asked Annie Mitchell questions about whether she's seen Celeste or is it just men that get the finger pointed at them and women who get to play the victim card? That's their ace, isn't it, only the two of us there, she says she's been followed even though I was just walking along, minding my own business, and everyone automatically assumes she's a helpless victim and I'm the big bad wolf.' William's voice grew louder. 'She's probably being offered counselling now, while you sit here, eating our biscuits, pointing the finger at me, when I've done nothing wrong.'

'I'm only asking if you saw Celeste, William.'

'I didn't. I didn't see Celeste. I saw the drunk guy in the park and Anne Mitchell, that's all.'

Noel felt the pressure of someone pushing to open the door from the other side and stepped back, letting go of the handle. Moira stumbled into the room, followed by Billy.

'We weren't listening,' said Billy, 'we just heard raised voices and wondered if we should maybe be in the room if there's something serious we need to know about?'

'Maybe I can make you another drink and we can all sit down and sort this out, whatever it is, together?' Moira added. 'He's a good lad, you know, officer, he's not a drinker, he doesn't do drugs or anything.'

Noel looked at Moira, the worry in her face. Different from the despair he'd seen in Yvonne but still the face of a mother trying to cope with something unexpected striding into her life and threatening her child.

'You're not wearing your necklace anymore?'

Moira put her hand to her throat, as though checking to see if it was there.

'It broke. It's like I said earlier, it was really old, I was just fiddling with it and the chain snapped. It's in the bin, not worth trying to fix it, something like that. I'd forgotten I had it until I found it when I was having a clear out earlier.'

'That's a shame,' Noel smiled.

'So, what is this actually about?' asked Billy. 'You know, he may be classed as an adult, but he's our son, living in our house, if there's something going on, we need to know really, don't we love?'

Billy turned to Moira. Moira glanced at him and turned back to Noel. 'Are you sure you don't want another coffee?'

Instead of answering Moira, Noel answered his phone with a polite nod and a finger held up to ask her to be quiet while he took the call.

It was Abi. 'They've found Celeste, She's in a bit of a state, but she's alive. I'm going to go straight to the hospital, the Royal Infirmary, can you meet me there?'

Noel sighed as the prospect of a warm meal and a doze through some Sunday evening TV with his wife slipped away from him completely.

'OK, just wrapping up here. I'll see you there.'

'Anything?

'I'll tell you when I see you.'

Noel looked up from his phone to see all three Keaveneys looking at him.

'So is that us finished?' asked William.

'Almost. You mentioned that the necklace was in the bin, Moira, which bin is it in? Can I have a quick look at it?'

'Oh, it'll be in the outside bin by now. It's bin day tomorrow, Billy always empties all the bins before bin day, don't you Billy? Putting the bins out is his job.'

'Yeah, but I haven't done it yet. Sorry love, I will get round to it.'

'So, we can still retrieve it? Could you get it for me do you think?' Noel smiled at Moira and glanced across at William, who was looking at the ground as though searching for something in the carpet.

'Erm, it's probably in the kitchen bin, I think. I'll just go and check.'

Noel followed her into the kitchen without asking for permission. 'Perhaps I could take William's trainers too?'

'Why?'

'Because we might be able to verify that William was in the park from the tread on his shoes and any soil still on them.'

'I've washed them, though.'

'Yes, he told me, but they still might be useful.'

'Useful for...?'

'Are they still in the machine? OK if I get them out?'

Noel opened the washing machine and took out the damp trainers, retrieving a plastic bag from his pocket to put them in. He turned to find Moira with her hand in the bin.

'Oh, it's OK, you don't have to go fishing for that, I can get it.' Noel walked across to the bin and immediately saw the necklace, lying right on the top, as though it had just been placed there.

'That's lucky, right at the top.' He took out another bag and popped the necklace in it. 'A shame it's broken, isn't it?'

'Why are you taking it? Surely you don't suspect me of anything, do you?'

'No, Moira, no, not at all. But you're certain it's *your* necklace?'

'It's just a stupid necklace. A piece of tat that I found lying around the house. I've got a tonne of ironing to do, if there's nothing else? William's a good lad you know. He's upset by all of this. I can see he's upset now, and he's not the only one.'

'No, nothing else. I'll leave you all to your evening now. Thank you for your time, and the coffee, and the biscuits. Really kind of you, an absolute lifesaver, I'll let you go. No need to see me out.'

Noel left Moira in the kitchen and stepped back into the empty hall. He looked into the living room on his way out, where the TV was switched back on and Billy and William were sitting watching it. 'Goodbye, both. You need to make sure you stay away from Annie Mitchell, please William.'

'With pleasure,' William replied.

23

Moira

Moira sighed as she looked around the room at the boxes surrounding her. It was as though she had set them up like a circle of wagons to defend herself from attack, but the attack had already been and gone, and it had come from within her safe space, not from outside it.

William was on remand in Bristol Prison, over three hours' drive away, along unfamiliar roads to a different world. It made sense to move closer to William, but that that wasn't why they were going. Moira did want to be closer to their son, so they could visit more often and more easily, but the real reason they were moving was to be away. To escape the place where it had all happened, and everyone knew who she was and what her son had done.

Their options for moving closer to William had been limited. Bristol had been too expensive. All the pretty towns and villages close to Bristol had been out of their price range too, particularly after they'd had to revise the estate agent's initial expectations on the sale price of their Manchester home to get it off their hands quickly. But their home had still raised more than they had imagined it might when they first discussed selling the week after William was arrested, and it had left them with a choice between a flat in Bristol, a shoe box in one of the less appealing market towns close by, a doer-upper, or a move across the border to Wales. Billy had also suggested that they might rent out their own home and rent somewhere close to William. They'd been warned that their son could be transferred to another prison at any time, and that a trial could still be months away, but Moira wanted a fresh start. She wanted to let go of their old life completely and trade it in for a new place where they knew no-one and no-one knew them. A place where they could begin again and somehow do things differently this time. Do things better.

So, they were moving to Wales, to a place Moira wasn't sure how to pronounce, not far from Merthyr Tydfil and less than 30 miles away from Bristol Prison. It had a lovely garden, and the kitchen diner she'd always wanted. And, most importantly, it was a world away from where she was now; surrounded not just by boxes, but by memories, regret and the averted gaze or cold hard stares of anyone she passed in the street.

In the days after William was arrested, Moira and Billy had been under house arrest themselves, confined to their own home, not by the police or the justice system, but by the media lined up outside waiting to hurl questions at them and push cameras in their faces. Billy had asked the police to help, and they'd said they would try to move the media on, but their efforts were minimal and the appetite of the media to get their story was voracious; even a picture of Moira in her dressing gown taking in the milk, or the supermarket delivery being handed over on the doorstep were snapped and splashed online.

They'd kept the radio off, and the TV permanently switched to Netflix too, avoiding the possibility of seeing their son's face on the screen or their whole lives reduced to sensationalism in the voices of newsreaders, or soundbites from shocked neighbours who couldn't believe that something like this could happen in a quiet neighbourhood like theirs. With the curtains closed, nothing but films and box sets on TV, and meals made only from whatever was already in the fridge, it had been like the two of them were on a mammoth sleepover. Except there was no fun. No conversation. Moira had cried, and hoovered, and cried, and done washing she couldn't hang on the line, and cried and cried and cried. Billy had sat in his armchair, watching films he had seen before, putting on comedies they both loved and staring at the screen without laughing.

James had offered to come home, and Moira ached to see him. She wanted to look into his eyes and check that he was still the boy she thought he was. She wanted to know that she had done something right with one of her children, that he was a good man, that he was still the same person she had loved all his life. But Billy had said no. Not just no, in fact, but a firm, uncompromising no. James mustn't come home, he mustn't tarnish his life at university with the turmoil his brother had caused at home. They would visit him as soon as they got a chance. They would come up with a plan.

And this was the plan. Move to Wales. There was a new home to make. New neighbours. New jobs. New lives. Moira thought about the friend who had tried to comfort her with 'everything happens for a reason' when her first fiancé had died in a car accident so many years before. The reason then had been so that she could meet Billy and have the boys, but she still sometimes wondered how life would have turned out if Paul hadn't died and they'd continued towards their happy ever after. The reason now? So that she could leave the city just as she'd always wanted and swap it for a new life in Wales? It was nonsense. There was no reason, what reason could there be for William to do something like that and cause so much collateral damage in the process? Nothing that had happened had been about building something new, she concluded, it wasn't for a reason at all. William had just shattered his own life into a million pieces, driven a juggernaut through the lives of a young woman and her family, and destroyed the lives of his own family in the process. There was mess everywhere, far beyond the half-filled boxes and the piles of clutter that needed to be sorted and packed or thrown out.

The press that had camped outside the house moved on after a few days, feeding off someone else's misfortune for a while, like migratory bison searching for the newest blade of grass as they grazed on misery from one location to the next. 'Last week's chip wrappers' Billy had called it, and gradually they were able to switch on the radio again and watch the news, without seeing their son's face or hearing the voice of Celeste's mother repeating the same words in every bulletin: *'He's a monster, and he wants locking up for good to protect other girls from going through the same ordeal he inflicted on Celeste. Our lives will never be the same again.'*

Our lives will never be the same again. The hugeness of everything that had changed was summed up in that sentence for Moira. The son she had thought she knew had been replaced by a man vilified by the media and despised by every young woman, every parent, every right-thinking, ordinary human who heard what had happened. She could switch the TV back on after a week or so, but the lack of headlines didn't undo the fact that their lives were now defined by a clear dividing line – everything before William had attacked Celeste and everything after that moment.

Even when the media had moved on, Moira still felt unable to leave the house. She had accepted the time off that work had given her, but how could she ever think of going back? She would always be the mother of Celeste's attacker. Every teacher, every child, and every parent connected to the school knew who she was, and whose mother she was. They might move on to other gossip in time, but they would never look at her as that nice Mrs Keaveney again; the lady who had worked in the office for a generation, who collected the registers and the dinner money, who passed on messages, looked after sick children until their parents came to fetch them, and handed over PE kits and lunch bags that had been dropped off late, having been forgotten at home.

In her old life, Moira had lived in a world where kids brought her thank you cards and drew pictures for her, which she'd stuck up proudly in the school office and taken photos of to show Billy when she got home. She had been a confidant for colleagues, a shoulder to cry on for stressed-out parents, a trusted grown-up for thousands of kids over the years. Now she was the mother of a violent sex pest. Her DBS check was unaffected, but her status had been switched from pillar of the community to pariah in an instant.

She sighed at the boxes again. What was the point in packing up all the old things to take to a new place? They needed a proper fresh start. A home where nothing of the past was present, where old mistakes and old memories were erased. Could she do that? She and Billy had already changed their names by deed poll. Billy had been reluctant at first, lamenting that the Keaveney surname had been brought across from Ireland by his great, great-grandparents during the potato famine and it felt like letting them down to swap it. But Moira had pointed out that those people had left their country behind because they'd had to survive a crisis by doing whatever it took. 'We need to do the same now,' she'd said. 'We need to protect ourselves and James from the stigma. We need to be able to start again without all of this following us.' She'd reminded Billy that she had changed her name when they'd married, she'd sacrificed that part of herself to build their future together. She was only asking him to do the same. They chose Raleigh as their new name, after Sir Walter Raleigh; a suggestion from Billy that they should chose a name after someone brave who went to new places.

The new place meant new jobs for Moira and Billy. School had been understanding, they'd sounded relieved in fact, when Moira had told them that she wouldn't be going back. They'd been happy enough to give her a glowing reference, even agreeing to use her new name in the correspondence. She would be swapping children for animals in her job as the admin assistant at a local vet in Wales, no more pictures to stick on the wall, but parents of a different kind to counsel and comfort. She'd promised to learn Welsh at the interview, that should be a useful distraction to take her mind off worries about William and the thoughts she was struggling to block out, whether she was busy or idle, awake or asleep. What could she have done differently? What should she have done? What had she missed?

Billy had got a job with a call centre. The hours were not great, with evenings and weekends included in his regular schedule, but it was local and full-time, and it had given them what they needed; enough income to take out a small mortgage on their new home so that they could press ahead with their move.

The GP had given her pills; pills to help her sleep and pills to help her get through the day. 'Think of it as using crutches while a broken leg heals,' the doctor had said. 'If you broke your leg, you wouldn't expect to hop around until it got better, would you. You'd say yes to putting a cast on it and yes to using crutches. This medication is there to do the same thing, it's just that it's not your bones that have suffered a trauma, it's your brain, your emotions. These few weeks, few months, are going to be tough, Moira. I can't give you a pill to make it all better, but I can give you medication that will help you cope with what you're going through.'

Reluctantly, she'd had to agree, and now it was hard to know whether she was finding it hard to focus on packing because the medication was fogging her brain, or just because it was hard. And perhaps it would be harder without the pills. 'There's only one way to get it done,' she said out loud, 'and that's to do it. Get on with it Moira!'

She'd started out with a system, using colour-coding to denote which room things belonged in with a sub-key of who it belonged to. If it was yellow and blue, it was destined for the living room and belonged to Billy, if it was yellow and pink, it was a living room item belonging to her. But the system was too complicated, and some boxes were overflowing while others lay mostly empty. They had argued about it, with Billy getting frustrated that he didn't know where to put anything, and Moira becoming annoyed that he was messing it up.

In the end, Moira had abandoned the system, and they'd agreed to defer the task of sorting their belongings until they got to the new house. But Moira was still angry and upset, because Billy was leaving her to it. He'd agreed to be the one to pack up William's room, and she'd been grateful for that, but she hadn't realised that her husband's offer to tackle their son's room had come with an implicit abdication from any responsibility to help with packing up the rest of the house. And they'd already agreed that most of William's things would be taken to the tip. Moira had declared William's stuff too toxic for the charity shop: even if people didn't know it was William's, she'd explained, it was still his. What if something of the darkness that had tarnished their son had rubbed off on his belongings, she'd argued, 'it would make us responsible for taking that shadow into someone else's house and I can't live with that, can you?' Billy had told her she was nuts, but agreed nonetheless. It was easier than sorting through, and meant that the only things he needed to retrieve from William's room were the few things their son had asked them to take to the prison for him, and the bits and pieces Moira had asked for: William's football trophies, the stuffed toys that he'd had since he was little – just the treasures and artefacts from the small boy she had adored. These were things she could keep to remind herself that he was once a beautiful boy who had been the centre of her world for all the right reasons.

Looking round at the disorder, Moira was tempted to leave everything. They could begin again like newlyweds with just an armchair and a kettle, and build up slowly from there. It's funny how much clutter you collect in a life lived in the same place for decades, she thought, and ridiculous how much of it you don't actually need. She and Billy had done tip run after tip run together; a ritual that needed to be shared as they both tossed items into different areas for recycling or landfill, hurling them like frisbees as far away as possible.

She looked at what was left to pack: books they'd already read or never would, ornaments she'd been given, or had collected as souvenirs, the odd keepsake from her mother's house and her grandma's, and frames containing photographs of the boys and pictures they'd drawn. She reached for a picture of the two boys, wearing their school uniform and siting side by side. James had his front two teeth missing, that would make him how old? Six? Seven? So William would be nine-ish. James was smiling as wide as he could to show off his big gap. William had a Mona Lisa smile, closed lipped, only slightly towards the happy side of neutral. Moira looked at their eyes in the image, was there anything in that moment that would give her a clue that William was different? Anything she should have seen at the time and tried to fix?

She jerked and dropped the picture as Billy entered the room with a loud 'I thought you were making a brew?' The frame landed glass side down on a vase in one of the boxes, breaking both things in one smash. 'Well, that's two less things to bring with us!' Billy smiled.

Moira looked at him, then the broken things, and for the first time in days she cried. Not the unstoppable, shuddering sobs she'd succumbed to in the first few days after William's arrest, but a quiet release of sadness that she couldn't keep pushing away with busyness. She had paused. She had allowed herself to think about the boy she had lost and the life she was leaving behind, neither of them perfect, neither of them ever staying the same for long as moments, days, years moved forwards, but a loss nonetheless. A sudden loss, a freak fissure, like the vase and the frame colliding at the exact point where both would break in unison.

'It will be alright' said Billy, zig-zagging through the boxes to reach his wife and wrap his arms around her. He kissed her forehead and wiped her wet cheeks with his thumbs. 'We have new adventures to look forward to, a new house for you to make into a home, new people to meet, new people to be.'

Moira smiled at him, allowing him to take comfort in his own words. 'It will be alright,' Billy repeated.

'It won't,' Moira thought, but didn't say. 'It will never be alright again.'

24

Yvonne

When Celeste had mentioned the idea of a thank you party for all the people who'd helped, Yvonne had thought it was a great idea and rushed at it with enthusiasm. She had no words that could ever be enough to thank everyone who had played a part in finding Celeste, but at least a party would be a gesture to acknowledge how grateful she was; how grateful they both were.

But now that the day was here, Yvonne wasn't so sure it was such a good idea anymore. Sending cards might be better. And maybe giving a donation to a charity or doing something for the community, like buying a bench, or planting a tree.

It had been a long three months. Days in hospital, followed by weeks of Celeste not leaving the house, having nightmares, barely speaking, tuning out and barely hearing anything Yvonne said, living a zombie existence. The party might just add to the problem, continuing to focus on the most difficult moment of their past, rather than the future. Yvonne had raised her concerns with her daughter.

'But we've invited everyone now,' Celeste had responded.

'We can just let them know, they'll understand. I'll just tell them you're not well enough.'

'But I am well.'

Yvonne didn't know how to reply to that. Life had not equipped her to navigate the narrow paths of the right and wrong things to say as she tiptoed around her daughter's fragile mental health following the attack. The doctor had been kind but unhelpful, telling her that she knew Celeste best and should just follow her instincts, trusting that she would know the right thing to say when those difficult moments arose. Those difficult moments were arising every day, and Yvonne never knew what she should say. She was fumbling her way through like a blind man in a maze, constantly bumping against unexpected barriers and wondering which way to turn.

Would it have been better to insist that they cancel the party? For Yvonne to follow her instincts as the doctor had suggested? Or was she right to do as Celeste asked and allow her daughter the agency to make decisions, even if she thought it was a choice that would do more harm than good?

Yvonne smiled as she assembled the electric mixer to whip cream for the Victoria sandwich and scones she'd prepared for the party. The question of whether to intervene or allow her daughter to make her own choices, right or wrong, was not just a question from today, or since the attack; it was a question that had vexed her for years. And she knew the answer, of course she did. But now, instead of a bad decision being as innocuous as money wasted, or time lost, or a broken heart, the wrong choice could trigger panic, anxiety, a set-back on Celeste's slow journey to recovering from what had happened.

Yvonne switched on the whisk and felt the vibration of its frantic rotations reverberate up her arm. People were coming, it would be lovely to see them. The house would be filled with people, voices, smiles – it would be good for both of them. It had to be good for Celeste, hadn't it? The children would be there, Sophie and Laura, Ivy and Lucas, there would be a reason for Celeste to talk, for her to smile, and maybe the thing that connected them all would not even be mentioned. She watched as the cream went from liquid to a soft cloud filling the bowl, transforming from one thing to another under the influence of the beaters and her own determination. Perhaps Celeste couldn't begin to heal on her own, or with just her mother to support her, perhaps she needed something else too.

Celeste appeared in the doorway in a black dress, holding a pink floral dress on a hanger and wearing a different shoe on each foot.

'Outfit choices,' she announced. 'I love the black one, but is it a bit funereal for a party?'

'No, I....'

'And is it a bit wintery for August? But will I be cold in the flowery one? Especially if we go in the garden? Have you put anything out in the garden? Do you want me to do it? Which shoes do you think? How long have we got?'

'I...'

'What time did we say? What time is it now? So, do you think the flowery one and the Gazelles? I can always grab a cardi if we're in the garden and it chills off.'

Celeste left the room again without waiting for answers. Not all questions need answers. Yvonne sighed; sometimes the question just needs to be asked and left to sit.

There was no time for sitting for Yvonne, nor any time for wardrobe crises for either of them. Everyone would be arriving in half an hour, and she still had to lay everything out. She was glad she'd dressed the table the night before with the nice linen tablecloth from the vintage fair that took ages to iron, and a vase of roses taken from the garden. She'd made party packs for the children – did people still do that? - a chocolate bar, a yo-yo, a tube of bubbles, a pack of bubble-gum and a pin badge each that she'd bought online: they were yellow enamel stars that said 'hero'.

Yvonne spread a thin layer of strawberry jam and a thick layer of cream on the bottom half of a vanilla sponge cake, and carefully placed the other half on top, making sure she didn't squidge any of the filling out of the sides. Then she used a sieve to dust icing sugar over the top, smiling as she did so at how the humble cake was transformed into something special just like that. She scooped the rest of the jam into a teacup, and the rest of the cream into another, and began slicing a plateful of scones that she'd baked earlier and left out to cool.

They crumbled a little as she cut them, and she popped crumbs in her mouth as she worked, without thinking. As she put the last piece of scone on a cake stand, Celeste appeared at the door again.

'Ta-dah! Do I look OK?'

Turning to look at her daughter, Yvonne was amazed and delighted to find that she looked lovely, full of life, happy even. What started as a smile in response to the question, became hard, uncontrollable crying before Yvonne could stop it. With Celeste standing in the doorway, Yvonne couldn't leave the room and protect her daughter from the emotion she'd been locking up ever since picking up a more fragile, quiet version of this girl from hospital. With the seal broken, weeks of emotion that had been expressed only as cups of tea, Jaffa cakes, home-made treats, shared TV programmes, small gifts and big, silent hugs was now spilling out all over the kitchen.

Celeste said nothing, but moved swiftly to put her arms around Yvonne and enveloped her, as though she were the mother and Yvonne were the child. They stood for a minute, with Celeste keeping her mother fixed in place with one arm, while stroking her hair with the other, and Yvonne bringing her sobs under control as though turning down the heat on the hob to reduce a rolling boil to a gentle simmer.

Eventually, Celeste released her hold and Yvonne stepped back.

'I don't want to ruin your outfit with my stupid tears,' she said.

'They're not stupid. You've been through a lot and been so stoic through it all.'

'No, you've been through a lot.'

'We both have, what happens to me, happens to you. Not in the same way, but it's still something that happened in both our lives. But the sadness ends today!' Celeste took a step back, paused and began again, as though delivering a speech at a political rally. 'Today we are yelling a big 'fuck you' to all that and celebrating all the good things and good people that came out of it. Today I am wearing a killer outfit, and eating cake, and playing with the kids, and laughing out loud. And if Orson actually turns up, which he might, or he might not, he will see that I am absolutely fucking fabulous and totally out of his league. I will make it clear how much that ship has sailed, and he's missed the boat. There is no room in my life for arseholes and fuckwits. I will say 'thank you very much for the vigil, but please take your giant ego with you when you leave.'

They laughed, and Yvonne marvelled at her daughter's knack for turning stress and heartache into humour, a talent she'd always had and never lost.

'And Esther?' Yvonne asked.

'It wasn't Esther's fault, Mum. I could have chosen to stay in the bar that night. I could have got a cab. I could have arrived home completely fine if it hadn't been for him. Esther didn't put me in harm's way, harm came looking for me, and there's only one person to blame for that. Thank you for letting me invite her. You will be nice to her when they get here won't you? And Dad, thanks for letting me invite him too, and same applies, you don't have to chat to either of them, just don't give them the evils.'

Yvonne laughed again. 'You know your dad might not turn up, don't you?'

'They all might not turn up, but the ones that do had better be ready to eat lots of cake. Exactly how much have you made?'

'Enough. I could do with a hand getting it all on the table. You can start with this,' Yvonne said, handing her daughter the Victoria sandwich.

They moved around taking cakes out of boxes and removing cling film from plates of sandwiches, with Yvonne giving instructions and both of them placing the food she'd prepared on the table she'd dressed for the occasion. They moved silently from kitchen to dining room, stepping out of each other's way as they crossed paths from room to room, with Yvonne leaving items on the kitchen table for Celeste to take into the other room, and rearranging items on the dining table so they looked just right. She had brought out all of her best vintage crockery and the cake stands that barely ever got used. When the last cake – lemon drizzle – had been sliced and placed on the table, they stood back to admire it.

'It looks beautiful, Mum.'

'It does, doesn't it?' Yvonne smiled.

'Thank you,' Celeste replied, taking her hand and squeezing it hard, with the force of a thousand thank yous.

'Wait there, I'm going to take a picture. We need to get one of the table, and one with you with the table and one with both of us before anyone touches it.' Celeste disappeared to find her phone, leaving Yvonne to look over the table and smile at the tableau in front of her. She had always offered tea and cake as a remedy for everything, not just for Celeste but for friends, for her own mother, for colleagues, for people she barely knew. Most of today's guests were people she barely knew, and yet, here she was, offering them cake with overwhelming love and gratitude.

'Right,' Celeste announced as she re-entered the room with her phone and stood on a chair to get a shot of the table from above.

'Be careful!'

'I'm Careful McCareful, Mum, stop fussing,' Celeste replied, getting down from the chair. 'Your turn next, stand next to your creations, baker extraordinaire!'

'But I look a mess! Look at me, I've no make up on and I'm still wearing my apron.'

'Well, that's authentic artisan. Shall we put a bit of flour in your hair and make you hold a wooden spoon too? Smile!' Celeste took multiple pictures then scurried across to stand by her mother, tapping the screen to reverse the camera and holding it out in front of them to take a picture. 'I'm not sure I can get much of the table in and both of us as well. That'll do, I'll ask someone else to take another one when they get here. Now off you go upstairs and get yourself cleaned up and party ready, you're a disgrace!' Celeste laughed.

As Yvonne opened her wardrobe to choose something to wear, she heard the doorbell go and the sound of Celeste walking through the hall and letting people into the house. She heard Celeste greet them with a loud, enthusiastic 'hello!' followed by children's voices.

'We didn't know if we should bring a present, because it's not a birthday...'

'But we wanted to bring one anyway because it is a party...'

'And Mum says you've been really brave, and you deserve a treat. She picked it...'

'But I helped...'

'We both helped...'

'Can you open it now...'

The voices got quieter as the first guests moved from the hall to the living room but, pausing to listen, Yvonne could still hear them.

'Are we the first?'

'OMG, look at all that cake. Look Grandma, look at the cake!'

'Balloons! Sophie, there are balloons.'

Eager to see the children and greet her guests, Yvonne hurried, choosing a dress and quickly changing into it, pulling a brush through her hair and applying mascara and lipstick. 'You'll do,' she said to herself in the mirror, and hurried downstairs, just in time for the doorbell to sound again as she reached the hall.

She opened the door to find Esther holding a bunch of flowers and accompanied by a young man.

Yvonne and Esther both paused before speaking and the young man filled their hesitation by stepping forward with his hand outstretched for Yvonne to shake it.

'Hello, I'm Tom, I hope you don't mind me tagging along with Esther? We brought flowers. Should have brought two bunches in hindsight.' He turned to look at Esther, who held out the flowers to Yvonne.

'Of course, that's fine,' Yvonne said, taking the flowers from Esther and smiling at Tom. 'There's tonnes of cake so extra help with eating it is good news. Celeste is in there with Sophie and Laura, you head on in.'

She stood holding the door for the couple to walk through it and, as they did, Ivy and Lucas filled the doorstep, with Ed and Lisa following behind, like bowling balls rolling onto the carousel ready for the next player.

There were more hellos, more instructions to go straight through to the room with the others, and Yvonne checked the street for signs of more arrivals before closing the door and heading to the kitchen with the flowers. She hurried to find a vase, discard the wrapper, cut the stems, and fill the vase with water so that she could join her guests in the other room, but as she walked back through the hall carrying the vase of flowers, there was a loud knock on the door. Robert, she assumed, and reluctantly put the vase down on the cupboard in the hall so that she could open the door. It was PC Noel Fisher, in his uniform.

'Yvonne! How are you. Abi sends her apologies, and I can only stay for a few minutes...'

'Come in, come in, it's lovely that you could come.'

'I can only stay for a few minutes. I'm on duty you see, it wouldn't be appropriate for me to come personally, but if I pop in while I'm on duty that's just a follow up while I'm in the neighbourhood. I can smell the cake, Yvonne. Smells amazing.' He lowered his voice, 'How's she doing?'

'Hard to know, really,' Yvonne said, 'she seems fine but who knows what's really going on. She's having counselling. The party was her idea, I...'

Celeste's head appeared from the dining room door, like a comedy player peeping round the curtain in an old-fashioned farce.

'I wondered who it was,' Celeste opened the door to the dining room, letting the noise of chat and laughter into the hall with her. 'Come on in! There's loads of cake. And sandwiches, you could take a whole packed lunch away with you. Come on in. Lovely flowers.'

Noel Fisher looked at the flowers, 'I didn't bring them.'

'Esther brought them,' Yvonne clarified.

Celeste turned to the room behind her, 'thanks for the flowers Est,' and then back to her mother. 'Give them here, I'll put them on the coffee table. We need plates, Mum. Everyone's dying to tuck in and we've got no plates. And more tea, I wonder if next door have got a spare tea pot we can borrow so that we can have two on the go?'

Yvonne handed the vase of flowers to her daughter and as Noel Fisher followed Celeste into the room, receiving a short burst of applause as he entered, she turned to return to the kitchen to get the plates, but was interrupted by the doorbell again.

She opened the door to Annie 'Mitch' Mitchell and her brother, both of them smiling, and Annie holding another bunch of flowers.

Annie stepped inside and hugged Yvonne. 'This is brilliant that you're doing this. I mean it's like a group therapy session isn't it?'

'But with cake!' added Adam, closing the door behind him.

'Everyone's in there, go and join them. Celeste will be delighted to see you. Thanks for these, I'll get them in water.'

Yvonne heard another cheer from the gathering of guests as the siblings entered the room and she returned to the kitchen to find the plates. She had bought paper plates, pink ones with silver butterflies on them. Three packets of ten so that they had plenty in case someone misplaced theirs or got jam on it and wanted a fresh one. She had thought of everything, but not a spare tea pot. And where had she put the plates?

Celeste rushed in with the teapot.

'It's so lovely Mum. I'm so glad we did this. The kids have just started on the cupcakes without a plate, I hope that's OK. I said they could. It seemed mean to make them look at them without letting them dig in. I'll put the kettle on, can you bring a fresh pot in when you bring the plates? You're a legend, Mum. Thank you!'

Celeste filled the kettle, emptied the dregs of the pot into the sink and added new tea bags, ready for Yvonne to complete the task.

'Ooh, more flowers. I'll sort those shall I?' She took a jug from the cupboard, filled it with water, discarded the cellophane wrapper and plonked them in.

'You're a star!' she called as she left the room with the flowers, repeating the phrase that Yvonne had used to express love for her daughter all her life.

Yvonne paused, allowing the enormity of everything to rush over her for a moment. Celeste was having counselling, but Yvonne was not. Yvonne had been stepping from one day to the next not knowing whether each hour would bring normal routine and busyness, or a moment like this, when she felt that she couldn't process a coherent thought, the space was too big, too cluttered. Her thoughts were too muddled and she just needed a sit down and a quiet space to slow everything down.

'I thought you'd be in here.'

It was Robert, and Yvonne was confused. Too confused to say anything. Had she let him in? It had been PC Fisher who had knocked, so how was it Robert walking into the kitchen?

'The door wasn't shut properly, I've closed it behind me now. What are you doing in here while everyone else is in the other room?' He placed a bottle of ginger beer on the table. 'I'm on the wagon, closest thing to an actual drink and I'm a bit addicted now to be honest.'

Yvonne looked from Robert to the ginger beer and back again, trying to remember why she had come into the kitchen.

'I need to make tea and find the paper plates. You go in. Have you said hello to Celeste?'

'I popped my head in, she was busy chatting to the police guy. I can help if you like. Shall I brew the tea?'

Without waiting for an answer, Robert pressed the switch on the already boiled kettle and it quickly rose to a boil again. He poured water into the pot, took a spoon from the drawer to stir it, replacing the lid.

'That's one job done. Plates you say?'

'I bought some paper plates. I can't remember where I've put them.'

'Let's have a look.' Robert began opening cupboards looking for the plates and Yvonne, stressed by his presence and his right-at-home self-invitation to rummage through her kitchen, stood and picked up the tea pot.

'Perhaps I forgot to buy them. Never mind. Let's take this tea in and I'll pop to the shop to get some.'

'Pop to the shop to get what?'

Celeste had appeared in the doorway and Yvonne explained that she'd bought paper plates but couldn't find them. Or perhaps she thought she'd bought them but forgotten.

'Can't you just use ordinary plates?' asked Robert.

'There's not enough for everyone, and what we have got don't match. And I bought some. I can remember buying some.'

'Mum, it's fine. I'll just nip to the shop. I'll be back in five minutes.'

Celeste took the teapot from her mother and handed it to her father. 'Can you take that in, Dad? There are cups and milk and everything in there, help yourself.'

When he'd gone, Celeste hugged her mother. 'I know it's a lot Mum, but it's fine. Today is nice and everything is OK. It's all OK. I'll go to the shop. You go and get a cuppa and I'll be back before you've drunk it. Make Dad pour it for you.' she glanced at the table. 'Ginger beer, nice. The kids will be chuffed with that, why don't you take it in with you.'

Yvonne picked up the ginger beer. 'Are you sure?'

'It's a five-minute walk. I'll be there and back before you know it, which is a good thing because there are people actually salivating in there. And I don't think PC Fisher can stay long.'

'Ok, take my purse, my card is in there if there's not enough cash.'

Celeste picked up the purse from the kitchen counter and they walked into the hall together. Yvonne hovered, watching her daughter as Celeste retied the laces on one of her shoes.

'I know how to tie my own laces, Mum. Just go in, there are compliments waiting for you for baking all that cake. I'll knock on when I get back – God knows where my keys are.'

Celeste tipped her head in the direction of the dining room door and Yvonne followed her instruction, lifting up the ginger beer and presenting it like an auctioneer.

'I love ginger beer!' declared Sophie, 'Mum, can we?'

Yvonne saw Robert look at her accusingly and heard the front door bang shut. Maybe she should have asked Celeste to get more ginger beer while she was at the shop. She could phone her. Or just text. Or just leave it.

'I've got a cup,' said Sophie.

'Then I'd best get pouring!' smiled Yvonne.

Celeste had been right, there were compliments on the cakes as she poured the ginger beer.

'I hope you don't mind me making a start while we wait for the plates,' said PC Fisher, holding a piece of lemon cake in one hand, with his other hand poised below it to catch any crumbs. 'My wife makes a nice lemon cake, but it's not as good as this.

Don't tell her I said that though, will you.' He took another bite, winking at her as he ate it.

'Could you pour me a cup of tea please Robert?' Yvonne smiled at her ex-husband as she filled the cup that Lucas held out to her. 'There you go Lucas. Ivy? Do you want some?'

Ivy wrinkled her nose in a 'no' and Robert presented a cup of tea to Yvonne, placing it on the coffee table with a 'there you go'.

There was a knock at the door. 'That'll be Celeste with the plates.' Yvonne went to put down her tea.

'You drink your tea, I'll get it,' said Robert, and Yvonne wondered if he was answering the door to be helpful or because he knew it would irritate her.

Robert returned with the new arrival, but it wasn't Celeste.

'Hello,' said the tall man, carrying a bunch of flowers. 'I'm Orson, Celeste invited me.'

He handed the flowers to Yvonne with a kiss on the cheek. 'Look at all this amazing food. Celeste told me you were a great cook.'

'Celeste has told me lots about you too,' Yvonne lied. 'Do you want tea? Or coffee? Or there's some ginger beer?' Yvonne responded.

'That's so kind. I don't do caffeine or fizzy drinks actually, but if it's not too much trouble, could I have this one?' he took an individually wrapped herbal teabag from his pocket and handed it to Yvonne.

'Looks fancy,' she said, and taking her own tea with her, left the room again to put the kettle on.

Yvonne looked at the clock as she waited for the kettle to boil. What time did Celeste leave? She should have checked the time so that she knew how long it had been. She could call her about the ginger beer and just make sure she was OK. She should wait. She should just make the interesting smelling tea and wait.

The kettle snapped off as the water boiled, and Yvonne filled the mug, releasing a scent somewhere between spa day and garden centre.

As she took the drink through there was another knock on the door. Yvonne opened it, and this time it was Celeste.

'Is that for Orson? Did he bring his own?'

Yvonne smiled and nodded. 'Was it OK?'

'He's such a high maintenance egomaniac!'

'Was it alright at the shop?'

'Fine,' said Celeste closing the door behind her. 'I mean, they only had boring white ones, but I got plates.'

Sophie and Laura appeared in the hallway, 'Plates! Did you get them? Can we have cake now?'

'We can,' smiled Celeste. 'And we will. Let's eat cake until our bellies pop!'

VIII

Celeste

I'm walking down a street that I have walked down a hundred times. A thousand times. More than a thousand. Returning from a shop I have visited most weeks, most days, since before I can remember.

Every house along the route is familiar. When I pass the house with the dog that always barks every time someone walks past, it barks. The house with the tear in the net curtains is still a gash that offers a little peephole into the room behind. The car that's always parked under a green protective cover, wrapped up like it's waiting for someone to come and reveal the surprise, is sitting there as usual on the drive. The window with brightly coloured glass ornaments of all shapes and sizes is displaying its rainbow of treasures as usual, with each of them crammed on the window ledge as though queueing round the block.

These are things that have stayed the same for years. Decades maybe. Things I have seen and known, but not looked at. I have been bored of noticing them. I have expected them to stay the same and they've done exactly as I expected. Nothing. No change here, can't be bothered, we've given up, we like the status quo. Boring you say? Thank you. We like boring. Boring is safe. Same is comfortable.

And it is.

Every house I walk past used to accuse me. Welcome back to Dullsville, Celeste, shame on you for getting stuck here. But now the same scene tells a different story. Welcome back to life, Celeste. Welcome back to a world where nothing has changed. We are still here, you are still here, everything is back to normal.

These streets were where I was trapped and I was so tired of seeing them. But I am walking to the shop to buy plates so that I can eat cake, made by a mother who loves me, to share with people whose kindness has helped me stay alive. I am alive. I can walk these steps and notice everything I've seen but ignored for so long. These are the streets where I am free. I will not be trapped by what happened, I will be freed by what didn't happen. I survived. I am alive.

And I will live. I will eat the cake, lots of it. I will stroke the dog, look through the gap in the curtains, rejoice for the days the car is unwrapped and missing from the drive, enjoy the museum of kitsch glass objects. This is home, and it is mine. He tried to take it from me, but he has given me the freedom to appreciate what I have. He took from me, but the Celeste he left behind is more than the girl he found sitting on a bench with her shoe in her hand.

I miss those shoes. But shoes are just things. What I have and where I am is not who I am. Who I am is not the same as it was; it is better. I have learned things. The power of kindness. The kindness of the right word, look, touch at the right time. The value of rest, of quietness, of leaving gaps for people to say the things that they need to unlock from inside their own heads. The comfort of the familiar, and the predictability of routine. The joy of small things, the sun on my face, the sound of my mum moving around in the kitchen when I wake up, the smile of the man from the shop who always says 'how are you?'

I have learned important things, and I have learned what's not really important. Thinking about what happened to me isn't important. Focusing on what didn't happen to me, that's the thing. That's the thing that will make me thrive. Will make me appreciate every day. I am still here. I am more present in my own life than I ever was before. I survived.

I am walking home from the shop with paper plates in one hand and my mum's purse in the other, but I don't want to walk, I want to dance. I want to cha cha, and samba, and polka. I want to skip and sprint. I jump off and onto the kerb like I did when I was a kid. I notice the trainers on my feet. Why not run the rest of the way? Why not run, life is waiting.

Acknowledgements

My sincerest thanks to Kevin and Hetha Duffy and the team at Bluemoose Books for their continuing faith, support and encouragement, and for their tireless dedication to finding new voices and championing great stories – as a writer and a reader I am eternally grateful.

Special thanks to Bluemoose editor, Lin Webb, for her knowledge, care and kindness – not just in the edit of this novel, but in all my work with Bluemoose over the past 10 years. With each editing process I learn more from Lin, and the way I chose to end this novel owes much to her gentle guidance on my previous novel, *Captain Jesus*.

Many thanks too to Fiachra McCarthy, whose design talent adorns this book.

For your considered feedback, suggestions, and encouragement, thank you to Manchester Women Writers; a community of wise women and talented writers who help each other improve and keep going, in writing and in life.

For answering my random questions about police procedure, thank you to Phil Machen and Elaine Brunskill.

For letting me witter on while I was working things out, and knowing when to leave me alone at my laptop, thank you to Gideon and Ingrid. And for the cups of tea.

I have dedicated this novel to my mum, but I also want to leave mention here for all the mums who have held each other up, brewed up, and checked in with one another: this is for you too.